# Werewolves:
## The Next Generation

by Kevin L. Delker

The contents of this work, including, but not limited to, the accuracy of events, people, and places depicted; opinions expressed; permission to use previously published materials included; and any advice given or actions advocated are solely the responsibility of the author, who assumes all liability for said work and indemnifies the publisher against any claims stemming from publication of the work.

All Rights Reserved
Copyright © 2023 by Kevin L. Delker

No part of this book may be reproduced or transmitted, downloaded, distributed, reverse engineered, or stored in or introduced into any information storage and retrieval system, in any form or by any means, including photocopying and recording, whether electronic or mechanical, now known or hereinafter invented without permission in writing from the publisher.

Dorrance Publishing Co
585 Alpha Drive
Suite 103
Pittsburgh, PA 15238
Visit our website at *www.dorrancebookstore.com*

ISBN: 978-1-6495-7156-4
eISBN: 978-1-6495-7665-1

# Introduction

Dave is a scientist that earns a living at a hospital lab testing for a number of illnesses. His specialty at the hospital is disease research, testing blood samples for disease and working on cures, when not busy testing samples.

Dave is one of the best lab techs in the hospital doing blood testing. But his night job keeps getting in the way of the hospital job. So, he works part time at the hospital now and devotes most of his waking hours to the lab in his basement.

The equipment in his personal lab was bought as the hospital upgraded to newer and better equipment and he watched the Internet, as well, for what he needed. He bought a walk-in cooler at an auction of a restaurant when it closed.

His relationship with his wife is rocky at best because of the night work in the basement lab. A lot of time is spent testing different samples that he has collected himself, as well as samples from zoos and veterinarians. This is how he manages to keep working at home and supports his research and the household.

Dave is very good at what he does and can have results quicker than most others. Usually by looking at the sample under a microscope. He has spent a lot of time looking at samples, "mapping" his findings, and comparing the test results to his findings.

There is one disease though that is challenging him and has him running many different tests trying, unsuccessfully so far, to find a cure. He is able to identify it under a microscope and believes it is a disease that many say is a curse straight from Satan himself: the werewolf.

See, Dave believes that it is not a curse but that it is a disease that can be cured. "As it is transmitted, so shall it be cured."

The intent is to cure the human host of the disease of the beast within. The biggest challenge is finding good samples; the hairs he recovers are human or beast. He believes there has to be an in between during the change. The blood samples have the same issue human or beast nothing showing the transformation phase of the disease.

He has been able to map the DNA structure of the beast. Both in beast form and human form and is comparing the structure of "none infected" with the results.

It has been six years now, going on seven since the existence of werewolves was acknowledged by local, state, and the federal government. With such acknowledgment come very strict curfew laws to try to "protect the public."

Work shifts are now twelve-hour shifts, daylight, and night shifts. Everybody caries a weapon to and from work. Most factories and many other businesses have hired security to protect the workers at shift change.

The over the road truck drivers mainly travel at night now. It's safer than walking through a truck stop parking lot in the dark. Though for some unknown reason the werewolves don't seem to bother the truck stops too much. Of course, there is the occasional attack but not enough to justify police protection. The armed security and armed drivers seem to do well for the safety of the truck stops. Another theory is the sound of the diesel engines running hurts the hearing of the beast or hinders its ability to hear, as well.

Rest areas on the other hand do not have armed security or police protection, all travelers are responsible for their own protection; attacks do happen at rest areas and along the interstate and smaller roads, as well. Which helps feed the theory of the diesel engines running, there isn't near the number of trucks in a rest area that is in a truck stop.

The infected area is all of the east coast, from Florida north through Canada. The west coast states are starting to acknowledge their existence and taking the precautions to try to protect the citizens of those states. California is the last state to acknowledge that the beast is real because most people figured it was the making of a movie and that Hollywood was behind it all, but the body count was on the rise and the number of missing, as well, was on the rise. The remains that were being found had to be DNA tested to be identified and it started like other states and known criminals were the first to be found and were treated as a regular murder with no suspects, but sightings grew and when the police asked the movie industry nobody was doing a werewolf movie.

Contrary to popular believe silver is not necessary to kill the beast in either form. It was a very costly battle with the silver and a very big risk to attempt killing a beast without the silver. Until one officer mistakenly had lead bullets loaded instead of the silver. The beast was still dead, and they didn't realize the mistake until the officer reloaded.

# Chapter 1
# The First Female

It's late September, about two days (nights) until the next full moon. It's ten minutes until ten in the evening when the phone rings.

Dave's wife Sarah looks at him and simply and sternly says, "Don't answer that."

Dave looks at her apologetically. "Sorry, dear, you know I have to."

Sarah allows her anger to start to show in her voice. "Bull! You want to!"

Dave picks up the phone and looks at Sarah. "We'll continue this after the call."

Dewight says, "You talking to me or to Sarah?"

Dewight is the night shift supervisor for the Hughesville Police Department.

Dewight went to school with Dave and they stayed in touch. They renewed their friendship when Dave started his basement lab.

Sarah gives Dave a look as she starts up the stairs to change for bed.

Dave continues, "Sorry, I was talking to Sarah. So, what's up?"

Dewight laughs briefly. "As if you didn't know. We have a body…" He doesn't finish the rest of his sentence.

Dave responds, "Dewight, yo! Dewight!" Raising his voice finally to a full yell, he says, "Hey, man! Dewight!"

Dewight says, "Sorry, dude, I spaced out. But you're not going to believe this. I'm looking at it and still don't believe it."

Dave's curiosity is rising. "Okay, you said something about a body. What body? Is it the real thing and not and imitator like last time?"

Dewight still in disbelieve about what he is seeing. "The body is going back to human form, and as for the imitator he was very convincing. You know about that group that dresses up like a beast to study their behavior at least until their discovered as impostors by the real beasts then the coroner gathers up what's left of their remains."

Dave, "Okay, but what about the body? How soon can I get it?"

Dewight still watching the body in its final stages of transformation. "The coroner is on her way now. But, Dave, you're not going to believe this."

Dave, with an almost mocking tone but more curiosity in his voice, says, "What the body stopped changing?"

Dewight does not acknowledge the mocking tone but simply answers the question, "No, the body… it's a female."

Dave is astonished to the point he almost drops the phone.

Dewight can't even hear Dave breathing, so he checks his cell phone to see if he lost connection. But connection is still there, so he calls out to Dave. "Dave are ya still there? Yo, Dave, snap out of it! Answer me!"

Dave snaps back to reality before the phone slides out of his hand. "Yeah, Dewight, I'm still here. Female, ya say? Interesting."

Dewight, "Yeah, and she looks familiar, too. Hey, Carla is here now, and they are ready to bag the body."

Dave, still trying to grasp the fact that they shot a female, says, "Good; she's bringing me the body, right?"

Dewight shakes his head in disbelief. "I can't believe you'd even ask me that. You're the only one authorized by Pennsylvania and Washington D.C. to receive the body of a werewolf or even the body of a suspected werewolf."

Dave is starting to get his thoughts straightened out. "Oh, yeah, sorry, I forgot that for a minute. I'll go and get things ready for when Carla gets here." He hangs up the phone without saying bye.

Dewight is unaware that Dave hung up. "The body is being loaded into the car now." He pauses with no response. "Dave, ya there?" He checks his phone and it's back to the standby screen. "I hate when he does that." With that he puts his phone away and tells Carla, "Dave will be waiting for you."

Carla looks at him and with a little chuckle. "I'd be surprised and disappointed if he wasn't."

Dave turns from the phone to see Sarah standing in front of the basement door.

She opens her robe to reveal the lingerie that she is wearing. "How soon are you going to bed?" She says in her sexiest voice, letting him know, without saying that she is interested tonight.

Dave looks at her, admiring the view that she is providing, especially since it's seen through and leaves nothing to the imagination. "As soon as I can, Carla is bringing a body, and I need to put it in the cooler for after work tomorrow."

Dave hates to refuse his lovely wife as she is a chronic pain sufferer. Most nights she is talking about her pain, so he leaves her alone and does not bother her for intimacy. But on the nights when she is feeling up to intimacy, he enjoys the time more then she believes.

Sarah looks at the clock as she closes her robe. "So, I'll be asleep when you finally go to bed."

Dave raises an eyebrow. "I hope not; this shouldn't take too long. The cooler getting to temperature will take longer, and it looks like I will not be waiting for it tonight."

Sarah goes upstairs as Dave starts unlocking the multiple locks on the heavy, steel basement door. After undoing the last lock, he looks up the stairs to see if Sarah is still in sight, but she is not, so he flips the light switch, opens the door, and heads down the stairs, closing the door behind himself.

Once in the basement, he turns on the rest of the lights and the cooler. Then he starts unlocking the multiple locks on the door to the outside entrance to the basement. He looks at the security monitor and realizes he has not turned on the cameras yet. He turns on the security cameras and the monitors, then goes back to unlocking the door and leaves one lock done. Then directs his attention to getting ready to receive the body; he prepares the table and looks at the monitor to see when Carla arrives.

As he is finished washing the table, he checks the monitor to see Carla backing into the driveway. He rushes for the door and unlocks the last lock, opens the door, turns on the exterior lights, tucks a handgun into his belt, and runs up to the driveway, throwing open the outer door at ground level. He then directs Carla back the drive and stops her at the access to the basement.

Dave reaches for the rear car door as she is stopping. Carla stops the car, puts it in park, and gets out as the police escorts exit the cruiser, with weapons drawn, to protect them while unloading.

Carla gets to the back of the car and smacks Dave on the back of his head. "When are you going to wait for me to stop before opening the door?"

Dave simply answers, "When there are no more werewolves."

Carla shakes her head in disbelief. "Then there will be something else you're looking to cure and be just as impatient."

Dave smiles and gives a nod, agreeing. "You're probably right. Are you ready to unload the body?"

They unload the body and carry it into the basement placing it on the table. Dave gives a quick look at the temperature of the cooler, and it's not cold enough yet.

Dave then escorts Carla back up the stairs to her car. And as she is closing the car door, Dave asks, "This one is female, right?"

Carla smiles and looks at him. "It was when we loaded it into the car."

Dave removes his pistol out of his belt line and holds it at the ready for a just in case needed. "Okay, I guess I deserve that one. It's just hard to believe after six years plus and now we get a female."

Carla puts her hand to his cheek. "Enjoy your examination. I hope you finally get what you are looking for, and you deserve more than that one."

They share a laugh over that remark. Carla finishes closing her car door, and Dave goes in the basement access, tucking the pistol back into his belt, closing the exterior door, and locking it. Going down the stairs, he closes the interior door to the driveway and locks the multiple locks on the heavy steel door. Then he watches Carla leave on the surveillance monitors to make sure her and the officers left safely. He then turns his attention toward the body and forgets to turn off the driveway lights. He returns the pistol to its place on the table, by the door.

Sarah is upstairs, in the dark, watching them unload the body and the interaction between Carla and Dave. She stands there and watches Carla and the officers leave, and she is secretly wishing to see Carla's car get attacked by the beasts. But then she regrets thinking that way especially since Carla is doing her job and she has no proof of anything with Dave. She closes the curtains and heads off toward bed, hangs her robe over the end of the bed, and gets in under the blankets. While lying there, waiting for Dave to come to bed, she starts thinking about whether she needs to worry about Dave having an affair or not, and if so, with whom. Then her thoughts start going over the process of receiving a new body.

Sarah worked with Dave in the beginning, but she couldn't stomach every aspect of the job that he does. She knows enough to be a great help in the lab. What bothered her the most was getting the DNA to identify the victims of attacks, especially when there isn't much recovered for identification. She helped on two of those cases and called it quits; one case was a missing child, and it was that case when she quit. What came to them couldn't be identified as any particular part of the body, just pieces of meat.

Now she tries to stay out of the lab and "out of his way" while working in the lab. She does get impatient and is trying to get him to quit testing bodies. She checks the clock and knows the cooler isn't cold enough for him to put a fresh body in it yet.

Dave decides to start looking at the body while waiting for the cooler. As he is unzipping the body bag, he watches the monitors to watch for any beasts that may be in the area. He has had a few sniffing around after a fresh delivery, but they never made it past the exterior door to be an issue. He has watched a few grab the door handle and try to open it but gave up once they realized it was locked. He keeps video like that to try and help understand their behavior better; he figures they maintain some human intelligence, but yet there are times they appear to be more animal than human.

He continues by removing the body from the bag, folding the bag, and putting it on a shelf by the door for when Carla makes the next delivery. As he puts it on the shelf, he realizes that she didn't pick up the last one. He thinks out loud: "Well, maybe she wasn't thinking properly either." Then turns back to the body, checking the cooler temperature on his way past it.

He pauses on the face and looks at her. "You do look familiar, but no time for guessing games." He continues, thinking out loud, "We know how you died, so that's not an issue tonight, and the reason you were brought to me is because of what you were at the time of death." He has forgotten about the monitors as he is focusing on the body and why she looks so familiar.

Dave starts looking at the bullet holes in her chest and abdomen. "Although because you're female, you could give me that piece to the puzzle that I'm so desperate to find." He grabs a magnifying glass to examine the wounds in her abdomen first.

"Let's see if I'm right. Any hairs, or at least the heavier and darker hairs, should be from beast form. Would you be so kind as to give me one good hair?" He manages to find some hair in the wounds. "Good, girl, now let's see if it's usable." Removing the hair with a pair of tweezers, he holds it up and looks at it through the magnifying glass. "Oh, yeah, that's a very good girl; the root is still there." He places the hair in a petri dish and puts it next to the microscope for later.

Something crashes outside, and he looks at the monitors to see a cat running from the area where the trash cans are sitting. "Stupid cat; now there's a mess to clean up in the morning. We should get plastic cans that the lids lock on; then maybe the cat will let them alone."

The cooler is at the temperature he wants now, so he places a sheet over the body and wheels her into the cooler. As he is leaving the cooler, he pauses before closing the door and stares at the body. He just can't shake the feeling that he knows her, and then he notices the stomach looks odd. Almost as if she started to bloat but she shouldn't have started bloating yet. At least, not noticeably.

While standing there thinking about all this, he hears something outside again. The sound reminded him of nails being pulled out and a metallic object hitting something solid, concrete or asphalt. He closes the door to the cooler as he looks at the monitors. He notices the basement stairway is exposed and the door is missing. He walks over directly in front of the monitors, which are on a shelf next to the breaker box. He looks for anything, then he sees the door on a different camera angle in front of the garage in the driveway. He is now hearing an odd sound from the driveway door. It sounds like sniffing, so he approaches the door and listens very closely. Shortly after reaching the door, the sound turns to a growl; it's a low and deep-sounding growl sending shivers up his spine. He has never heard a growl like that before it does sound dog like but different somehow. The volume of the growl grows and manages to get deeper, as well. Dave just starts to back away from the door in amazement and fear. He believes that what is at the door is that what he seeks to cure: the beast itself, a werewolf.

He stops a few steps back from the door and stands there listening for the growling and is surprised that he can still hear it. Then there is a loud bang from something hitting something else, but it's hard to guess what was hit and with what, so he listens and looks at the monitors to see if the cameras are seeing anything. The noise is repeated again and again and again, but there is nothing on the monitors. He turns back toward the door to hear a pause in the banging, but the growling tone has changed. His curiosity rises and approaches the door fear is replaced by his desire to listen and try to figure out the difference in the tone. He is right next to the door, ear turned to the door, listening very closely to the growl, and the banging starts again. Right in his ear, he is startled and jumps back, looking straight at the door. Now he knows what the sound is, the beast is beating on the door. He watches the door as the beating and the growling continues, the growl sounds angrier and perhaps more desperate as the beating goes on. The hits sound like they are growing in strength. He is amazed and wonders just how strong is this beast? How much stronger can the hits get? His full attention is on the door watching and listening, the door appears to be moving slightly and Dave isn't sure if he's seeing what he thinks he's seeing. So, he looks at the door locks and the loose hanging handles that some have, they jump with every hit and he sees not just the door, but the door frame moves, as well. Dust falls from the door frame with every hit on the door, and it does not retreat back as far as it is being knocked out, the door is now starting to show dents on the inside that he can see easily. His amazement in this creature continues to grow. The door makes one big jump inward, the frame does not retreat at all, and the dent visibly grew when hit.

Dave finally realizes that what is on the other side of the door is a real threat and is not going to stop until it gets in. He walks over to a switch on the wall, and there is a pause in the beating of the door. Dave says, "Let's see how you like this." The growling gets louder and angrier, the beating starts up again with more strength, and Dave pauses at the switch in awe of the increase in strength, but the door jumps and brings him back to reality and he flips the switch, electrifying the door. The next hit the beast gets a small jolt as the electricity builds in the steel door, and there is a pause and the growling stops. Dave is wondering if the electricity worked as he had hoped when he had it installed. His hope is crushed as quickly as it started to form in his mind as the growling started again and got louder. Dave grabs his .44 Magnum revolver and holds it at the ready. If the door gives way to the next hit, he is standing to the side, anticipating the door flying straight when it gives.

The pause has allowed the electricity to build up to a full charge for the next hit and it's not a long wait for the next hit. The beast hits the door and receives a full charge of electricity from the door, the impact of the hit seems to have been diminished by the electricity, or perhaps fatigue was setting in, or it was using a test hit to check the door, but either way the hit didn't have the strength of the previous hit. The door barely moved when hit, the beast however was not as fortunate as the door. The beast took the full charge and the sound that it made was a mixture of surprise and pain, as Dave figured.

Dave looks at the monitors in time to see a dark blurred streak exit the basement access. The beast disappears into the shadows, but as Dave watches the monitors, he sees eye shine across the street reflecting from his driveway lights.

Dave saves the recording from when the beast first entered the camera view, through the eye shine. He turns off the basement lights, double checking the doors and the windows are locked and turning on all the switches that electrify the steel bars on the windows, doors, and even the steel bars on the chimney.

The use of steel bars on the windows, doors, and even chimneys are common practice now, any place that is considered "vulnerable" to a beast gaining access to the house. To electrify those steel bars is not common. Dave is one of a few houses that has electrified the bars. It's not widely used for a few reasons one is cost, it's costly to wire the bars for electricity, not to mention the cost of the electricity itself.

Second is that nobody knows for sure if electricity will actually work to turn the beast away. There are arguments to support both sides of the debate and even real cases that support both sides some that it worked and some that it didn't work to stop the beast. There is also a group that says it depends on how badly the beast wants in and if it wants in the electricity will not stop it.

The third reason is nobody knows how much voltage it would take to repel a beast, or how much they can take and still proceed to enter at will. Like anything there are several theories but nothing to support those theories. The voltage that worked at house number one may not be enough at house number two.

However, tonight the voltage that Dave has wired up to the steel seems to have been enough, at least for now. Or the beast was just caught off guard at the full one hundred fifty thousand volts that was put into the steel, either way it worked tonight, and Dave is grateful.

Dave pauses at the base of the stairs and looks at the basement door and the locks verifying they are all locked, looks around the house for any lights he may have missed then heads upstairs for bed. On his way upstairs he realizes he is not carrying a pistol, most nights it's not an issue but tonight a beast tried to enter. He stops at the door to the bedroom and thinks why tonight, what is different tonight that one would try to enter the lab? He goes into the bedroom believing Sarah is asleep and still thinking about the beast and what is so different tonight, a thought comes to mind and he feels a bit dumb founded for not seeing it sooner. "Duh… it's a female" he whispers to himself.

Sarah rolls over to face him. "What is female, and what was that ungodly howl that I heard?"

Dave looks at her and continues to get changed for bed. "Oh, sorry, dear, thought you were asleep. The body in the basement is female, and the howl was a werewolf trying to get into the lab." He answers her question very calmly and is not looking at her to see the terror on her face. His tone was as if this is a normal occurrence.

Sarah sits up and looks straight at him and with a mixture of anger and scarred tone in her voice. "Hold on, back up here for a minute. Did you say female? The new body is female, and a beast tried to get in tonight?"

Dave tries to reassure her. "Honey, the steel door and the electricity stopped it, and it ran off into the darkness, howling in pain."

Sarah's voice is angrier, still with obvious fear. "So, it took both; you had to electrify the door to prevent entry." Her fear is starting to show physically.

Dave is still trying to reassure her that they are safe. "I electrified the door as a precaution." Thinking out loud, he continues "Although after seeing the strength that it displayed tonight, I doubt the steel doors will hold them out for long. Definitely not without the help of electricity, and even then, I'm not sure for how long the doors would hold." He gets up and moves to the window wearing pajama bottoms and no top as usual. "Especially if there are others as strong or stronger than that one tonight." He is completely unaware of the shear horror on Sarah's face mainly because his back is to her.

She watches him cross the room to the window, and when he stops at the window, she asks with fear dominating her voice. "What do you mean the steel doors won't stop them? Do we need thicker doors, more voltage into the steel, or something else?"

Dave doesn't turn around; he just looks out the window into the darkness and calmly continues the conversation, "No, the beast had the whole door frame moving when it hit the door. Granted it took several hits to get the frame to move, but it did move."

As he is speaking, he sees the stray cat from earlier move into the street that is lit by the streetlight. The cat stops and stares into the shadowy area under the tree across the street so he to watches the shadows as he speaks. The cat appears to be taking a defensive stance and is still very closely watching those shadows.

Sarah realizes he is looking at something because of the way he's looking out the window very focused. Not like most nights where he goes and just stares out the window at nothing or trying to see something. "What are you looking at out there, or would I rather not know?"

Dave stays focused on the cat and the shadows. "A cat in the street." Sarah gets up and joins him at the window. "A what, where?"

He points out the shadows that the cat is watching and they both keep watch with the cat. They also watch the cat at the same time, as best as possible.

The cat starts backing away from the area while continuing to watch the shadow. The cat arches its back. Dave and Sarah both simultaneously look to the shadowy area under the tree. They see movement, they can't tell what it is moving, but they can tell it's big.

The large object steps into the light cast by the streetlamp. It's walking upright on two legs, but it looks like a dog, a very large dog.

Sarah is so scared, not just for Dave and herself but for the cat, as well. She can't even scream, as much as she wants to, she is scared to the point of staring in silence.

Dave looks at her and quietly puts a finger to his lips making the "be quiet" sign but not sounding it out. Sarah sees the motion and gives a nod in acknowledgement.

They both watch the beast that they both know is a werewolf.

The werewolf is focused on the cat. It starts to slowly lower its upper body forward, reaching for the ground and never breaking eye contact with the cat.

Dave is amazed at what he is witnessing and is wishing he had his video recorder within reach so he could record this. He has no idea who, if anyone would believe him, there is no recording of the beast being on all fours, there are rumors but nothing verifiable.

Once on all fours the beast starts to crouch for the attack as a dog preparing to attack its favorite toy. When settled into position the werewolf looks up at Dave and Sarah, making eye contact with both of them. Sarah instantly screams, loud and long. Dave considers plugging his ears with his fingers but instead watches the beast with the curiosity of a scientist. The question on Dave's mind is. Who is the target the cat or us? Is the cat merely a diversion to make us think we are safe?

The cat takes advantage of the beast's attention being elsewhere and runs to the nearest tree.

The werewolf, still looking at Dave and Sarah, licks its lips as dogs do so commonly. Then looks at the cat running and springs toward the cat in the same instant.

The cat narrowly dodges the beast's snout by jumping to one side while running.

The werewolf tries to adjust as quickly as the cat but instead looks clumsy. Dave tries not to laugh at the site of the cat making the beast look big and clumsy.

Dave continues to watch not as a spectator but as a scientist trying to get some information on the creature that kills any who view it and the beast is killed on site.

Sarah on the other hand is openly routing for the cat with every breath.

The cat is completely unaware of the audience watching its attempt to survive.

The cat makes it to the tree by jumping the last couple of feet landing on the trunk and climbing almost instantly.

The werewolf jumped at the cat while airborne but once again missing his target.

The werewolf turns and watches the cat climb the tree. Then turns to look at Dave and Sarah again. Dave got the impression, just to see if they were still watching, but then thinks why would a beast, a werewolf, which is apparently more beast or wolf than human… or is it? Why would it keep looking at us? Dave continues thinking is it wanting us to do something? Is it looking for approval? Dave's thoughts keep going trying to answer any of these questions and observing the beast with the cat. Sarah though is not only watching but she is a bit more exited, or perhaps animated would describe her better. The way she is bouncing around as if trying to control the cat with her body movements.

The werewolf sees Dave and Sarah are still watching at the window and the look it gives is like excitement, pleasure, and a large dose of Evil, shining in the eyes. It appears to acknowledge them with a wink, but Dave isn't sure due to the poor lighting in the street and does not ask Sarah figuring she is worried enough. The beast turns back to find the cat sitting on a branch approximately twenty feet of the ground looking down at it. The werewolf stands upright on its hind legs and reaches for the cat falling short of course.

The cat hisses at the attempt and gets ready to strike at its aggressor.

The werewolf jumps up at the branch but makes no attempt to grab the cat or the branch. The cat turns to face the trunk of the tree again. The beast jumps again this time harder and mouth wide open. Dave figures the cat is a snack this time. The cat jumps onto the trunk and climbs to a higher branch as the beast's jaw is clamping down on the limb. The cat narrowly escapes the grasp of the jaws again but this time the teeth had more than air to grab and it bit through the three-inch branch effortlessly. The beast and the branch fell to the ground without the cat who is now perched on a higher branch looking down at the werewolf again. Neither one makes a sound just looking at each other, as if sizing up the other. The beast empties its mouth while watching the cat, giving Dave the thought of more human than beast in that moment as it watched its target while doing something in preparation, to catch the cat.

Dave and Sarah are starting to think the cat is safe for the night, but to their amazement the werewolf starts climbing the tree. Not as graceful as the cat but easier than a human. It doesn't reach around the tree as a bear or a human would but instead digs its claws into the tree as a cat. It's tearing the bark off the tree and leaving deep gouges in the trunk.

Dave is watching this canine beast climb a tree and is really regretting not having his video recorder within reach. Who would actually believe this? He knows he wouldn't if someone were to tell him of this ability. He would admit the possibility of the beast being able to climb, but not believing it until it can be proven.

The beast is now within reach of the cat. As the beast reaches for the cat, the cat goes around the tree and heads down the opposite side. The beast growls at its missed attempt again. It sees the cat running across the road toward Dave and Sarah's house.

The beast jumps out of the tree from about twenty-five feet, Dave estimates, and it lands on two feet upright. Then starts running, and as it's running, the beast lowers itself to all fours and its speed increases greatly. It catches up to the cat and reaches out to grab the cat with its muzzle, the cat narrowly makes it to Dave and Sarah's garage. It runs through an opening at the base of the garage door, the cat did lose some hair off its tail where the beast actually grabbed its tail. Just the tip of the tail is all it managed to grab. The cat did lose hair off its tail and got some scratches from the teeth of the beast.

The beast realized where it is at and who's garage it is. The beast stopped short of the door trying not to touch it, remembering the basement door and being shocked. It turned its head to avoid the garage door not wanting shocked again. Instead, it backs away and lays down watching the whole the cat went in and just lays there quietly.

Sarah looks at Dave. "Do you think the cat made it to a safe place?"

Dave starts walking toward the door as he answers, "Don't know, but they went through the driveway, and the cameras are on and recording."

Dave goes straight to the basement lab and Sarah follows not saying a word.

Once they get to the video screens, they see the werewolf is laying in the drive watching the garage. Dave tells Sarah to watch him while he checks the recording. Dave transfers the image to another monitor to view the recording without disturbing the images that are still being recorded. He finds the cat being chased and the narrow escape that was pulled off, he shows Sarah the recording of the cat escaping, and she is relieved to know the cat is safe.

Sarah starts for the stairs to go back to bed and realizes Dave is not following her, so she goes back to him and just stands quietly behind him.

He's checking further back in the recording and finds that one camera recorded the beast trying to get the cat in the tree and the beast climbing the tree. Thinking out loud, he says, "This is great. I got it all." He saves it to the computer to transfer to disk later.

Now he stands there still unaware of Sarah behind him, looking at the cooler and the monitor with the image of the beast watching the garage and thinks aloud in a normal tone. "Why are you still here? What is your connection to her? What possibly could she mean to you? Are you even the same one from earlier?"

Sarah speaks up now with a raised voice from anger and disgust at him still standing there. "You can ponder those questions tomorrow; right now, we need to get to bed. Besides, I don't think it's going to answer you, at least not in a manner that we would understand. It can't even hear us, so you may as well just save your breath."

To their amazement, the beast sits up as a dog and looks straight into the camera and nods yes. Sarah's mouth just drops in amazement and Dave smiles at the prospect that this creature may be able hear and understand them.

Dave keeps watching the monitor as he asks in a volume comparable to Sarah, "Can you hear me?"

The beast nods in a yes motion and continues to look at the camera.

Sarah can't believe what she is seeing, and she doesn't want to believe it either.

"Dave, stop, this has gone far enough." The fear in her voice is unmistakable.

The beast shakes its head side to side as if to disagree with her.

Dave smiles. "I agree not far enough."

Sarah, not knowing what else to do and not wanting to see anymore, says, "I'm out of here; this is just ridiculous, and I'm not taking part in it any longer." She then leaves and heads for the stairs.

Dave never looks away from the screen. "Night, dear." She does not respond, and he hears her going up the steps.

He continues with the experiment and asks, "Was this female special to you?"

The beast simply nods yes.

Dave's amazement grows and the scientist in him urges him to continue. "Was she a sister?"

The beast responds no.

"Was she perhaps a mate?"

The response surprises Dave. The answer is yes. Dave thought it possible, but now there is no doubt.

"Is that why you tried so hard to get in here tonight?" Dave figured its worth asking curiosity urges the question more than anything else.

The beast looks at the camera, and Dave wonders if it heard him but before he can ask again, he gets the answer. Yes, then a pause, and he thinks about another question and the beast shakes its head no.

Now Dave is confused. "What do you mean… yes or no?"

He gets the same response yes and no, but this time its head is making a circular motion as it responds.

Dave thinks and asks, "Do you mean maybe?"

The beast nods yes with no delay.

Dave looks at the screen, a bit puzzled at the response and his curiosity continues to urge him to keep going even after he realizes it is now midnight.

Dave asks, "What do you mean? Maybe either she was or wasn't your mate?"

The beast just stares at the camera not moving or making a sound.

Dave then asks, "Was that an attempt to recover your mate?"

The beast nods yes and no again.

Dave's patience is starting to wear thin and begins to be reflected in his voice. "Alright, what is with the maybe? She is the only one in here."

The beast nods no, then licks its muzzle.

Dave isn't sure he wants to ask the next question. "Was you after me, as well?"

The answer doesn't really surprise him, but it does concern him; the answer is yes.

Dave decides to end this now. "Okay, last question: We've established that was you at the door. We also know that you were after her and me. But why me? Is it because the bodies come to me?"

Yes is the motion made. With the response done, the beast gives one more look at the garage then gets up and walks away upright on two legs.

Dave saves the recording and makes sure he has the questions written down in the order they were asked. There are more questions floating around in his head, but they will have to wait and see if the opportunity occurs again. He looks around the basement and realizes that a window to the driveway was slightly open. "So, that is how you heard me, sad I was thinking your hearing was much better than that, but then to it's a relief to know your hearing has limits."

Dave leaves the window open and double checks the locks and turns off the lights on his way upstairs. As he's locking the basement door, he remembers he still is not carrying a pistol. He shrugs his shoulders and thinks out loud, "Oh, well, we should be safe for the night." He continues on to bed.

Once in the bedroom, the lamp on his side of the bed was left on for him. As he lays down and turns off the light, all the thoughts and events from the night are still going strong in his mind. He is thinking about old theories and which ones were dismissed tonight.

# Chapter 2

# The Accident Victim

Dave lays there with his thoughts listening to the sounds of the night that are so common now. He listens to the barking and the howling of werewolves and domestic dogs of all breeds. But they sound different tonight. But what is the difference? He lays there and listens and decides they sound sad tonight as if they are grieving. But could it be, is it possible that they are grieving the death of the female beast? He knows that animals do grieve but not to the extent of tonight. He finally drifts off to sleep listening to the beast's vocalizations of the night.

The alarm goes off at five o'clock, and Dave gets up and goes downstairs to the kitchen and starts the coffee pot, then goes back upstairs to get dressed for work.

Dave is still tired as it was almost one o'clock 'til he got to sleep.

Like any other morning, it's quiet outside as sunrise is close. Dave looks out the bedroom window and can see the fallen tree branch that the beast bit through trying to get the cat. He knows that it was real and not a dream. He continues getting dressed for work and looks out the window at various times. As the sun lights up the street, he can see more damage. The neighbor's wooden fence across the street is broken; it looks like something went through it. Some neighbors have yard damage, though it's hard to see what may have caused the damage. He speculates that the beast from his driveway is the guilty party for the destruction, though he has no proof and did not even hear anything let alone see it happen.

When he is dressed, he kisses Sarah and goes downstairs. The coffee is done, so he pours a cup then gets a bowl of cereal for breakfast. When he finishes his cereal, he fills a travel mug with coffee for the ride to work. He finishes his cup of coffee, then heads to the garage with his travel mug and removes the basement door from in front of the garage door. He opens the garage door and gets into his car and leaves for work.

The ride to work is as peaceful as any other morning, but he can't shake the feeling that something is wrong. He sees more than usual, things that had been there for six months or longer now seem out of place for some unknown reason. So, he sips at his coffee and continues on to work trying not to dwell on the odd feeling he has this morning.

He pulls into the parking lot at the hospital and finds a parking spot. Once the car is parked, he grabs his mug and heads in. On his way to his work area, he greets everyone from doctors to the janitorial staff with a hello. There are a few that do not return the greeting, but he continues to greet them anyway.

He gets to his workstation and gets signed in for the day. Then he checks to see what is on the schedule for testing.

He begins the first test promptly at seven o'clock… no later and no sooner. Start time is seven, so he spends the few minutes before preparing for the day.

At about five minutes after seven, Dave's supervisor comes out with someone new.

The supervisor looks at him. "Dave, put down what you're doing and greet your new assistant, Ashley Marie Thomas."

Dave doesn't even look up or stop what he is working on. "First of all, Allen, you know I'm not going to stop a test I've already started, especially to greet someone that may not even last a month here, let alone with me. If she is to work with me, she needs to get used to it now." He pauses and looks up at them. "Don't you agree?"

Ashley answers, "I do agree."

Dave acknowledges her with a nod and goes back to work.

Allen looks at Ashley. "This is your workstation; sorry about your partner, but it's the only opening we have. If you have any problems, you know where my office is."

Ashley thanks him and continues, "I'll be fine. I've dealt with people like him before."

Dave does not look up or acknowledge her remark and keeps his smile to himself.

So, with that said, Allen wishes her luck and goes to his office.

Once Allen leaves, Ashley asks, "What can I do to help?"

Dave doesn't look up as he responds, "Start the test on the next sample; the paperwork is with the sample." He looks at her. "You do know how to read the test request form, don't you?"

Ashley responds with the same attitude he used, "I use to be able to read them, but this looks Greek to me. I can read English and Spanish."

Dave smiles as he looks back to his sample. "Okay, as long as you can read."

Ashley picks up the sample and the paperwork for the tests and begins the tests.

Like Dave, she doesn't look up from her work when she speaks, "Dave, right?"

Dave simply responds, "Yes."

She continues, "My friends call me Ash, but you can call me Ashley Marie, seeing how we are not friends."

Dave smiles and continues with his job. "Very well, and you can call me Dave. I'm not too fond of being called David."

Ashley asks, "Are you David Stone?"

Dave responds, "Yes, why do you ask?"

Ashley tries not to sound star struck. "Well, I've wanted to work with you since I've heard about you and the research that you do."

Dave looks at her. "What research is that?"

She smiles and looks at him. "The werewolf research. Or dog man, as some are called."

Dave still working, says, "I don't do that here, and I'm not sure I need help. Besides, I can't pay an assistant."

Ashley continues working. "Well, I'm not asking for a paycheck. That's why I work here; I just want to help you find the cure."

Frank speaks up, "Ah, excuse me, miss, but I work at the station right there behind you, and I couldn't help but overhear you mention finding 'the cure.' Don't let him sucker you into believing that nonsense. You're too pretty and too young to waste your life and your career as David did."

Ashley looks at him as she speaks, "Wait one minute, old man. I'll decide what I want to study. And as for my age, yes, I'm younger than you but the same age as Dave."

Dave had stopped working to stand up for Ashley, not knowing she would do it herself. He is impressed with her. Most new people don't stand up to Frank. A lot of people that worked with him for several years still don't stand up to him when he challenges.

Dave knows Frank is getting ready to say more so he speaks first. "Frank, you should just stop and walk away. She just demonstrated to the entire lab that she will not back down from you. And she doesn't need me or anyone else to fight a battle for her, so just go back to work."

Frank gets irritated. "So, why are you speaking up now, David?"

Dave keeps his calm, which bugs Frank even more. "Because she doesn't know you and that you hate it when someone stands up to you to defend themselves and that she doesn't need me or anyone else to fight a battle for her, so just go back to work."

Frank looks at Ashley, then back to Dave. "You know, David, this is not over yet."

Dave smiles. "I know."

Frank goes back to his workstation.

Ashley looks at Dave and, with a hint of anger in her voice, says "Thank you, but I could have handled that myself."

Dave looks at her. "I know, but he will not give up. You need to be working instead of arguing with him or anyone else."

Ashley's anger is getting harder to hide. "So, I should let them win? I shouldn't defend myself, my believes, friends, family?"

Dave still calm, says, "No, I'm not suggesting that. Just be more careful about when and where."

Ashley apologizes for getting angry at him.

Dave looks back down to his work. "It's okay; you're new, and I've seen new people argue with Frank and get fired by the end of the week because they wouldn't stop. Frank or the other person. See, Frank has been here longer than any of us… even Allen. Frank was offered the supervisor position and turned it down saying he didn't want the headache."

Ashley asks, "How old is he anyway?"

Dave pauses a second. "He's pushing retirement age; that's the best guess I can give. I've never asked and was never that interested to know. But what I've heard over the years, I figure late fifties, early sixties."

Ashley smiles. "So, he's at least old enough to be our father."

Dave looks up. "Yeah, but I think I would have run away from home as a teenager."

They both laugh and continue talking while they work.

A few minutes before lunch, a nurse brings in some samples to Dave and Ashley's table, saying that these samples are to be rushed.

Dave points to a space on the table and tells her to put the samples there and they will get to them after lunch.

The nurse gets irritated with his response but manages to stay calm. She repeats herself and emphasizes the urgency of these samples. "Dave, I was told to give these to you for immediate testing. The state police requested you by name and need these results now."

Dave wonders why he was requested by name anyone can rush the tests they want. He looks up from his current test. "What's so important about these samples?"

The nurse is thinking she is getting through to him. "These samples are from an accident victim that was dead on scene. Apparently, he hit a tree at a very high rate of speed."

Dave is getting curious now. "Okay, is the officer's badge number, name, and contact phone number on the paperwork?"

The nurse is now insulted, as well as irritated, and it starts to show in her voice. "Of course, you fool, do you think this is my first time?"

Dave looks at her and tries to keep his temper in check. "No. I've seen you in here before, but I could see about making this your last trip in here."

The nurse puts her hands on her hips. "You don't have the authority."

Dave smiles. "You're right, but I know who does."

Allen has been standing behind the nurse from the time she walked by his office and has listened to the entire conversation.

The nurse is completely unaware of Allen as her full attention is on the conversation with Dave. "Who do you know with that authority?"

Allen speaks up, "Me."

The nurse's expression changes instantly. It goes from a cocky confidence to an "oh, nuts, it can't be." But she recognizes the voice as Allen and is hopeful she's wrong. She knows that all work orders are to go through Allen and didn't give this one to him, and she's not sure what his response will be. Yeah, she's heard rumors of the consequence but never knew anyone whom he has dealt with for ignoring his rules. That is until now, and she will learn it first hand and not through the grapevine.

Dave and Ashley just smile as the nurse slowly turns to face who is behind her and find out for sure if it is Allen. As if the look on Dave and Ashley's face left any doubt as to whom it could be.

The nurse looks at Allen. "Oh, Allen, nice to see you. When did you get back from lunch?" Sounding cheerfully surprised and as convincing as she can be, especially when she saw him in his office sitting at his desk.

Allen doesn't even pretend to buy her ignorance defense; instead, he looks at her and very sternly says, "Cut the bull; you completely bypassed my office intentionally… you and I both know it. I watched you walk by, and you even looked into my office. As well as you know, I eat my lunch at my desk for this exact reason."

The nurse takes on an apologetic tone. "Sorry, but the state troopers asked for Dave specifically to do the testing. They told me to give the samples directly to Dave and nobody else."

Allen remains firm. "I royally don't give a flying fig what they told you. You've been in here enough to know that even special requests and rushed requests still come to me. They have other samples to test that went through my office."

The nurse keeps her apologetic tone but adds some confidence. "Sorry, Allen, but I'm doing as I was told. They want a full test done, everything they said, and they were certain Dave would understand the request. They want to know why he would take on a large oak tree with a jeep wrangler at an estimated speed well over one hundred mile per hour. They were amazed the man is still in one piece."

Dave's curiosity rises with the more he hears, and some ideas are forming as to why he was requested by name.

Allen tells the nurse, "They will get to the sample after lunch and not before they finish the samples they are currently testing."

The nurse decides not to continue arguing as she figures her point got across. She agrees and hands Allen the samples and paperwork. "Thank you, Allen." She then leaves the lab and returns to the emergency room where she is to be for her shift.

Even though the nurse sounded agreeable and nicer when she thanked Allen her body language displayed her anger for all to see as she walked away.

Allen tells Dave and Ashley to go to lunch and Dave can show Ashley how to rush sample tests and to get to this sample after lunch.

Dave and Ashley finish the tests they were working on then go to lunch.

By this time in the day, they found out they are the same age with the small chat they would engage in through the day. They also discovered Dave was born and raised in Pennsylvania while Ashley was born and raised in Wyoming. She moved to Pennsylvania for the job and applied because of the opportunity to work with him. They also both believe in a cure for the werewolf and that the cure isn't death they just haven't found what they need yet.

On the way to the cafeteria, Ashley looks at Dave and thinks he seems occupied on a thought. But then she just met him today, so she doesn't speak up, instead she continues with the small talk. She asks, "Is Allen usually like that if someone doesn't give him the test samples directly?"

Dave appears to have not heard her but then he answers but doesn't look at her. "Yeah, he can be worse, depending on how many times the individual passed his office."

Ashley uses a joking voice, "Oh, you are listening? I thought you were lost in a thought."

Dave simply answers without looking at her again, "I am."

Ashley looks at him and asks, "Want a second opinion?"

Dave gives her a brief look and then looks away before answering, "Not yet. I'm still thinking and trying to figure this out. I don't even know how to word a question from my thoughts yet."

Ashley takes offense to the remark and wants to hit him but instead tries to hide it. "Okay, but remember you have a partner now that you can talk to."

He looks at her. "Thanks. I forgot that I could talk to you. Done this by myself for a while, ya know."

Ashley smiles. "I understand."

They go through the line in the cafeteria and get their lunch and as they get to a table Dave asks, "Where are you staying?"

Ashley smiles and responds with a flirtatious voice but trying to keep a joking tone, "Why are you asking?"

Dave finishes sitting down all at once and lands on the chair, hard. "Oh, sorry, I don't mean any offense. I was just wondering if you're with family, friends, or a rental."

Ashley laughs a little. "It's okay, I'm actually staying at Big Daddy'Os Hotel just outside of town."

Dave looks down at the table, trying not to choke on his food and shakes his head in disagreement.

She gets curious and concerned at his apparent disapproval of her choice in hotels. "Is there a problem with the hotel? Is there a better hotel?" She's trying to look into his face by getting hers closer to the table as he has not looked up yet.

Dave doesn't look up as he pulls out his cell phone and turns it on as he speaks to her "Well, I'm not sure how much my opinion will mean to you."

Ashley, still concerned, says, "More than you know; you're from the area and know what is or isn't safe."

Dave lays his phone on the table and looks at her. "Well, I need to run my idea past my wife first and make sure she is okay with it and not blindsided. Besides, you should be safe in the hotel for at least one more night."

Ashley's gaze followed his when he looked up, her eyes open a little wider at his response and her concern mixes with fear. "What do you mean safe enough. at least one more night."

Dave looks at his phone as he accesses the numbers in his contact list and speaks with an emotionless tone. "Well, I'm not sure how to say this nicely or softly, so I'll just say it. Hotels in general seem to be unable to prevent attacks. The beasts pull the bars off the windows or bust through the door or a wall. But you should be safe for at least tonight because the beasts shouldn't know your helping me yet."

Ashley is confused. "What does me helping you have to do with my safety? And where would I stay if not in a hotel?"

Dave pushes the call button as he found the number he was looking for. "I'm working on the place to stay. As for helping me affecting your safety…" He stops there because his call went through and was answered.

Sarah wonders who is calling at lunchtime as everyone knows Dave works today and she don't normally get calls in the day. So, she looks at the caller ID and sees Dave's cell number and wonders why he would be calling because that isn't normal for him to call at lunch break or at all in the day.

Sarah answers the phone with curiosity and caution in case of an accident and his phone is being used to call her. "Hello."

"Hello, Sarah, it's Dave."

Sarah isn't sure whether to be mad or not. "Okay. What's going on that your calling in the middle of the day?"

Dave remains pleasant. "I got a new partner at work today."

Sarah now begins to get irritated, "Okay, and this affects me how? Usually, you wait 'til you get home to tell me that kind of news."

Dave simply responds, "Well, she needs a place to stay. She's currently in a hotel and has no friends or family in the area."

Sarah gets more irritated and starts moving toward anger. "So, why should I care if she's in a hotel or not? And would you even be asking if she was he?"

Dave is offended by her question and tries not to show it as he has learned it just encourages her to continue. "Actually, I would if I could stand to be around the individual and he had no place to stay."

Sarah, "Okay, and I'm supposed to believe you no questions just blind faith. How many times in the past have you made this request?"

Dave doesn't hesitate, "I haven't because they either had a house rented, an apartment or was staying with friends or family and not in a hotel, let alone the Big Daddy'Os Hotel."

Sarah is surprised and loses some of the anger in her voice. "Is that really the hotel she's staying at?"

Dave hears an opening in her voice. "Yes, dear, that is where she is really staying."

Sarah says, "But they have the worst safety record for guests in the area. Why in pray tell would she choose to stay there?"

Dave remains calm. "I suppose the same reason everyone else does; she didn't have that information. And most likely cost."

Sarah shakes her head as if he could see her. "Would she be helping you in the lab at home?"

Dave says, "Maybe; we haven't discussed that yet."

Sarah's anger is almost gone. "What is her name?"

Dave allows a small smile. "Ashley."

Sarah holds on to her partial anger. "I can't believe that I'm going to say this aloud. I'll probably regret this, but I suppose she can have the spare room."

"Now, why would you regret helping someone?" Dave's curiosity is more obvious than fishing for information about her mistrust in him.

Sarah's tone doesn't change. "I'll see even less of you now. Because now you'll have help in your lab, and I'll probably have to take your meals to you in the lab."

Dave tries to ease her concerns a bit. "But you do that now. I don't foresee too many, if any, changes happening."

Sarah does not relax her concerns. "I do. I foresee you and Ashley talking about lab work upstairs in the living room while relaxing, in the dining room at the supper table, and I'm left out of the whole conversation."

Dave didn't realize just how deep her jealousy ran. "Honey, I include you in those discussions as much as you allow me to. Instead of walking away from it and our guest at the time join in the conversation and be sociable. Instead of making me come up with an excuse, why you walk away."

Sarah is offended and mad that he would point that out. "How dare you? I don't leave when you include me in those conversations."

Dave doesn't stop, "Should we call Dewight or how about Carla or any number of people we've had over?" He was maintaining his temper and keeping his voice at a normal level.

Sarah is still steaming over the fact that he is pointing this out to her but decides to drop it anyway. "Alright, fine, I still say that I don't do that, but I'm not continuing this argument over the phone or this call for that matter. Bye!" The line goes dead, and he turns off his phone and puts it away.

He looks at Ashley as he turns off and puts his phone in his pocket. "Well, she agreed to let you have the spare room."

Ashley speaks cautiously out of fear of offending the one person she has wanted to work with for a long time, ever since she found out about him and his studies four years ago. "Your call seemed like she wasn't too enthusiastic about a house guest."

Dave looks at his watch as he finishes chewing a bite of food before speaking. "No. It's not so much her objecting to a guest. It's an objection to a female guest and that I work with you here and perhaps at the house, as well. I knew she was jealous, but I didn't know the extent or how far she was willing to go."

With a mix of concern and curiosity in her voice, she says, "What do you mean?"

"Well," Dave begins and is thinking how to explain as he speaks, "My wife Sarah has thought for years now that I've been having an affair. She just will not say it or even whom she suspects. Now it's looking like she may be willing to sacrifice someone else's safety due to her mistrust."

It's harder for Ashley to eat as her concern grows. "What do you mean sacrifice someone's safety?"

Dave checks his watch again. "It's time to head back to the lab. I'll try to explain on the way."

As they get up from the table, Ashley says, "You'll need to do better then try." Dave responds with a nod in agreement.

They dump their trash and return their trays and head toward the lab.

Once in the hall, Ashley waits for Dave to start explaining.

Dave begins speaking when Ashley is ready to ask again. Still thinking as he speaks, he begins to explain, "My wife is willing to allow you to stay at the hotel knowing full well that it's the one with the worst safety record for guests in the area. I believe it's mainly because of her jealousy. If I knew how to put her mind at ease, it would undoubtedly fix a lot that is wrong. Most likely not everything, but a lot of it anyway. She may even begin to trust me again."

Ashley stops and grabs him by the arm to stop him and get his attention, as well. "Maybe in return for the generous invitation to stay, I can help you in that area."

Dave looks down and shakes his head in disapproval and begins walking again. "I don't even know if she's interested in saving anything between us. I mean, one minute she's acting like she wants to work through whatever it is, and then the next she acts like she doesn't care and is very mistrusting again."

Ashley steps in front of Dave just before going into the lab. "Do you spend more time with your wife or with your experiments?"

He looks at her a bit confused and again thinking while speaking, "Well, I do try to even out the time with both and more with Sarah when I can. I thought that she understood that she was more important to me than the experiments. Besides, I had that conversation with her, and she said that she understood and was okay with it as is."

Ashley smiles slightly. "We'll find out; something must be bothering her the way you have described her."

Dave returns the slight smile. "I agree, but she will not discuss it with me."

Ashley's smile remains the same, "Maybe some girl talk will help."

His smile relaxes. "Maybe, but I wouldn't hold my breath if I were you."

Her smile relaxes as well now. "Okay, oh, and you may now call me Ash."

His smile returns larger than before. "Thank you."

Seeing him smile makes her smile, as well.

Dave looks at her as the smile leaves his face. "When we are done here, we need to get you packed and out of the hotel quickly."

She just simply nods an agreement, and they walk into the lab and to their workstation, where the samples and the paperwork are still waiting for them.

They look at the request form, and Ashley starts the tests for drugs while Dave does the tests for poisons.

While waiting for those tests to finish, Dave looks at a sample of blood under the microscope. For nothing more than to settle his own curiosity and perhaps the officers, as well.

He sees something, but he's not sure, so he increases the magnification and focuses on the sample. He looks more intently and is shocked not amazed at what he sees. It was, after all, suspected.

Dave is trying to hide his excitement as he calls Ashley over. "Ash, you need to see this."

Frank turns his head slightly to listen without them knowing.

Ashley is confused as to why he would call her over to the microscope. "Okay," and she looks in the microscope at the sample.

Still trying to hide his excitement, Dave asks, "Do you see the anomaly in this man's blood?"

Now she knows what she is looking for, "Yeah, yeah, I see it, but what is it I've never seen it before."

It's harder for him to hold his excitement as she looks up at him. "It's the dormant stage of a werewolf, or the human stage, if you prefer." With the largest smile Ashley has ever seen on anyone, let alone Dave, up to this point, he says, "That is the anomaly that I have only seen in the blood of known werewolves; it's similar in both forms with a little difference but close enough to say the same creature."

Her eyes, then her whole face light up with the same enthusiasm as Dave; actually, more as this is her first time seeing werewolf blood at all in any form. She's just better at hiding it than Dave is.

Dave asks her to get the results of the other tests while he verifies the discovery for sure.

While Ashley gets the results, Dave searches his briefcase for his notes and finds the notebook as Ashley retrieves the last of the results.

Dave compares his notes to what he found under the microscope, then asks Ashley to do the same. They agree that what they saw matches the notes.

They check the results of the other tests to rule out other possibilities for the accident, then Dave looks at the time.

It's about two o'clock, and Dave decides to run one more test just to verify the conclusion that is suspected.

They begin the final test to identify the DNA structure in the sample, just to label the blood, human, animal, or both with no further identification desired. He does a DNA test because a test that he has developed is not approved for use to identify Werewolf infection in blood samples. The FDA still has not approved it and therefore the hospital will not permit the test to be done. But DNA will at least tell him if the blood is human or "contaminated" with something else.

While waiting for the test results, Frank tries to pay attention to them and their conversation without them knowing. He manages to succeed as they are so focused on the test that they are not aware of him listening in.

Dave is explaining that time is of the utmost importance tonight. "If this is what I think, we need to get the body to the house and into the basement as quickly as possible. You'll leave your car here, and we will take mine."

"Why would I leave my car?" she asks curiously.

Dave responds, "My car is faster, and the police know my car."

She looks at him. "Oh, and what makes you think my car is slow?"

Dave looks at her. "I didn't say your car is slow; I said my car is faster, unless yours can do two hundred-plus, we take mine."

Ashley is caught off guard. "Sorry, I've never had a reason to find out if it's capable of that kind of speeds. I highly doubt that it would go that fast anyway."

The test result is ready. As Dave retrieves the results, he continues, "Good. Now that we have that out of the way, we will take my car and get yours tomorrow."

As Dave looks at the results, he begins to smile. He shows Ashley, and her mouth drops in amazement.

Ashley asks while looking at the results, "How did you know?"

Dave just keeps smiling. "Experience, my dear. I've looked at these samples for six years, now almost seven."

She looks at him. "This is the first time for me to even see the DNA structure on paper, not to mention the anomaly through a microscope. Now what do we do?"

Dave gathers all the results while keeping his smile. "Now we go to Allen with everything."

They take everything to Allen's office and present him with their findings. Allen looks at the results as they stand there waiting. He looks at them and says, "They're all negative."

Dave leans in and points to the DNA test. "Not all were negative."

Allen looks at the test and isn't happy at all; not entirely angry with them but still disappointed and that is coming through in his voice. "This shows a contamination with canine origin. Besides, who ordered this test?"

Dave very politely answers, "It's in the request form, and it's also a new law that anyone shot dead, a suicide, or killed in a car accident must have this test performed ASAP. You also know that we do not have a complete structure of werewolf in human form. This test always comes back as contaminated."

Allen just blankly looks at Dave. "Okay, so, I guess that means you will need to leave early and take the body with you?"

Dave just keeps smiling. "It would be greatly appreciated. I will need Ashley released at the same time as I am her way home tonight."

Allen is a bit confused as why she is riding with him. "Okay, how early and why Ashley?"

So, Dave gives a brief explanation, "I spoke with Sarah and Ashley is going to use our guest room and work with me in my lab at home. So, it is important that she leaves when I do."

Allen picks up the phone as he responds, "Three thirty you may leave, and I'll call the morgue and have the body released to you when you get there."

They both thank Allen and head back to work.

Frank is at their workstation when they return. "So, you found a werewolf, did ya?"

The smile leaves Dave's face. "Yeah, so what of it?"

Frank sounds very sure of himself, "Oh. Nothing, but I suppose you'll be leaving early today, correct?"

"Yeah," he says, wondering what Frank is up to.

Frank doesn't keep him wondering long. "So, that means your new friend will be here alone." He keeps his gaze on Ashley while speaking.

Ashley speaks up, "No, I'm leaving at the same time. I'm going to help Dave with his studies and experiments."

Frank looks at Dave and smiles. "What's your wife think about your new assistant moving in, or haven't you said anything yet?"

Dave smiles. "Sarah is all for it and actually is looking forward to meeting her." Frank is caught completely off guard with that response and is at a loss for a comeback.

Ashley smiles. "Frank, would you excuse us, please? We have work to do."

Frank just turns to walk away, keeping his head low. As he turns, he removes his hands from his pocket, and the knuckles on both hands are bruised and scabbed over.

Upon seeing that, Dave asks, "Frank, aren't you afraid of contaminating yourself with a disease or creating a dirty sample with your scabbed hands?"

Frank stops and looks at his hands and doesn't turn around to answer. "No," he says, then continues to his workstation.

Dave thinks no more about Frank's response. That's Frank, and he has been like that since Dave met him many years ago. He just figures Frank does as he would and doubles his synthetic gloves wearing two pair instead of one.

Dave and Ashley watch the clock as they continue working.

About 3:20, they start cleaning up, and Dave calls the morgue to make sure he is receiving the body.

The morgue director assures him that all the required paperwork is done and awaiting his signature.

Dave politely informs the morgue director that he is done at three-thirty and should be at the loading dock by 3:40 at the latest.

The director agrees. Most people, the morgue director included, have learned not to deny Dave of much especially a body that he is interested in.

At three-thirty, Dave and Ashley clean up their work area. The sample of "contaminated" blood got put into the refrigerator with a label werewolf contamination, then they remove and hang their lab coats on the way out the door. Neither one gives the sample another thought.

Frank speaks up as they reach the door, "Dave, do you expect the body to rise from the dead, or do you just want it for your studies?"

Dave pauses long enough to respond, "Not sure; I'll figure that out later." Then he walks through the door without looking back and before Frank responds. Ashley is through the door, already waiting for Dave.

Frank gives a wave as Dave walks away as if to wave off Dave and/or his response.

Frank's assistant says, "Well, now he's not very polite, is he?"

Frank does not even look at his assistant. "Ah, shut up."

"Neither are you apparently."

They both return to work and restrict their conversation to work only.

In the hallway, Dave and Ashley start walking at a fast pace.

Ashley is trying to keep up but isn't sure about the pace or the reason for it. "Why are we walking so fast?"

Dave doesn't look at her, nor does he slow down as he responds, "Perhaps I wasn't clear earlier when I said time is of the utmost importance tonight. We need to get to my car, get the body, call Diane for a police escort, get your stuff at the hotel, and still have time to unload and set up before dusk."

"Oh." She looks at him, still not fully understanding but figures he's been doing this longer and he knows what he's doing so she goes with him at his pace.

They continue into the parking lot and to the car without speaking.

Once outside Dave turns on his cell phone and continues to the car before calling Diane.

In the car Dave puts the phone in a holder and activates the blue tooth to call Diane. He pushes the speed dial number that is assigned to that office, then backs out of the parking stall as the phone is dialing.

He's headed across the parking lot when the phone is answered at the other end. "Hello, Dave what's up?"

"Diane I'm headed to the morgue to pick up a body that was killed in an accident and has the blood markers to be a werewolf."

"So, why are you calling me? Oh, let me guess… you want a police escort, right?"

Dave has grown accustomed to her remarks and doesn't even pay attention to sarcasm anymore and definitely takes no offense. "Now, Diane, you know me too well. I do need an escort to the house, and I need the officers to meet me at the Big Daddy'Os Hotel. You have the description of my Crown Vic and the plate number and send officers that can keep up."

Greg is standing there and starts laughing. Diane, however, takes offense and tries not to let it show. "Now, wait one minute; an escort is to lead not follow. That is then a pursuit."

Dave stops her there. "Diane, I'm at the dock to receive the body. I need to go."

Diane, regaining her composure, says, "Okay, I'll send the escort to the hotel." There's no response. "Dave, hello, Dave!" The line is dead; she finally gets a dial tone.

She looks at Greg. "He hung up on me."

Greg laughs. "I've heard he does that a lot."

Diane hangs up the phone. "Yeah, but it still gets to me every time he does it."

She then contacts the dispatch to send a pair of officers out to meet Dave, and she specifically asks for a pair of experienced officers.

Dave is out of the car as soon as he pushed the end button on his phone; he didn't wait to see if it disconnected or not.

He was on the dock before Ashley was completely out of the car.

Ashley is coming to the back of the car as the morgue director is pushing the gurney with the body.

Dave calls to Ashley to get her attention. "Ash!" He tosses her the keys as she looks up at him. "Unlock the trunk while I sign the paperwork."

She agrees and opens the trunk of the car.

With the paperwork all signed, the director assists Dave loading the body into the trunk.

The director asks, "What do you think will happen with the body? I assume it's werewolf if you're taking it."

Dave closes the trunk and looks at the director. "I honestly don't know what to expect, but I have a theory I've been wanting to test for a while now. This body is my best chance to test that theory."

The director looks at Dave and nods his understanding. "May I ask as to what that theory may be?"

Dave motions to Ashley to get in the car, and he starts toward the driver door. "You may ask and if I had more time, I'd explain it to you, but I'm short on time now."

The director looks at his watch and nods. "Wow, I guess you are short on time, aren't you? Okay, maybe another time, then, or I'll read it in the paper in a couple of days."

Dave opens the car door as the director is speaking and responds before closing the door. "Thanks for understanding and for your help with the body. Maybe we can speak another time."

Dave starts the car as he closes the door. He puts his seatbelt on as he puts the car in gear and tells Ashley to do the same. She then realizes hers is not on, so she puts it on as the car is starting to move.

Dave tells her to hold on and no screaming as time is short.

She agrees and doesn't question why. But she does look at him confused at his request to not scream and hold on.

Dave pulls away from the dock and gets to the street.

On the street, he accelerates very quickly. The only thing slowing him down is traffic and not being able to pass right away. He waits for a chance to pass and gets a one finger salute a lot and some horns blowing as he passes.

Once on the four-lane highway headed out of town, he weaves in and out of traffic at speeds well above the posted limit. There just happened to be no speed traps this particular afternoon.

From the direction he is coming from to get into the hotel is a U-turn onto the street to the hotel, then a short distance later is a left into the lot.

As the hotel comes into view, he asks, "What is your room number?"

She tells him the number and the location of the room, second floor far end from office.

He tells her to hold on.

She looks at him, and the speed odometer that is currently reading ninety. The concern is obvious in her voice. "You are going to slow down, aren't you?"

Dave smiles and does not take his focus off the road. "Some."

Dave slows enough to take the turn sideways as the intersection is empty, and he didn't need to worry about hitting another vehicle or pedestrian.

As the car is making the corner and he is applying more throttle to power the car through the turn, Ashley is not sure where to hold on to stay in her seat. She holds the dash with her left hand and her seatbelt above her shoulder with her right, saying, "Oh, my" and nothing more. They are through the turn and into the hotel lot before she lets go of anything.

Dave parks in front of the stairs to the second floor and tells her, "Let's go."

They get out of the car and, once again, Ashley is playing catch up. She's just not as fast as Dave, and he is trying to be patient but still trying to get her to understand the importance of hurrying.

In the room, he asks, "What is ready to go? Anything?"

She points to a couple of suitcases in the corner. "I haven't unpacked those yet."

Dave grabs one per hand and heads for the door. "Just hurry; we need to get out of here now. Just throw your stuff in a bag, and let's go."

He takes those two bags to the car and puts them in the back seat, seeing how the trunk is occupied.

He gets back to the room as she is making her final check to make sure she has everything. "That looks like everything. Just these two bags and we're out of here."

Dave smiles. "Good; you travel light, don't you?"

They each grabbed a bag and head for the door.

She answers as they leave the room, "Yeah, I try not to take more than I know I need or that my car can carry."

They laugh and head to the car. "Just throw it in the back seat and get in."

Dave tosses his bag in the back seat and opens the driver door as he closes the back door. Ashley is not that quick. She closes the back door before opening the front door and Dave has the car started before she is in her seat.

He begins to back out of the spot before her door is closed. She is surprised to say the least, and a bit ticked off. "Hey, what's the idea? Let me at least close my door first."

Dave is already out of the spot and looks at her. "Keep your hands and feet clear of the door, and I'll close it." She pulls her hand in, and he floors the throttle, slamming the door closed from the sudden acceleration.

He stops at the office, and she goes in to check out. He tells her to hurry; the sound of the police sirens is audible now and steadily getting louder as they are getting closer very quickly.

The state police escort arrives before she is out of the office.

The driver stops with window down to speak to Dave.

"Are you David Stone?"

"Yes."

The driver smiles at Dave. "Good; we'll turn around and you follow."

Dave shakes his head in defiance. "I need to wait for my assistant. She's checking out now. Then we'll see who follows whom."

The trooper looks at his partner, and they both smile. He looks back to Dave. "So, is it true then? Your car is capable of out running a cruiser?"

Dave smiles slyly. "It's been known to beat newer police cruisers."

The driver and his partner are very excited. "We've wanted to test that for ourselves for a long time since we heard about you beating the rookies."

This pair of officers are in the newer Dodge Charger police interceptor and not a "stock" cruiser.

Ashley comes out the door, and Dave looks at her and back to them. "You better turn around, or you will not stand a snowballs chance in hell to keep up. This is my assistant now."

The trooper looks at Ashley and loses his train of thought until she opens the car door and Dave is reaching for the shifter.

The troopers partner actually nudges him back to reality.

The driver then puts the cruiser in reverse and backs around and puts the car in drive and floors it to stay in the lead. He has heard the stories about Dave's Crown Vic and is not taking chances.

Dave is laughing at the troopers attempt to stay in the lead, so he allows Ashley the time she wants to get in and fasten her seatbelt.

Dave pulls out right behind the cruiser. "Hold on; Diane did good with this escort."

"What do you mean?"

Dave, still smiling and keeping up with the troopers, says, "They actually want to race and make a name for themselves."

Ashley is confused. "What do you mean make a name for themselves?"

As they enter the interstate, Dave explains, "My car is known to outrun police cruisers. They've apparently heard about the rookies, but not the others."

Ashley smiles with the thought of a car the police can't catch. "Is it possible to tighten my seatbelt?" She looks at where it mounts to the side post.

Dave laughs. "No, just hold on, relax, enjoy the ride, and trust that this is not my first time."

She smiles. "Okay, then what?"

He just simply laughs. "Watch this."

They are already doing 130 miles per hour and staying with the cruiser. Dave gets in the passing lane and floors the accelerator. The speed increases to 140 then 150 as they pass the state troopers.

The troopers look at each other in amazement that his car is capable of speeds over 130. The passenger gets on the CB radio as they speed up to pass. "Just how fast can your car go?"

Dave responds, "As fast as I want it to; now don't hold back, or you will not get another chance to pass." Dave allows them to take the lead back.

The troopers are a little embarrassed and a bit ticked. They increase their speed to 170, and Dave is right there. They up it to 190, and he is still there. The driver asks, "Do we go full speed and see if he can keep up?"

The passenger looks at the speed odometer and then behind them. "Go for it. He can keep up at this speed; let's see if he can go full speed." They laugh, and the driver puts it to the floor and maximizes their speed.

Dave keeps up even at full speed when the cruiser has reached its maximum speed.

He tells Ashley to take his phone and call speed dial number two.

Ashley agrees and calls the speed dial number. She put it back in the holder, and the blue tooth is still activated.

Dewight is on patrol and actually sitting in a speed trap when his phone rings. He looks at the caller ID and it's Dave. "Hello, Dave, what do you need?" He hears the police sirens in the background. "I'm not getting you out of a ticket this time. If you want to toy with the staties, then pay the price."

Dave speaks evenly and calmly, "Shut up and listen. I have a body in transit in the trunk of my car. I've got it legally and am taking it to the house. The staties are actually my escort, and I need you to meet us at the Muncy exit."

Dewight is used to Dave and the way he speaks when it is a study subject. "Okay, how soon?"

Dave, still with no emotion, says, "Five minutes or less. We just passed Milton exit."

Dewight is putting stuff away and activating his lights and sirens. "I've told you I need more notice than that." He hangs up and heads that way.

Dave smiles. "We will pass them on the off ramp and not only take the lead but keep it."

Ashley smiles and nods her agreement to his statement, although she isn't sure if he can deliver on his statement. After all, the only car faster than a police cruiser isn't what he is driving, but it's nice to dream, and besides, he said he's done it before.

As he suspected, the trooper started to slow once on the exit ramp onto Interstate 180.

Dave stays in the travel lane and passes them before getting into the exit lane. He doesn't slow down until he gets closer to the actual ramp and needs to slow down for the turn.

The trooper gets on the radio and says, "Dave, you're going too fast for the ramp."

Dave responds, "I know my car and what it can do. How well do you know yours?"

The trooper says, "I thought that was a police interceptor."

Dave chuckles on the radio. "It is with some upgrades that I did."

The troopers look at each other. "What upgrades could you have done to a car that was already upgraded for police work?"

Dave's response is delayed as he is going through the turn on the ramp and has both hands on the steering wheel for control. He begins to accelerate out of the turn and then responds once it is safe to do so. "If one knows where and how to, it is possible to upgrade."

The troopers are coming through the turn, and their tires are squealing through the turn, signaling top safe speed for the turn is very close if not starting to be exceeded.

As they come out of the turn, they begin to accelerate, as well, in an attempt to catch up.

Dave tells Ashley, "I'll let them catch up, then pull ahead." So, he backs his speed down to 190 until the troopers catch up, then like he said, he pulled away as they tried to pass.

Dave gets on the radio and says, "Meet you at the Muncy exit."

The passenger tells the driver, "Floor it; let's go."

The driver watches Dave pull away. "It is floored. This is it; she has no more."

Dave gets on the radio and says, "I have Dewight meeting us at the exit if you just want to head on back to the station."

The troopers say, "No, we were told to escort you all the way home."

Dewight had radioed the office and demanded that the streets be blocked as they come through town.

Dewight sees the exit ramp and is relieved he made it there before Dave. Just then, Dave's car comes down the ramp.

Dewight grabs his radio mic and calls to Dave. "I see you on the ramp. Dave, keep it coming. You're clear at the bottom, no traffic. How close are the state troopers?"

Dave answers, "Thanks, and I can see them in my mirror."

The troopers respond, "Keep moving. We'll catch up."

Dewight responds, "Roger that, and, Dave, I'm going to flip a U-ey right here."

Dave responds, "Okay, do it, and I'll get behind you."

Dewight then gauges the traffic and spins the car around in the middle of the road when safe to do with traffic. He has his tires smoking during the turn spinning the back of the car around and on the throttle to accelerate through the turn. Then trying to get back to a speed that will prevent Dave from rear ending his cruiser.

Dave is slowing down to allow Dewight the time and space he needs, which allows the troopers a chance to catch up. They, in turn, slow to fall in line behind Dave.

Dave decides to harass Dewight a little. "Come on, Dewight, the troopers caught up; let's go."

Dewight gets on the radio. "Okay, Dave, I'm moving as fast as the car can pick up speed. You know, I need to regain my speed, and it's not as quick as your car."

They are getting back up to 190 miles per hour as the roads allow.

Dave laughs. "I know, and I'm sure you're aware I'm just teasing, and we do need to move as time is running out on us."

Dewight is controlling his temper. "I'm aware of the time and the distance and that you enjoy giving me a hard time." He then changes his tone and to whom he is speaking and says, "Dispatch, are the roadblocks ready?"

The dispatcher says, "I've been informed that all are in place."

"Wonderful; we're coming into town now. Dave, we'll be slowing down to seventy as long as I see the roadblocks; otherwise, we slow down more."

Dave shakes his head in disagreement. "Okay, you're leading."

Dewight sees the officers blocking the side streets to allow them to pass without interference. Until he sees the intersection of Main and Route 118, there's no officer visible and no cruiser, either. He immediately slows and is on the radio. "Is anyone at 118?" No response. "Who is at the 118 intersection?" Still no response, and now his temper is no longer hidden.

"Dispatch, you said all were covered!"

Before dispatch can answer, an eighteen-wheeler starts to very slowly pull out into the intersection.

Dewight is immediately on the CB. "Driver, truck driver, stop! Now look to your left and stop!"

The driver stops and responds, "Sorry, didn't know where you were; that's why I progressed so slowly trying to find you."

As they go around the truck, Dewight responds, "That's okay. My people were supposed to be there blocking the road, and I will take it up with them. Thanks for stopping and for holding traffic for us."

The truck driver smiles. "No problem; glad to have been of service. Again, I apologize for not knowing where you were coming from."

The dispatcher gets back to Dewight. "Sorry, but they told me that all roads were covered."

Dewight says, "We'll take that up later. We need to be thankful that it was an eighteen-wheeler and not a car that wouldn't have thought about it and just pulled out."

The other roads were blocked as reported, and the convoy picked up their speed as they headed out of town.

As they approach Picture Rocks, they slow down and make the turn onto the street that Dave lives on.

Once at the house, Dewight pulls ahead, and the troopers stay behind while Dave sets up and then backs into his drive, backing to the exterior basement access.

Dave hands Ashley the keys. "Open the trunk and unload your luggage. Dewight and the troopers will help. I'm going to go around and open the basement. Dewight knows the process and can help unload the body if I'm not out here in time."

She takes the keys. "Okay, are you sure the cops will help?"

As he walks away, he says, "Yes, they don't want to be out here any longer than necessary. Especially this close to dusk. "

Dewight and the troopers getting out of their cars after pulling into the driveway. Dewight is the first in the drive, and he actually backed in as he will guard the troopers when they leave.

Dewight calls to Dave, "Dave, hey, Dave!"

Dave just keeps walking at a fast pace just short of a full run.

Ashley opens the trunk and is in the process of unloading her luggage from the back seat when Dewight and the troopers get to her.

Dewight extends his hand. "Hi, I'm Dewight."

Ashley takes his hand and shakes hands with him. "I'm Ashley. Dave had told me that you and the troopers would be willing to help me unload."

Dewight looks at the troopers and laughs. "He did, did he?"

"Yes, and he also said that you know his procedure for the body." She sounds confident but not too much since she doesn't know the officers and doesn't want to seem disrespectful.

Dewight looks at her. "Well, he usually has the door open when I get here." He looks at the exterior entrance. "Oh, it's already open." Then he realizes it doesn't look right. "Wait. The door is gone."

Ashley looks at the entrance. "I don't know anything about that."

The troopers are looking at the entrance, as well, and one of them sees what might be the door by the garage in the yard. He gets the attention of the others. "Is that the door there?"

Dewight and the troopers start toward the door, and Dave is coming out of the basement.

"Where are you guys going? I told Ashley you would help. Now, let's go. I need this body inside now, and we are losing time and daylight very quickly." Dave is sounding irritated, angry, and disgusted that they would not help.

The officers all walk back to help.

Dewight's curiosity gets the best of him and he asks, "What happened to the door?"

Dave looks at him. "Help me with the body, and I'll tell you."

They reach into the trunk and grab the handles on opposite ends of the body bag and remove the body from the trunk and begin down the steps into the basement.

Dewight is getting impatient waiting for him to explain the door. "Okay, you going to tell me about the door or not?"

Dave looks at him. "I said I would tell you; I didn't say when."

In the basement, Dave says, "Over there in the cell" with a nod of his head.

They place the body on the cot in the cell, and Ashley and the troopers are bringing in her luggage.

Ashley speaks up, "Dave, the car is empty, the trunk is closed, and the luggage is in."

Dave looks at her and gives a nod. "Good. Now we need to get this ready." He unzips the body bag; Ashley comes in to help, and Dewight steps out of the cell and waits.

They get the body out of the bag and place it on the cot in the open and cover the groin with a towel to keep the privates covered. Dave hooks up a heart monitor to the body so they can watch for a heartbeat or see the lack of a heartbeat in this case.

They exit the cell; Dave closes the door and makes sure it's locked.

He sets up and checks an HD video camera to ensure correct placement and focus on the body. The HD capability allows him to see the bruises on the body easily.

As Dave is turning around to face Dewight, he sees the door is still open to the outside. He runs over to the door and closes it.

He looks at everybody. "This door is to be closed when not being used, no matter the time of day."

Dewight looks at Dave and is trying to keep his patience with him but is quickly losing it. "Dave, settle down; it's not quit dusk yet. Besides, you were going to explain the door to the outside."

Dave glares at Dewight and rubs the dents in the door. "Do you see this?"

"Yes." Dewight, trying to figure out where he is going with the obvious damage to the door, says, "Looks like it got hit by something heavy."

Both troopers walk over and start looking at the door.

Dave laughs and points to the door frame where it started to separate from the wall.

"Yeah, it was hit by some*thing* heavy. Repeatedly hit by the same *thing*." Dave is frustrated that the officers are still there.

Dewight says, "What do you mean?"

One of the troopers calls to Dewight, "Dewight, you need to see this."

Dewight and Dave pass going in opposite directions.

Dewight and the troopers look at the damage to the door and discuss what could have caused it. One of the troopers mentions that "the door outside at drive level appeared to have been ripped off the frame."

Sarah had come downstairs and while the officers are looking at the door. Dave introduces his assistant to his wife.

Dave is able to clear most of the frustration and anger from his voice. "Sarah, this is Ashley, my assistant that we spoke about."

Sarah is looking her up and down from head to foot and back. She is being very judgmental as she is looking at Ashley.

Ashley extends her hand and says, "Hi."

Sarah takes her hand, and they shake hands. "You are kinda pretty."

Ashley smiles. "Thank you, so are you."

Sarah gives a sly smile as if she is thinking something else. "Oh, thank you." She's thinking to herself how two-faced Ashley is.

Dewight is looking at the door. "Dave, come here."

Dave turns slowly with an angry look on his face. He heads over. "Yeah, what do you want?"

Dewight rubs the door. "What exactly did this?"

Dave looks at the damaged door. "Do you really want to know or just curiosity?"

Dewight just looks at him. "If I had to guess, I'd say a beast was beating on your door."

Both troopers agree.

Dave answers, "Well, you'd be right. And you know about my theory of beasts existing in daylight. That those are the ones referred to as dog men. That is why the door needs to be closed."

Now Dewight takes the angered look. "Why didn't you call the office or even me directly about the beast beating on your door? And you are yet to prove your theory, so keep that in mind when speaking to new people and even me."

Dave just looks at him. "I didn't need anybody to protect the house, and besides, the door held, and the beast would have been gone by the time you got here."

Dave doesn't acknowledge Dewight's comment about his theory; he just lets it go.

Sarah jumps into the conversation and says, "Hold on. What do you mean you didn't need them to protect the house? I, for one, would have appreciated their help." She isn't hiding her anger in the least.

Dave looks at her. "The door held."

Dewight jumps in. "Barely," he says as he rubs the door frame.

Dave says, "That's fixable."

Sarah is getting angrier now. "What do you mean it's fixable?"

Dave does not raise his voice. "Just what I said… it is fixable. In other words, it can be fixed; repaired, if you prefer."

Dewight steps in between them and says, "Hold on, you can continue the argument after we leave, but right now, Dave I need to know that we will be called next time."

Dave looks at him. "Okay, does that mean you are going to have someone nearby every night and not ten minutes away or more?"

Dewight glares at him. "My officers have a specific route that they are to patrol."

Dave smiles. "Okay, but if I call like last night, the beast may be gone. By the time your officers get here."

Dewight looks at him. "Call anyway. We can at least keep track of their movements and actions, timeframe. All that happy hoo-ha boring stuff. It will help us with our patrols."

Sarah speaks up, "I'll call if he doesn't and if I'm aware of what is going on. Last night I had no clue."

Dewight looks at her and smiles, then looks at Dave. "At least one of you understands the importance of calling us for help and for your safety."

Dave looks at her and smiles. "Suck up."

She smiles and sticks her tongue out at him.

Ashley is trying not to laugh out loud but finds it difficult to hide her smile.

Dewight says, "Now, look, children; enough. Just as long as we get called when and if another beast tries to get in."

Dave and Sarah both agree that they will be called next time.

Ashley joins in, "Dave, you mean a werewolf was beating on the door last night? Is that the beast you guys are referring to?" There is more curiosity is in her voice than fear.

Dave looks at her. "Yes, we refer to werewolves as beasts; it's easier."

Ashley, still with curiosity in her voice, says, "So, you had a werewolf… ah, a beast at the door last night. That is so cool. I wish I could have been here for that."

Dave smiles. "Be patient; you will get to see one up close, possibly closer than you ever expected."

Dewight says, "Hold on. What do you mean she will get to see one up close? What are you not telling me?"

Dave looks at him and smiles. "You know as well as I do that the beast will return. Granted it learned about the door and the electricity in the door. I must say the beast did not like the voltage."

Ashley is smiling as Dave is speaking. Keeping her smile, she says, "Do you have any idea when the beast will return?"

Sarah speaks up, "If it's smart, it will not return. But if it does, and I see it, I will kill it without prejudice. Well, maybe with discrimination but no prejudice about shooting it or where I hit it as long as it dies."

Dave is smiling partly because he knows Sarah will unload into the beast if giving a chance, but to hear her say it is just more than he could keep a straight face for, even though he didn't flat out laugh he was able to keep it to a smile.

He looks at Ashley. "If my expectations are correct, the beast will be back tonight; whether or not we see it is another question. It may decide to stay hidden. After last night, that would not surprise me either."

Dewight calls Dave to the door and says, "Is this what I think it is?"

Dave and Ashley both look at what Dewight is pointing at and look at each other and Ashley speaks up before Dave, "What do you think it is? Dewight, isn't it?" Wanting to make sure she got his name right.

Dave lets out a chuckle and pats her on the back for the question.

Dewight looks at her and shakes his head disapprovingly. "And so it begins. You've already worked with Dave too long; you're starting to sound like him. And, yes, my name is Dewight; thank you for remembering. To answer your question, I believe it to be blood."

Dave puts a finger up toward Ashley as a gesture to not answer and she acknowledges with a nod. Then Dave answers, "It does appear to be blood, but there is only one way to tell for sure. If this is blood, then this is a sample I've been after for a long time: blood from beast form. Do not touch it any more than you may have already touched it, and I will get my things to collect samples for testing."

Ashley looks at her watch, then outside through the now open door and then asks, "When were ya all looking to leave? It's getting dark now, isn't it?"

Dewight looks out and then at his watch as he looks at the state troopers. "Maybe you should both go up and keep watch, and I'll be along shortly, then we can get out of here."

The troopers agree, and they head out to keep guard 'til Dave is done, and Dewight heads up the steps giving the all clear.

Dave returns and notices the lack of daylight outside. "I'd better do this quickly, so you can go and I can close my door and lock it for the night."

Dewight answers, "Take your time; the staties are upstairs keeping guard, so you can get what you need."

Dave continues taking his samples as he responds, "That's great, but I'd still prefer to get this done quickly, so I can secure the house."

Dewight agrees verbally since Dave is not looking at him but at what he is doing.

Ashley is as excited as Dave but a whole lot less controlled about showing it than he is, and she is having trouble standing still while he collects the samples.

Sarah calls out to Ashley, "Ashley, honey, if you need to use the restroom, I'll show you where it is."

Ashley looks at her. "Thank you, but actually, I'm just excited to the point that I can't stand still."

Sarah just shakes her head, and she looks at Dewight, and he's trying not to laugh and smiles when he looks at Sarah.

Dave gets the samples, and Dewight leaves.

Dave closes and locks the door behind Dewight, and as he turns to walk toward the counter with the testing equipment on it, Sarah screams. Loud enough that Ashley jumps, and Dave almost dropped the samples.

They look at Sarah and Dave asks, "What is it?"

She just points to the body in the cell.

Dave and Ashley both look at the body and walk over to the bars, then Dave asks again, "What is it? What happened?"

Sarah is terrified to the point she is shaking. "That guy is dead, right?"

Dave says, "Yes, as dead as every other body that has come in here."

Sarah says, "Well, maybe you should tell him. Because I just seen him move his hand."

Dave is staring at the body.

Ashley, too, has been staring at the body, studying it, and looking for anything that might be different, no matter how small of a change. Then she thinks she notices something and points it out to Dave. "It looks like the bruising is going away; it's not as dark. Some of the deformities from the broken bones are not as obvious… at least that's what it looks like to me. Do you agree, Dave?"

Dave does not look at her; instead, he maintains his focus on the body. "I believe you are right. Or I'm having the same delusions that you are."

He looks at Ashley and Sarah and says, "You know what this means? If we are seeing what we think we are, do you know what that means?"

Sarah speaks with the fear dominating her voice, "Yeah…we are not safe in here now."

Ashley looks at him. "If this is what you thought, then the beast lives even after the human side dies, and it will reawaken. As a dog man as they have been called before being known as werewolves."

Dave says, "Yes, but now, if my theory is correct, when it reawakens, it will be only beast day and night. The human side is dead, and until the beast is killed, the body will live as a beast, and it will be interesting to see if it retains any humanity. Or is it going to be all beast?"

Sarah is just not happy about this arrangement at all. "What do you mean 'interesting'? It will be a beast, and in beast form that is all we need to know." She grabs a nearby pistol that is a .357 Magnum, and she does look at the barrel stamp to verify that it is a large enough caliber for the job. "This should do nicely, though I think at this point, I'd prefer your .44."

Dave turns to see her coming with the pistol in hand, checking the revolver to ensure all six rounds are loaded and live and that none have been fired. She closes the revolver, satisfied that all rounds are present and live.

Dave stands in front of her. "Just what do you think you are going to do with that?"

She looks at him in disbelief that he just asked such a stupid question. Ashley goes to the other side of the room for more of a comfort zone and to another pistol if needed for self-protection.

"I'm sure you know full well what I intend to do with this, and if not, then you are not as bright as you and so many others think." Sarah has very little fear showing in her voice; it's more like determination coming through.

Dave looks at her and extends his hand to receive the pistol. "You will not shoot him. You will not destroy the one chance to prove this theory one way or the other. You will give me the pistol, and you can pray that my theory is wrong and that once the body is dead, it stays dead. Now, give me the pistol, and go relax upstairs or on the other side of the room away from any weapons."

She hands him the pistol and laughs. "Where can I go in this house to be away from weapons?"

Dave points and says, "The cooler."

She looks at the cooler door. "You're nuts; there's a body already in there, unless you got rid of it already with the receipt of a fresh one."

Dave gives a sinister smile. "No, it's still in there."

Sarah goes to another corner and sits down while Ashley comes back over to Dave.

Dave looks at Ashley. "Okay, now we need to start the testing on this blood to see if there is any DNA in it that is not too degraded. Then see if there is anything else to learn from this sample."

Ashley points to the body. "What about him?"

Dave simply says, "He is being videotaped, so we don't have to watch him. And the bars should contain him if he awakens."

She is put at ease knowing this, but Sarah speaks up, "You did catch that he said, 'Should hold,' didn't ya?"

Ashley looks at her. "Yeah, I caught that. But with the weapons here, we can defend ourselves, if needed."

Sarah looks at her, shaking her head. "You obviously have never seen these things move; they are fast and in such confined space one could kill all three of us before one of us could grab a weapon… let alone fire one."

Dave starts to lose his patience. "Okay, that is enough. You are concerned about things that you shouldn't be, and you're trying to scare Ashley now."

Sarah sits a little taller. "Well, she needs to know."

Dave looks at Ashley. "We need to start the testing. Don't pay any attention to Sarah; she's afraid of the dark and any shadows that appear to move."

Sarah says, "With good reason, and you know it. You've seen what those things can do and how fast they are."

Dave and Ashley begin the testing and ignore Sarah totally who just ends up sitting and watching the body in the cell.

Dave forgot about the car in the driveway and about the heart monitor on the body. The monitor is on silent, so no sound is to be heard from a heartbeat or the sound of the flat line of no heartbeat, which is what nobody wanted to hear.

## Chapter 3

# The Pack

Dewight gets back to the office and is informed of phone calls that started coming in after dark.

The calls seem to be warning him of a large migration of beasts headed in his direction.

The troopers that left him earlier call him on his cell phone. "Dewight, you may not believe this, but we observed many beasts headed your way. They are not acknowledging anything else. They appear focused on the direction they are headed."

Dewight says, "Thanks. I've been informed we started getting calls like yours after dark."

The trooper tells Dewight, "We'll let you know if anything changes." With that said, they hang up, and they check in with Diane, the night shift supervisor at the state police station in which they are based.

About fifteen minutes pass, and Dewight is being told he has an urgent call on line three.

He asks who it is, and the dispatcher tells him "Diane."

He looks at her as he picks up the phone. "Hello, Diane, to what do I owe the honor of your voice tonight?"

Diane says, "Cut the bull, Dewight. I've lost contact with a cruiser. The troopers are not answering their radio; the same troopers I had helping you earlier. When they checked in, they were five to seven minutes out; that was almost fifteen minutes ago now. They said they had called you personally to inform you of some out of the ordinary movement of werewolves."

Dewight says, "Yes, they called me on my cell and told me directly they didn't tell me anything else."

Just then Diane gets interrupted. "Excuse me, Dewight. I've got some information coming in. Could you hold please?"

Dewight says, "Sure, take your time."

A minute later, she's back on the phone. "Dewight, the trooper's car was found by a couple other troopers. It doesn't look good; the car has been torn apart. It looks like they hit *something*, but my other troopers couldn't find anything, only blood all over the car inside and out. I've lost troopers to the beasts before, but tonight is different, and I called all my people in off their patrols until we figure out what is going on out there. I suggest you do the same, especially since the beasts have been seen headed your way."

Dewight, with a mournful tone in his voice, says, "Sorry to hear about your men, and I will take your advice into consideration. I need to find out what my people have seen and make a decision based on all the information."

Diane says, "I understand, and I would do the same, but remember it appears to be a migration in your direction. Goodbye and stay safe."

Dewight says, "Goodbye and you stay safe, as well."

They hang up, and Dewight sits at his desk, thinking of what to do then he walks out to dispatch. "I need to know what everyone has observed so far tonight."

The dispatcher nods and puts the call out to check in and report activity for the night.

The calls start coming in almost immediately.

Most of the responses match with all quiet, and no signs of a single beast to be found. One officer adds that in itself is odd usually you see something.

There is a few that report seeing beasts moving toward Picture Rocks.

The expression on Dewight's face looks like a light bulb turned on; it changed that quickly.

"Oh, for pity sakes, Dave and Sarah, the beasts are headed there tonight," he thinks out loud looking at the dispatcher.

The dispatcher asks, "Do you want me to send officers over there?"

Dewight looks at her. "No…No…call all cars back to base. We need to regroup and come up with a plan to help Dave and Sarah. Praying that I'm wrong may help, but I fear I'm not wrong. Dave even expected the beasts tonight." As he turns away, he says, "Although, he only expected one beast, not an army of them."

The dispatcher nods as she puts the word out on the radio, "Calling all cars; calling all cars. Return to base."

The cars check in and report heading into base, except one car that calls in saying they will swing down Dave's street on their way in.

Dewight turns and takes the microphone. "Ben, you and Carl head straight back to base. Do not, I repeat do not, go past Dave's place. I believe the beasts are headed that way. More than you two can deal with and live. So, for your families' sake, *do not* go down that street."

Ben and Carl look at each other, then Ben picks up the microphone. "Sorry, we're already halfway down the street and, so far, all clear."

Dewight, shaking his head, says, "You guys get back here and let me know if you see anything out of the ordinary."

Carl nudges Ben as he is looking in the rearview mirror. "Look behind us and tell me what you see, and would you call that out of the ordinary?"

Ben looks at him, confused. "You're the one with the mirror, not me." He turns in his seat to look behind them, then he turns back to face Carl with a dumbfounded look on his face because he can't believe what he saw either. Carl points to the front, not saying a word. Ben looks and sees what Carl sees. Now they are both as white as can be, and considering Ben is African American, or black, if you prefer, that's pretty scared.

Ben picks up the microphone again and calls dispatch. "Is Dewight still there?"

Dispatch says, "Yeah, hold on."

Ben says, "As long as he can hear me. He wanted to know of anything out of the ordinary. I have a big out of the ordinary for him. We have been surrounded by werewolves to the back of us and to the front of us so thick that's all we see. With the shadows moving to our sides, I bet they are in there, as well."

Dewight grabs the microphone from the dispatcher. "Ben, you guys need to figure out a way to escape and get back here, so we can regroup and think up a plan of attack." He is doing his best to remain calm.

Ben continues scanning the area front, back, and both sides as fast as he can turn. He picks up his microphone. "Okay, Dewight, we'll try."

He then looks at Carl, who is also scanning the area. "Any ideas?"

Carl keeps scanning. "None how about you?"

Ben looks around. "Oh, look to the right; we have a beast approaching us walking upright. I must say, for a beast, I'm not liking the look on its face."

Carl looks at it and agrees with Ben the beast has a different look on its face tonight compared to other nights they have seen werewolves. This one just looks different somehow.

Ben looks at Carl. "Man, sitting here doing nothing isn't getting us out of here alive. If we're moving, we're at least trying."

Carl agrees and starts moving the car forward as the car starts to move the beasts to the rear follow the car. The beast to their right dropped to all four and charged the car jumping onto the roof before either officer realized it was even on the move.

The beast lands with a loud bang and shaking the car at the same time.

Ben and Carl look at each other, and Ben asks, "What was that?"

Carl looks past Ben and with a voice that does not hide his fear very well. "You really don't want to know."

Ben looks out his window. "Oh, my… I hope it wasn't the missing beast."

Carl looks in the mirror and realizes the group behind them is following. Then he sees what he thought was a tail at the top of the rear window. Before he can say anything, they both hear a deep low growl… or what they believed to be a growl.

Ben speaks, and the fear is now starting to show in his voice. "Please tell me that was the car and not what I think it was."

Before Carl can answer, they see something like a stream of water running down the windshield in a single line.

Carl says, "Better call Dewight and get help out here. I do believe the beast is on the roof." The fear in is voice is obvious.

Ben grabs the radio microphone, and he is no longer hiding his fear either. "Dewight, ya there?"

Dewight answers, "Yeah. What's wrong? Can ya get outta there?"

Ben answers as the beast is growling, "Can you hear that?" He holds the microphone up toward the roof of the car. He pulls it back to himself to speak. "It's not looking or sounding good."

Dewight says, "What was that sound?"

Ben says, "As far as we can figure, there is a beast on our roof, and that was the beast growling."

Dewight doesn't key the microphone. "Heaven help them. They need more help than we can give at this point."

Carl looks at Ben, and with some hope in his voice, says, "What about Dave? They can call Dave and ask him to shoot into the crowd of beasts in front of us and give us a chance to escape."

Ben smiles as he keys the microphone. "Dewight, can you call Dave and ask him to fire some shots into the crowd in front of us and give us a chance to get outta here?"

Dewight answers, "I don't even know if he would answer his phone. We escorted him home earlier; he had a new body for a different experiment, and I would rather not call him if we can get you outta there and keep civilians out of it."

As Dewight was answering, the beast started to scratch the roof applying more force with each pass. They can actually see the path the claws are taking by the indentations on the inside.

Ben pulls his 9mm service weapon from its holster and chambers a round and moves the safety selector to fire. Then he puts it back in his holster for quick access and takes the microphone. "Dewight, the beast is clawing at the roof of the car. Tell our families that we love them if we don't make it out of this alive." When he lays the microphone down on the center console, it lays on the button, and the office can hear all that happens and is said.

The beast growls louder now; there is no mistake what they are hearing. The stream on the windshield is still flowing and appears to have gotten heavier.

The growling stops, and the stream that they believe to be drool stops flowing.

They hear a sound above them as the beast forced its claws through the metal. It then begins to peel the roof apart, making a whole that it can see them, and they also have a much closer look a werewolf than either of them has ever had before. The car is shaking violently as the roof is being torn open. Ben and Carl are being tossed around in the car, and one of them bumps the switch, activating the lights and sirens.

The beast arches its back, howling in pain with its eyes closed and covering its ears. The sound and lights were more than it could take.

Carl says, "Use the shotgun and kill it. Shoot it. At least get it off the car."

Ben reaches for the 12-gauge shotgun mounted to the dash. The car starts shaking and rocking violently again as the beast tears the light bar from the car. They see the light bar hit the ground to the left of the car and the growling starts again loud and deep. It's looking at Ben who is still trying to remove the shotgun from its resting place in its mount. The siren also stopped; it got shorted out with the removal of the light bar.

Ben continues trying to get the shotgun, and the beast reaches in and grabs the shotgun mounting bracket and all just rips it all out away from Ben who jumps back out of the way.

Dewight and the others are listening to all of this, and Dewight is telling them to "Release the button so we can talk."

Dewight is getting frustrated not being able to speak to the officers. He thinks one of them may be holding the button or leaning against it if they didn't hang it up properly.

Dave heard the siren and saw the lights of a patrol car. So, he looked out the window of the other cell he has set up in case he may be able to capture a live specimen to examine. He sees the patrol car and the rider on top of it. He grabs his cell phone and calls Dewight on his cell phone.

Dewight answers, "Hello, Dave, how may we help you tonight?"

Dave responds very calmly, "Start by telling me who is in the patrol car on my street."

Dewight drops his head. "It's Carl and Ben. They wanted to make a pass on your street before coming in after I called all cars back to the office. We've been getting reports of werewolves heading your direction; well, our way. All night we were trying to find out where they were headed. Now we know and it may cost me two good officers."

Dave, still watching out the window, says, "Sarah, get me the .30-06 and the .308. Ashley, gather up the pistols and whatever rifles and ammunition is in the basement."

Dewight jumps into the conversation and says, "Hold on; you don't need to risk your household or yourself to help. We are working on a plan to get them outta there safely."

Dave remains calm. "Remember I said the beast may return tonight? Granted, I didn't expect that many beasts to show up."

Dewight says, "Hold on; you can see how many bests are out there?"

Dave says, "More than I can count. The shadows are moving, and the one on the car is apparently the leader of the pack. The others are staying back as he tears the car apart; it's amazing in that form. They seem to have a leader."

Sarah and Ashley return with everything asked for as Dewight responds. "Hey, they are friends and good officers out there, so how about focusing on and helping me figure out a way to save them instead of admiring the beasts that are after them?"

Dave smiles. "Yes, sir. I'll shoot into the crowd in front of the car and try to open up a hole for them to drive through, just let them know." Then he hangs up before Dewight starts arguing over the plan.

Dewight speaks, not knowing Dave hung up, "We already explored that option and not sure it will work. You're one person shooting at an unknown number of beasts." He gets no response and looks at his phone and sees Dave hung up. He shakes his head. "Should have known."

Dave looks at the ladies. "We are in for a long night once they find us shooting at them."

Sarah's fear is obvious in her voice: "Normally I'd say leave them alone, but we need to help the officers in the car. Did Dewight tell you who is in the car?"

Dave doesn't look at her, just sets up on his first shot as he answers, "Carl and Ben."

Sarah says, "I like those guys. Why couldn't it be someone I don't like?"

Dave asks Sarah to turn off the basement lights with the hope of not being seen right away or as easily.

Dave studies his shot, thinking of how low he can shoot and still kill the beast. Hit the first low and as the bullet travels forward and upward it will kill a few more. His idea is to kill as many with one shot as he can and get the angle right so not to hit a neighbor's house if his idea of the bullet lodging in a beast is wrong. He steadies his shot with the windowsill and the bars, taking careful aim, and says a silent prayer: *Lord, steady my hand and allow me to shoot straight and true.* He then fires.

He watches six beasts drop dead or dying, and the others spread apart until the one on the car barks. Then they regroup and surround the ones that are dead. The one on the car is looking around and doesn't see Dave or the rifle out the window as he has only the tip of the barrel outside the window. The beast, however, seems to know where the shot came from as Dave watches. It is staring at the house. The beast focuses its attention back to the car, and Dave lines up another shot. He saw the beast remove the shotgun from the car, so he knows they only have their side arms for protection.

Dave watches the living beasts remove the dead by throwing them to the side of the road with a one-handed throw. He is amazed at the strength as the bodies have not returned to their human form and therefore are still heavier.

Dave has another shot lined up and checks the car first and the beast isn't watching, so he gets back in the scope and fires. Again, he watches six drop to the ground, but this time, he sees a seventh grab its head but doesn't drop. Again, the beasts separate, and the one on the car barks and they regroup.

Again, the living throws the dead to the side. Dave does not know if it is to keep from tripping over the dead, or if there may be a different reason for the action.

This time the one on the car scans Dave's side of the street as if knowing the shots are coming from that side of the street. It has teeth showing in a low growl as it looks at each house and pauses on Dave's house longer, as if expecting to see movement.

Realizing the beast is distracted, Ben taps Carl on the shoulder and points to the roof of the car.

Carl looks up and realizes the same thing and makes an attempt to remove the beast. He floors the accelerator pedal, but the beast manages to hold on.

He then slams the brakes for a quick stop; again, the beast remains on the roof. It digs its claws into the roof of the car, both front and back claws.

Carl uses his hand to signal Ben to shoot the beast with his handgun, by making the shape with his thumb and fore finger pointing at the roof.

They look at each other while the beast refocuses on them.

Loud, deep growling as the beast looks into the car through the whole it made in the roof.

Ben is slowly removing his pistol from its holster as he watches the beast.

Ben points the pistol at the whole in the roof and fires. He hurried the shot and narrowly missed the beast's head.

The beast dodged to the right and reared its head back as the bullet passed by its left ear.

The beast very quickly regains its focus and reaches into the car through the whole in the roof and grabs Ben's pistol, hand, and all. It begins to squeeze and crush the pistol and Bens hand with it.

Ben is screaming in pain, as the beast continues to squeeze slowly as if it enjoys causing pain.

Carl has no idea how to help his partner and is starting to panic, as well.

Finally, the beast decides play time is over and gives a short, low growl, and in one, swift motion, rips Bens arm off at the shoulder, just separated it at the socket.

Ben's pain is now different, of course, and his scream changes, as well. His scream now reflects not only pain, but in the horror of his arm being torn off.

Blood sprays Carl, and he also begins to scream at the horrific site and sound of Ben's arm being torn off. Carl has now lost control of his emotions and all his fear of not making it out alive is added to his scream.

The beast throws Ben's arm to the crowd of beasts to the right of the car.

The arm doesn't even hit the ground before they are fighting over it. Beasts are fighting like a combination of man and animal. Biting, scratching, even what appears to Dave who is still watching, throwing punches.

Dave takes aim at the group in front of the car and fires.

Again, the beasts separate briefly as the dead and dying fall to the road.

The separation was not as long this time. And again, upon regrouping, they throw the dead.

Dave is thinking aloud, "Come on, guys, make a break for it before your both dead."

Sarah in a demanding voice, says, "Which one has it killed?"

Dave doesn't look at her. "Listen…You still hear two screams? I do."

Sarah listens. "Okay, I hear two screams, so the beast has not killed either one of them, right?"

Dave is taking aim for another shot. "It would appear that way."

The beast on the car let out a bark and a growl after the last shot. Ben and Carl didn't hear over their screams.

Carl starts to regain some composure and motions to Ben to calm down. Ben is able to calm his screams enough to hear Carl's plan. Carl tells him next time Dave fires, and the beasts open up we shoot for the opening.

Ben nods his head in agreement.

The beast on the car turned its head as if to listen to their conversation. Then it barks a couple quick barks and a short howl.

Nobody gave any thought to the beasts barking or howling.

Dave takes his next shot and as the beasts drop. Carl puts the throttle pedal to the floor.

But the expected opening didn't happen this time; instead, the rest stood still and even closed the gap that was caused by the fallen. They do not even remove the dead this time.

Carl hits the brakes, realizing the opening isn't happening.

Dave is in shock but then begins to think the one on the car told them not to move. Dave begins thinking he is the leader… or at least a higher-ranking beast.

As Dave is thinking and slowly pulling the rifle barrel back in the beast on the car barks, and Dave realizes a large number of beasts turning toward him.

The beasts start moving toward the house, and Dave sees one last possible shot before they are to close. He takes aim at the beast on the car.

Carl sees the beasts headed for Dave's and tells Ben, "We're on our own." Carl says, "Last shot, buddy; we're just going to drive through them."

The office is still listening and all praying that it works. They are not aware of everything going on; only what they can hear over the radio.

Dave takes his shot before it's too late. At the same time Dave pulls the trigger, Carl is flooring the accelerator pedal to drive through the crowd.

The bullet grazes the beasts back enough to cause pain and take hair and some skin but not enough to knock it off the car, let alone kill it. The bullet also missed the beast's spine.

The beast howls in pain and digs its claws into the car as it accelerates.

The beast growls low and deep from anger and pain and reaches in and grabs Carl's neck and rips his throat out in one, quick move. Carl never knew he was grab it was so fast.

Ben sees movement out of the corner of his eye and looks to see Carl's throat missing.

Ben knows he is about to die, as well, and makes one last effort to take the beast with him. He reaches across to Carl's service pistol with his remaining hand and removes the holster lock strap as the car is crashing through the beasts, who are trying to stop the car at the same time.

The beast on the car sees what Ben is doing and allows him to get a hold of the pistol. But as he is removing the pistol from the holster, the beast ends the game it was playing and reaches in and removes Bens head with one, very quick motion.

The beast jumps from the car holding Ben's head and looks at Dave and holds out the head as a trophy then tosses it into the crowd. Again, the other beasts begin fighting over the piece thrown their way.

The car crashes into a big oak tree on the corner and the beasts begin tearing it apart. As they pull the bodies from the car and fight over the bodies, others keep destroying the car. At some point, the fuel line starts leaking, and a spark is caused when a piece of the car strikes the asphalt at the correct angle causing a spark and igniting the fuel, which then the car explodes.

Dave sees many beasts flying when the car explodes. Then he is quickly reminded of the others when the apparent leader barks.

Now the entire group of beasts is headed to the house, except the leader. He stays back, and before Dave loses all sight of him, it seems to be smiling. Dave thinks he may be seeing things. For how can a canine beast smile?

Dave steps back as he fires into the group, and beasts fall to the ground. The living beasts grab the dead and throw them out of the way and keep moving to reach Dave.

The beasts are reaching in through the window trying to get anyone but reaching nobody.

As Dave keeps firing into the group, Sarah calls Dewight. Ashley keeps rotating weapons for Dave; an empty one for a loaded one. She is reloading almost as fast as Dave is emptying them.

Dewight answers his cell phone, "Hello Sarah."

Sarah, scared beyond any previous level she has known, says, "Dewight, you gotta send officers to help. The beasts are attacking the house. They killed Ben and Carl and are trying to get in here now. Dave is shooting as many as he can, but they keep coming."

Dewight, the sorrow obvious in his voice, says, "I know, or at least suspected. We could hear everything over the radio; they never released the mic button. We heard everything up to the explosion. I don't know how we can be of any use at this time. I need to call for help from the state police and the other towns. And even then, I don't know if we could help." He then realizes he is talking and not just silently thinking to himself. "Sarah I will make the calls, and we will be out to help. We will get you through the night alive."

Sarah, not sure to believe him or not, decides to believe him and thanks him, figuring a little hope is better than no hope.

Upon hanging up, Dewight calls Diane.

Diane is told of his phone call, and it is transferred to her office. Diane answers, "Hello Dewight. Have you figured out the out-of-ordinary movement in your direction tonight?"

Dewight, still with a sorrowful tone in his voice, says, "Yes, and it ain't good."

Diane perks up a little. "What do you mean yes and it's not good? Explain."

Dewight tells of the large number of beasts at Dave and Sarah's house and how it cost him two, good officers tonight. He goes on to tell her of the current battle Dave is in at his place and that Sarah had actually called him for help.

After listening to Dewight fill her in on all that is going on, she asks, "How do you think we can help them? I mean, if there is more, then we can kill we put our people at risk, as well. This opens up possible attacks with the more officers we lose."

Dewight, with his head down while on the phone, says, "I know, but I have no plan as yet and would appreciate any ideas that you may have."

# Werewolves: The Next Generation

Diane is thinking, and before Dewight asks if she is still there, she responds, "I'm not sure how we can help, but I have a friend that has studied the beasts' behavior, and I don't mean Dave." They share a brief laugh. "He's a retired Green Beret and has been close to the beasts. I'll call him and get him here, so we can start making a plan."

Dewight answers, "Thank you, Diane. I'll be awaiting your call."

They hang up the phone, and Dewight looks at the others. "We're not waiting for her to call; we will start making a plan now." They all gather around the conference table and start looking at a map of Picture Rocks and start talking out loud with ideas.

Diane starts looking through her personal phone book for the number. She calls to her receptionist to search her desk for the number, as well.

Diane calls to her receptionist, "I found it. Thanks for looking."

The receptionist responds, "You're welcome."

Diane picks up her office phone and dials the number in her book.

The phone rings, and she counts the rings. One. Two. Three. Then there's an answer, it's a male voice with a Mexican accent. "Hello."

Diane asks, "Juan, is that you?"

Juan answers, "Yes, it's me. Why are you calling, Diane?" He is smiling as if he already knows.

Diane tries to stay professional. "Well, we have a problem with werewolves."

Juan laughs and speaks before she explains, "That's an understatement."

Diane stays calm with her response, "I don't know what you are referring to, but I need you to come to the office now or sooner to discuss the situation."

Juan answers calmly and professionally, "I'll be there as soon as I can. I am not about to forget what is out there and what they can do."

Diane rolls her eyes into the back of her head before answering, "Very well, but make it as fast as you can as we do have a serious situation that we can use your help with."

Juan says, "Very well; as fast as I can."

Juan hangs up his phone and grabs his keys a jacket and a bag with his firearms and ammunition and then heads for his car, taking care to look for any movement before opening the door, let alone going out the door.

Dewight tells the others that Diane is calling in outside help.

Brook asks, "What do you mean 'outside' help?" She uses her usual tone that sounds a bit rough and even challenging to those who do not know her.

Dewight looks at her, and in a plan voice, says, "Juan, I suppose."

Brook looks at him as do the others with surprise and disappointment in their eyes.

Brook asks, "Did she actually say his name?"

Dewight says, "No, but she left no doubt as to whom she referred to when she said he studied the beasts and has been close to them and retired green beret. Who would you," he looks around at everyone, "think she referred to? Anyone?"

Brook looks around the room and everyone seems to be nodding in agreement with Dewight. "Looks like we all agree; it most likely is Juan that she is calling. But I don't understand why she would call him. Do you think she forgot he started the whole craze of people dressing up like a beast and trying to walk among them?"

Dewight shakes his head disapprovingly. "I doubt she forgot that, but she is grasping at any and all possibilities at this time as are we. Now, let's get back to putting together a plan to help our friends."

They all go back to looking at the map and discussing ideas as to how to get in there to help and get everyone out alive that is left alive.

Back at Dave's, the beasts keep coming.

He kills one, two, and three at the window. The living beasts grab the dead and throw the bodies to the side or behind. They just grab and throw and move in on the window. They remove the bodies so fast that the change from beast form has not even begun.

Dave sees Sarah is off the phone. "So, can Dewight get help out here or not?"

Sarah, looking down, and sounding depressed, says, "He said he needed to call for help from the state police and the other towns, then they will be out to help."

Dave looks at her, then back to the window. "Fine, until then." He fires into the window. "Turn on the power to the window bars." He fires again into the group at the window.

Sarah lights up with new hope and runs for the control box and turns on the power to electrify the window bars and the doors to the house.

In between shots, she tells him, "The power is on."

The electricity builds slowly, and the beasts are not sure about it. Then one gets the full charge and howls in pain. It is still being electrocuted when another grabs it to remove it from the window and that one is now being electrocuted.

It keeps snowballing like that. The beasts at the window connect with the bars and get electrocuted, and the next one grabs to remove the one being shocked and gets electrocuted.

In a very short time, a large number of beasts are howling in pain. The sound is so deafening that Dave can't even fire; they are all covering their ears. The sound is even penetrating the ear plugs they have in because of the shooting.

What they can't see is the one from the car standing in the street opening and closing his hands as if they were stiff or perhaps sore and trying to work it out.

The beasts being electrocuted are now starting to smoke, and the smell is overpowering the urge to cover their ears. They are now trying to cover their face to breath. Dave realizes the beasts at the window, at least, are dying. He kicks into scientist mode, and although the sound and smell are horrific, he manages to watch.

Once the beasts at the window die the current no longer has the proper connection to continue to flow through the group, at least not strong enough to bother the other beasts. They let go of the dead beasts and move backwards away from the window and to the sides as to allow the one in the street to see what has happened.

The one in the street stands silently as it looks at the smoking remains at the window.

Dave looks at Sarah, and Ashley and puts a finger to his lips to make the quite sign as he listens to what maybe going on outside.

They all listen and hear nothing for a while.

Some of the beasts that were being shocked are rolling on the ground in pain. Some are just lying there, but none are making a sound. What Dave and the others can't see is how quickly the beasts are able to function again after being electrocuted for so long. They are not completely healed but have most of their strength back and are able to move around and be a part of the pack again.

Then the beast in the street, as if reawaking, jerks and stops working his hands in and out of a fist. He barks and the beasts retreat to the street as the one starts toward the house.

Dave, Sarah, and Ashley all heard the bark. Sarah starts to ask a question, "Wha—" but Dave puts his hand over her mouth before she is done with the first word.

To state the obvious, she is not happy with him. But before she can remove his hand to voice her anger, the beast is sniffing at the window, sniffing the smoldering dead. It moves to the next window and sniffs. The window above the suicide victim Dave brought home.

The beast barks and waits barks again and waits.

The beast looks in the window and locks eyes with Dave and starts growling.

Dave looks past the beast when it looks at Sarah. He's looking at the others in the street. Not a single one has moved, not even a shuffle.

Now Dave's curiosity is raised and waving a big red flag.

The beast stands after making eye contact with Ashley, as well, then turns around and looks at all the dead, in the yard, in the street, and by the burning wreckage of the car.

It lowers its head as it starts walking toward the street.

At the street, it stops, turns toward the house, and looks again at the dead then howls. A sorrowful sounding howl, low and long. Then the others join in on the howling, just as sorrowful as the first.

Ashley grabs the key to the cell without Dave seeing her. She extends her hand to the cell door with key in hand. Dave then grabs her hand and shakes his head no, and again raises his finger to his mouth for the quite sign.

He takes the key, and they all watch beasts and listen to them howl in harmony.

The beasts stop howling. Then the one barks, and they all leave, except the one from the car. He stays as the others leave. He stares at the house.

Once the last beast is out of sight, he drops to all fours and is gone before anyone can blink.

Sarah in shock, says, "Oh, my, where did it go? Which way did it go?"

Dave staring at the suicide victim. "I don't know. But I'm willing to bet it didn't go too far."

Ashley, with curiosity in her voice, says, "Why did you not want me to open the cell? We could have gotten a better look at what was going on outside."

Dave, still looking at the body in the cell, says, "Mayhaps, but don't you want to know why the beast barked at the window above him before we go in there?"

Ashley smiles and nods in agreement. "Yes."

Sarah, on the other hand, looks at Dave. "Oh, no you don't think. No, you do think it, that's why you put the camera and the EKG machine on him. Now you're thinking that the beast at the window has somehow justified your suspicion."

Ashley looks at her. "What makes you think all that?"

Sarah smiles. "I used to help him in here, not to mention the years I've been married to him."

Ashley looks at Dave with a curious look. "Is she right?"

Dave does not look away from the suicide victim. "Yes, she used to help me here in the lab, and we been married many years."

Sarah smiles, trying not to laugh out loud.

Ashley rolls her eyes and her head before looking at him. "No, I mean her thoughts about what you're thinking with this dead guy."

Dave just simply asks her, "Are you sure he's dead?"

She now looks at the suicide victim differently, watching to see if there is any evidence of him breathing. "Yes, I'm sure he's dead. I see no movement of his chest."

She asks Dave, "Did he just breathe?"

Dave says, "Yes. Look at where the injuries were. The bruising is almost completely gone. The compound fractures that he had are no longer obvious. Look at the EKG printout; it has been registering a heartbeat."

Sarah speaks up with a mix of fear and anger in her voice, "He is dead. How could his body heal, let alone be breathing? Unless he wasn't dead when you brought him in."

Dave goes and gets a broom and reaches the handle into the cell to the printout.

Trying to hook the paper and stretch it out to read hoping for a timeline, he manages to hook the paper and begins to carefully stretch it out toward the empty cell where Ashley is waiting.

He gets it to Ashley, who carefully grabs the paper, being very careful of the bars as the electricity is still on. She is getting it stretched out as Dave heads her way.

Ashley finishes stretching it out to read as Dave gets there.

Ashley, not believing what she is looking at, says, "He was dead when we hooked him up, look. Nothing until sunset tonight, then a heartbeat. It's been getting stronger all night."

Dave heads to the video recording of the dead guy.

Ashley and Sarah stand there beside him as he rewinds and watches it in fast forward mode. Neither one is happy with him watching it in fast forward.

Dave stops the recording. "Here, watch this."

He rewinds the recording, then with them watching he plays it in fast forward mode. As they watch from the beginning, the ladies now see what he has seen: the bruises and the obvious broken bones that could be seen seemed to disappear.

There seems to be movement of the hands, fingers, and arms, and even appears as though the head moves. The chest appears to rise and fall as if he is breathing.

In the recording, Sarah points out that it looks like he is getting hairier.

Dave rewinds, and they all watch and agree that the guy does appear to be getting hairier.

Ashley speaks up, "Rewind it again."

Dave rewinds it and asks, "What did you see?"

They watch it. Ashley says, "Right there—stop."

Dave and Sarah are looking at the image and still not seeing what Ashley is seeing.

Sarah says, "I don't see anything."

Ashley points at the screen. "Right there; it looks like his hands are changing. Maybe even the face a little bit."

Dave rewinds and plays forward until he and Sarah both see what Ashley has seen.

They all agree that the body is changing and that the power will stay on to the bars of the cell. The full moon is the next night. If Dave's theory is correct, the body will awaken and in beast form.

Sarah gets the .357 Magnum revolver. She comes back to the cell and starts to raise it.

Dave grabs the revolver and prevents her from raising it any farther.

Sarah is not happy at all. "What are you doing?" She is not trying to hide her anger at all.

Dave asks calmly, "What exactly are you intending on doing?" As if he didn't already know.

She just looks at him. "I'm going to kill it before it wakes up and kills us."

Dave looks at her, takes a hold of the revolver, and begins to pull on it, hoping she will release it to him. "Sarah, sweetheart, if we kill him now, it is murder. He is in human form, and we still cannot prove he is a beast."

She releases the pistol to him. "I still think we need to kill him before he awakens. He is obviously a beast in human form. How else would you explain his recovery?"

Dave shrugs his shoulders. "I don't have an answer babe. But we need to be 100 percent certain before killing him. There can be no doubt as to what he is."

Ashley is staying to the side and out of the way. She still is not sure of Sarah's mental stability, but she is willing to give Sarah the benefit of the doubt since they only met tonight and have already battled the beasts together.

Chapter 4

# New Discovery

At the police station, Dewight's dispatch has been getting calls about the beasts in the neighborhood and the police car exploding. The battle at Dave's house with the gun shots and the number of beasts being too many to count.

The dispatchers tell the callers that they are aware of the situation and are currently working on a solution. So, they don't let Dewight know about the calls until he asks. They inform him that they told the callers it is being addressed and he tells them "good job."

Dewight and his officers are discussing what to do and how to do it when one of the dispatchers calls to Dewight.

He ignores the dispatcher, but he doesn't give up. He keeps calling to Dewight, "Sir you need to take this call."

Finally, Dewight says, "What or who is so important that you can't take the call yourself?"

The dispatcher looks at him. "This person has information you may want to hear, sir." No hint of anger in his voice.

Dewight takes the call. "Hello, this is Dewight. How may I help you tonight?"

The caller just simply responds, "Oh, but chief, it's not how you can help me, it is how I can help you."

Dewight says, "Who are you? What do you mean you can help me?" He is trying to not let his anger show as he does not know with whom he is speaking, as yet, even though he suspects it is Juan. But yet there is no sound of a Mexican accent.

The caller stays calm and does not give his name. "I am one of the people who lives on the same street as Dave. I saw the beasts leave. They all left the area. I do not see any beasts on the street. Other than the dead."

Dewight, sounding a little nicer but still unsure of the caller, says, "Will you give me your name and address for my report? And are you sure they left?"

The caller stays calm. "With all due respect chief, I would like to remain anonymous. I'm sure you will respect that request. I don't usually get involved in these matters, and if you don't respect my request I never will again."

Dewight says, "Okay, you will be anonymous. But what makes you think the beasts left the area?" He is still trying to recognize the voice.

The caller responds, "Well, let's see. I watched them leave. I do not see any beasts in the area at all. The burning car is lighting up the area better than the streetlights. Looks like the tree is starting to burn, as well."

Dewight, sounding a little surprised, says, "Wait—what tree?"

The caller says, "The tree your officers hit after being killed by the beast."

Dewight isn't being as calm as the caller now. "So, do we need to get the fire department out there to put out the fire? Or will it be contained until daylight and we can get them there to put it out then?"

The caller looks at the tree. "No, I'd say they need to get out here sooner than later. The tree is definitely burning; it may fall onto one of the houses in that vicinity."

Dewight thanks the caller and tells him that he will alert the fire department to get there for the fire. The caller in return thanks him, and they end the call.

Dewight says, "Shit—now we need to get out there to protect the fire department."

As Dewight is calling the fire department, Brook asks, "Why do we need to go out there? What is burning?"

Dewight finishes dialing and is waiting for a response on the other end. "The cruiser hit a tree, and now the tree is starting to burn with the cruiser."

The fire chief answers his phone, "Hello, Dewight. Do I even want to ask why you are calling?"

Dewight, sounding sorrowful, says, "No, but I will tell you anyway. At the end of Center Street there is a police cruiser that hit a tree. The car burst into flames and is now burning the tree it hit. I will be sending officers there, as well, to protect your crew as you work on the fire."

The fire chief agrees, and they hang up so he can get everyone around.

Brook looks at Dewight and, not holding back her concern, says, "What do you mean we are going out there? Why are you sending the fire department out there? Okay, so a tree is burning. What about the lives of those that will be going out there?"

Dewight looks at her. He does not lose his temper. "The caller had said the beasts left the area. I will be going out there with anyone who will volunteer to go. I am not dispatching anyone that does not want to go. I will call Diane on the way and hope she can send other officers, as well."

The officers look at each other.

Brook and her partner Julie agree and volunteer to go.

The rest of the officers all volunteer, as well.

Dewight thanks them all, and they head for their cruisers and then to the scene.

Dewight calls Diane as he said he would.

Diane answers, "Hello, Dewight. So, what have you called about? Juan is here now, and we have just started looking at ideas to get in there."

Dewight, trying not to allow his anger to show, says, "Diane, we are heading out to the scene now. My whole police force and the fire department. There is a fire they need to deal with immediately, and we are heading there to protect them."

Diane cuts in there. "Hold on. You are risking your force and the fire department personnel? The sheer number of beasts alone will kill all of you. There is no chance of survival."

Dewight stays calm. "Diane, I received a call that stated the beasts all left. If you would like to send officers to assist in protecting the firefighters, we all would appreciate the assistance."

Diane agrees. "I am sending Juan out with officers, as well."

Dewight says, "Okay." He is doing his best to not show any anger or disgust.

Diane tells Dewight to be nice. She knows he does not approve of Juan and his desire to be with the beasts.

Dewight and his officers get to the scene and secure it so the firefighters can get in there to fight the fire.

While the fire department is putting the fire out, Dewight takes a walk around the area. He is looking at all the dead. He does not believe what he is seeing. The other officers stayed with the firefighters, except for Brooke and Julie. They refused to allow him to walk around without back up.

They are not speaking to each other, just looking and shining their flashlights around into each dark area they see.

Dewight grabs his cell phone and is getting ready to call Dave when the state police show up with Juan. He puts his phone away.

Juan joins Dewight and so do the state police officers, just looking around not believing or understanding exactly what they are seeing.

Juan asks, "Have any of you seen this before?" His voice is shaky as he speaks.

The fear is obvious.

They others just shake their heads to say no.

Dewight speaks up, "This is new to me. How about you, Juan? Ever see this before?"

Juan says, "No."

Dewight grabs his phone again. This time he calls Dave.

Dave says, "Hello, Dewight. Everything has calmed down now. So, I don't think you need to come out here tonight."

Dewight says, "We are already here, Dave. We had a call about the tree burning and came out to protect the fire department."

Dave jumps in and says, "Why did you come out? Okay, a burning tree; that is great. You know that just because we don't see the beasts don't mean they can't see us."

Dewight stops him. "Dave, just stop. We got a call about the tree, and the danger it presents. The caller also said the beasts left the area. The caller watched them leave. So, we all came out to check out the area. You know that the beasts are rarely active after such a large attack. They usually go hide for the night, and we don't get bothered again for a day or two."

Dave starts to calm down. "Okay, Dewight, so why call me now? We are getting ready to start the autopsy on the female Carla dropped off."

Dewight, disbelief in his voice, says, "Dave, you need to come out here. This is not what I expected to see."

Dave, staying stubborn, says, "Dewight, I don't want to come out yet. I would like to start this autopsy."

Dewight is persistent. "Dave, if you don't come out, we will come in and drag you out in handcuffs."

Dave is set back by that statement. "What do you mean?" Dewight stays on him and doesn't let up. "Just get out here now."

Dave, not used to Dewight talking to him like that at all in all the years they have known each other, says, "Okay, I will be right out."

Dave hangs up and starts to power down the doors, so he can leave.

Sarah is not happy and allows it to show. "What are you doing? That is keeping the beasts out."

Dave doesn't even look at her. "Dewight needs me outside now, not after sunrise. Honey, he threatened me with arrest if I don't go out."

Sarah gasps. "He never has threatened to arrest you before. This must be serious. I'm coming out, too."

Ashley agrees and decides to go, as well.

They get out to the driveway where Dewight is waiting. Brooke and Julie are at the corner of the house in the driveway. The state troopers and Juan are still out front, looking around.

Dave looks at Dewight. "Okay, what is so important that it can't wait until sunrise?"

Dewight looks down at the ground and back up to Dave. "You are sure you only shot werewolves?"

Dave is confused by the question and even offended that his longtime friend would even consider asking such a stupid question. "Yes, every one of those people was a werewolf when I shot them. Why? Who is out there?"

Dewight, trying to stay calm, says, "You will not believe me if I tell you. You need to look for yourself."

Dewight leads them to the front of the house to see what has everyone so confused.

There, on the ground, is what was expected: naked humans that were once in beast form. But there is also some in beast form that never changed back to human form.

Dave looks at these figures. "I suspected this could happen. My theory is the human side died. Most likely suicide, but the beast didn't die it lives without the human host. I suspect this is what is called dog man in some areas; this is what they have seen and nobody realized it. Mainly because it wasn't believed to exist at that time."

Dewight takes Dave's shoulder. "No, my friend, not those bodies." He points farther into the street and down from the house. "Those bodies."

Dave's mouth drops when he sees what was pointed out. Sarah and Ashley are just as stunned as he is.

Not even Dave expected this find. He never thought it possible. But here lays the proof spread out in front of him and the others.

The bodies that shouldn't be but that lay there are everyday house pets: dogs of every size and breed.

They walk over to the dead dogs and look at them, some with a bullet hole where it was shot. Others that have no obvious injury to have killed it.

Dave looks at the dead dogs. "Dewight, ask the girls there were no house dogs out here tonight." His voice has an almost panic quality to it.

Juan speaks up, "You know, this may explain why some act different."

Dave looks at him. "What do you mean?"

Juan says, "You know how some are more dog than others. Some are more human." He is speaking with confidence.

Dewight not being patient at all with Juan. "Nobody wants to hear about your hair-brained ideas."

Juan keeps his calm and speaks with confidence, "But you know I was with them for the night. Three months before, I think they know I human not beast. I see lots of things, lots of behaviors that did not make sense but now makes little more sense. Seeing pet dogs can be the beast. Look a Chihuahua, a miniature poodle. A wiener dog… What are they called? Oh, yeah, a dachshund, and many large breeds, as well. It looks like they are all here."

Dave keeps Dewight from speaking up. "You are the one I have heard about that spent time as one of them and lived. Perhaps we can help each other?"

Dewight shakes his head to disagree. "I don't see how you two could help each other."

Dave continues, "He could help me to understand behaviors that I don't understand now; help me to learn about new behaviors that I don't know about at all because I have not observed them as yet."

Sarah speaks up letting anger show, "Hold on, you are not going to ask him to help you spend time with them as one of them, are you?"

Dave smiles and looks at his wife. "Well, to be honest, I didn't think about that until you suggested it."

Sarah looks at him and angrily says, "Don't you even think about it."

Dave looks at her. "It's nice to know you still care. But I think it would be better to have him come in and talk over dinner one night."

Juan agrees that would be best. He adds, "Since the beasts discovered me, I haven't tried to go back into the dark. But I would like to have dinner with the Mr. David Stone and see how we can help each other understand the beasts better."

Dave smiles. "I have wanted to meet you for quit a long time, as well."

Dave goes back to scientist mode and tells Ashley and Sarah that he needs blood samples from the dogs. "A sample from each dog and the breed listed on the sample, please."

Sarah asks, "Why do you need the breed listed on the sample?"

Dave looks at her. "You of anyone should understand that better, my dear, so we can see if there is a difference in how the infection affects the different breads."

Sarah says, "But you already know that they become the beast… just like the humans do. So, what do you think would be different?"

They are heading into the lab to get the needles and syringes to get the samples.

Dave looks at her and back to where he is walking. "I don't know that is why I need to know what breed the dog is and to compare it to the other dogs and to the human infection. I'm sure it is at least close; otherwise, it wouldn't infect canine and human. But we need the samples to see."

They retrieve the materials needed and, once outside, Juan asks if he can help.

Dave agrees and gives Juan some needles and syringes to collect samples, as well. "Thank you for your help, Juan."

Juan says, "You are welcome."

Dewight goes to Dave after Juan has left. "Are you sure you trust him? You only met him tonight. He is, after all, infatuated with the beasts more then you. He wants to live among them. I would be concerned that he would keep a sample and inject himself later."

Dave smiles at Dewight. "If you are concerned, then watch him. I can use his help now and will not say no to someone willing to help collect samples. Besides, he is trying to understand the beasts as are we. He is doing it differently."

Dewight is still concerned, and it is obvious to Dave. "Okay, I suppose you are right, but I will watch him anyway. I just don't trust he is over the idea of being one of them."

Dave shrugs his shoulders. "Whatever."

The four of them are collecting blood samples from the dead dogs. They are listing the breed of dog each sample is taken from. Per Dave's request, they are only taking a sample from each breed and not every dog. The dead dogs that are in the area of the firefighters working on the fire; they wait until the fire chief says they can go in there for the samples.

Dewight keeps his gaze on Juan and manages to be scanning the shadows whenever Juan looks toward him. It's not intentional as in he looks away when Juan looks his way but, just by chance, he is looking around and shining his light into the shadows when Juan looks up.

They had divided the areas up, so they could cover the most ground in the shortest amount of time.

The fire department has the fire out before they are done collecting samples.

They collect the samples from that area, and they all leave. The firefighters leave the area first, then Dave and his team go into the house as the police officers are keeping guard.

Brooke is shining her flashlight around into the shadows. She notices Julie is shining her light, as well. So, Brooke shines her light onto the rooftops in the area. She sees what she believes to be eye shine, but the flashlight just isn't strong enough to show anything else at that distance. So, she goes to her cruiser and gets the portable spotlight. She returns to the spot, and Dewight asks why she grabbed the spotlight. She tells him she thought she saw eye shine on the roof. Brooke shines the spotlight onto the roof she saw the eye shine.

What they saw is what none of them wanted to see. The light showed the full body of a werewolf, just sitting there, watching them. Julie went for her side arm. Dewight grabbed her arm, "No, don't even pull it out. The beast isn't moving. If the others are still close, we are all dead before it hits the ground."

Dewight looks around. "Is everyone accounted for?" he shouts to the officers.

They all answer yes.

Dewight says, "Let's get out of here now."

Dewight stands beside his cruiser as he sees the others leaving. Once he is sure all his officers left safely, he gets into his car and starts to leave.

A lone beast jumps into the street about a half block from him and in front of his moving car. His thoughts go to Ben and Carl and what they had went through. He gets on the radio to the other cars. "A beast jumped into the road in front of me. Do not come back in case this is another trap for us. Keep going to the office and secure the office."

One of the state troopers gets on the radio. "Dewight, we can turn back and assist you. Perhaps Juan can help to identify the behavior of the beast."

Dewight stays calm but allows some anger to show. "No, I am the ranking officer here, and you will continue on your current path to leave. This is not open to discussion, do you understand? Juan and you will be of more assistance alive than dead."

The trooper responds and agrees to continue on the departure.

Brooke slows down, and Julie doesn't question why. They are the last car in the convoy out of the area. Brooke doesn't say a word to Julie until she looks in the rearview mirror.

Brooke gets a look of uncertainty and fear on her face. "Julie, look behind us and tell me if you see what I think I see in the mirror."

Julie turns and looks. Her jaw literally drops open she gets a look of terror on her face. She turns to Brooke. "Do-ooo-oo you see many werewolves behind us?"

Brooke says, "Yes, that is what I thought I saw in the mirror."

Brooke speeds up to catch back up to the convoy. She gets on the radio. "We have many beasts behind us. Keep moving; we cannot go back, even if we wanted to. There are way too many to drive through. It doesn't look like they are following us at this time."

Dewight hears Brooke on the radio and stops his car. He was thinking about driving through the one blocking his escape route, but he now knows he has many more beyond that one. He just stops the car. He is thinking about his options as he is watching all the way around his car. So far he only sees the one in front of him.

He thinks to himself about making a run for Dave's and taking refuge there for the rest of the night. But then he realizes the distance to the house and knows there is no way he could make it there before the beast is on him; not to mention getting Dave to open the door in time.

Another thought is to call Dave and have him shoot the one in the road. No, that won't work either if the others would come running to investigate the shot. Then it starts the whole battle over again.

He has another thought. He calls Dave.

Dave looks at his cell phone and sees its Dewight calling him. "What could he want now?"

Dave answers the phone with a bit of curiosity in his voice. "Hello, Dewight. What can I do for you now? I thought we had everything done for the night."

Dewight is still calm but does sound concerned; just enough that Dave picks up on it. "Dave, just listen to me. I have a beast blocking my escape. Brooke radioed that the road is blocked by many more behind this one. I can't just drive through them; there is just too many. I have one chance to get out of here. No matter what you hear." He raises his voice and says, "DO NOT do anything. If you look outside, still do nothing. I have one chance here, and if we do anything wrong, I'm dead. You may be dead by daybreak, as well, if you get involved this time. Do you agree to do nothing, my friend?"

Dave looks out the window and sees Dewight's cruiser in the street. "You do know that what you ask is not easy, my old friend."

Dewight says, "I know, that is why I am demanding and not asking you."

Dave lets out a little chuckle. "You of all people know I don't listen when told to do something. But in this case, I will honor your demand as I have faith in your decision and that you know what you are doing."

Dewight says, "Thank you, my friend. If I don't make it remember you were one of my best friends."

Dave says, "Thank you. You are one of my best friends, as well."

He gets no response. He hears tires squealing and sees Dewight in reverse at a high speed.

Dave checks his phone, and it is on the main screen. "Well, how do like that? He hung up on me this time."

Dewight spins the car around in the street; one fast move that he doesn't need to do often, but tonight, he hoped he didn't miss any gears or make a wrong move during the maneuver. He manages to pull of the maneuver successfully and is moving forward when the beast starts chasing him.

He looks in the mirror and watches the beast drop to all fours to chase him.

The beast lets out a couple barks as it begins the chase.

Dewight is trying to watch the beast and where he is going, as well.

Two beasts appear out of the darkness in front of Dewight. He puts the throttle pedal to the floor, ramming the two beasts at a high speed. The beasts go flying to opposite sides of the road when hit by the car.

The werewolf chasing him barks again. More beasts appear in front of Dewight. This time he cannot count how many there are. He turns onto another street instead of heading for the pack.

The beast chasing him appears to shake its head in disapproval. The beast barks again and follows Dewight onto the new street.

The beast is gaining on Dewight. He doesn't realize it as he is watching his path of travel. He is travelling about sixty miles per hour in a twenty-five zone. He slowed down for the turn after hitting the two.

Dewight can see the main road ahead of him about two blocks. A beast comes out of the dark and runs at him. He checks his rearview mirror and realizes the beast chasing him is almost close enough to jump onto his car. He accelerates, and the beast coming at him doesn't adjust for his increase in speed and collides with the cruiser. It started a jump too late and was hit in the lower body. It flipped over, and its head was hit with the light bar breaking the light bar. The beast lands on the road behind the car and in front of the one chasing the car, tripping the beast that is already chasing the car.

Dewight looks in his mirror to see the beast get tripped. He looks ahead again then back in the mirror to see the beast that was chasing him attack the other beast that lays on the road. Other beasts appear and do nothing but watch.

Dewight makes his turn onto the main road and continues to travel at well above the speed limit. He catches the convoy before his headlights go out. Somehow his headlights were able to work long enough before blowing out. Perhaps it is because the beasts hit the guard on the front of his car more than the headlights.

They position his car in front of Brooke and Julie, so he can see the road from their headlights.

Back at Dave's, he could see what was happening until Dewight made the turn onto the other street. Dave watched the two beasts go flying of the side of the road after Dewight hit them. He thought to himself, "He may get out of this yet."

Dave looks at his phone to see if maybe he missed a call.

It shows no missed calls.

He goes to the table and he, with the help of Sarah and Ashley, sort the samples by breed size of the dogs, with the small dogs like chihuahua, miniature poodle, dachshund, and similar small breeds on one side of the table and the medium breeds like German shepherd, husky, in general, in the center of the table. The large breeds like St. Bernard, great Dane, and mastiff go to the other side. But one category that was not created at first was the wild breeds like coyote and wolf. When Dave sees these samples, he asks, "Who took these samples?"

The ladies look at each other. "Not me," they both said.

Dave goes to the window again, looking into the darkness where Juan was taking samples. He can't see far enough to see if it was mislabeled. But he thinks to himself, "Juan must know what he was looking at. After all, he was studying the beasts for a while before they discovered him. I'm sure he knows the breeds of dogs."

He goes back to the table and separates those two samples.

Dave looks at the samples. "These will be the first two we look at; actually, the wolf will be first."

Ashley nods in agreement.

Sarah speaks up, "You see it is eleven-thirty now, don't you?"

Dave looks at the clock. "I do now; thank you."

Ashley asks, "What about the time is so important?"

Dave starts to put the blood samples in a rack, making sure to keep them separated. "The importance is that we have work in the morning and need to get packed up so we can get sleep before needing to get up for work."

Ashley sounds a little surprised. "Oh, I wasn't even thinking about work tomorrow."

Sarah smiles. "That is why he has me to remind him of his schedule at the hospital."

Dave agrees. "Without her knowing my work schedule, I'd be down here all night when I have a body to study. I wouldn't make it to work the next day."

Sarah helps put the samples in the refrigerator. But she refuses to help with the body. Actually, the only reason she helps now is that she doesn't trust Dave alone with Ashley. But she doesn't tell them that.

Dave looks at Sarah. "Thanks, honey, for your help. It's been a while since you even offered to help. I take it you are feeling pretty good tonight."

Sarah smiles. "Yes, the pain is manageable tonight. But I'm not feeling that good tonight."

Dave looks at Sarah. "You can head up to bed, and I'll be up as soon as the body is in the fridge."

Sarah looks at him then Ashley and then at the stairs. "Umm…I don't want to go upstairs by myself tonight, not after all those beasts were here. Are you nuts? I can wait and we go up together."

Dave shrugs his shoulders. "As you wish, dear."

They get everything put away. The female body is the last thing to put away. Dave looks at the body in the cell and doesn't see anything obvious for a change. So, they all head upstairs to the first floor, turning off the lights and double-checking locks on the way from basement to bedroom.

Dave and Sarah help carry Ashley's suitcases to her room, so no one is alone in the hallway.

Ashley enters her room, and Dave and Sarah drop off the bags and then goes into their room.

Dave looks out the window as Sarah changes for bed. Sarah asks with curiosity, "What are you looking for?"

Dave doesn't look at her. "Just looking like most nights, except tonight I see a lot of dead out there."

He sees something that he couldn't see from the basement. He isn't sure if it is or not, so he grabs the binoculars.

Sarah letting some fear show in her voice. "What do you see?"

Dave looks through the binoculars and answers, "I think I may see the dogs Juan listed as wolf and coyote."

He is looking in the area Juan was collecting samples. "Yes, there they are. It looks like he labeled correctly. But there are more than just one of each out there."

Sarah has her pajamas on and goes to the window. "How many dead wolves to you see?"

Dave says, "I'm not sure, but so far, I've seen five in the same area, four coyotes in the same area. As if they stayed in their pack even as the beast, they appear to have stayed close to each other."

Sarah lets curiosity take over. "What do you think that might mean?" Dave puts down the binoculars, and Sarah takes them to look.

Dave gets his notebook to make the notes of his observation. "I don't know just what to think, sweetheart. But if they do stay close in beast form and are from the same pack as dogs, then they can be very dangerous; more so than any other canine turned into beast. They could be as dangerous, maybe more so, than a human turned beast."

Sarah is still looking through the binoculars at the dead dogs. She is looking at all the dead out there not just the wolves and coyotes. "Why would you think they could be more dangerous than a human turned beast? Wouldn't the human type be more dangerous with the human capability to think?"

Dave doesn't look up from his notebook; he just keeps writing his notes. "No, honey. The wolves and the coyotes that work together in a pack in their canine form can take that to the beast form, making them more dangerous than the human type. Sometimes the wolves and coyote packs take humans for food not in beast form. They are capable of learning and taking whatever they see as prey."

She drops the binoculars and runs to the bed.

Dave looks at her. "What is wrong? The wolves and coyotes are not usually human hunters unless very desperate."

She looks at him and points to the window. The fear is obvious in her voice. "I saw beasts."

Dave goes to the window. He is looking out into the darkness. "Where?"

Sarah says, "I am not getting out of this bed before daybreak. They were in the shadows Two houses to your left."

Dave looks and keeps his eyes on the shadows in the area she said she seen the beasts. He sees movement.

Sure enough, he sees one step out into the light. It resembles the one that he figures must be the leader.

He keeps watching the beast as it moves around the dead, sniffing each one. Every so often, it reaches down and nudges at one of the dead.

Dave thinks out loud, "Interesting."

Sarah asks, "What is?"

Dave says, "Sorry, I was thinking out loud. But the beast is checking the dead."

Sarah stays in the bed. "So, a lot of animals check their dead. Some think they morn their dead. Or, in this case, maybe it is looking for something to eat."

Dave keeps watching the beast. "I'll agree with the morning of the dead theory. Because it isn't making any attempt to eat any of the dead."

As he gets done with that statement, the beast looks at the house, and its gaze travels up toward the window where he is standing.

Dave is still watching, trying to figure out what the beast is thinking. He doesn't tell Sarah because he doesn't want her to be concerned about the beast looking at him.

The beast stares at Dave. It watches him as it moves to a spot across the street from the house. There it sits and stares at Dave.

Dave is confused as to why this beast is watching him. There are other beasts out in the light now checking the dead. As this one sits and stares.

The beasts gaze is drawn from Dave briefly.

Dave looks and realizes the cat is in the driveway. Dave looks back to the beast.

The beast seen that Dave looked at the cat. The beast now bares its teeth as if growling but Dave hears nothing.

The beast lunges in the direction of the cat. Dave looks as the cat runs for the garage again.

The beast returns a short time later without the cat.

Dave smiles, figuring the cat made it back into the garage safely.

The beast looks at Dave and appears to know he is smiling.

The beast is walking upright on two legs. It looks around and barks a couple times; a short howl. All the beasts leave the light and return back into the darkness. It looks at Dave on last time before it disappears into the dark, as well.

Dave looks around at the dead. He thinks something is different but what. He keeps looking. "Oh, shoot, their gone."

Sarah asks, "Who is gone?"

Dave sounds surprised and maybe a little mad. "The wolves and the coyotes. They are all gone."

Sarah isn't sure to believe him. "Are you sure? You not just looking in the wrong place, are you?"

He grabs the binoculars. "No, they were right there. Now they are gone. Now I understand why it was watching me."

Sarah asks, "Who was watching you?"

Dave realizes he just screwed up. "Oh, sorry, there was a beast that was watching me from across the street. It chased the cat again and apparently missed again."

Sarah is allowing anger to show in her voice. "Wait, there was a beast watching you? And just when did you figure on telling me?"

Dave puts the binoculars away and looks at her. "Sorry, babe, I didn't want you to worry about it."

Sarah says, "Well, you did a very poor job of that."

Dave agrees as he gets changed for bed.

Sarah asks, "Did you find the wolves and the coyotes?"

Dave simply replies, "No."

Dave doesn't sleep very well. He keeps waking up to every sound, and he keeps thinking about the animals that disappeared in the dark. Why did they remove the wolves and the coyotes? This is a question he keeps going over in his mind.

At the police station, everyone looks at Dewight's car.

Dewight says, "Okay, let's get inside before we get ambushed here."

Juan sees blood on the car. "Mr. Dewight, I think Dave would like to have that for his samples." He points to the blood on the car.

Dewight looks at the blood and at Juan. "I suppose you are right." He tells one of the officers to go get an evidence kit so they can get a sample for Dave.

While the officer is inside getting the kit. Dewight keeps watching Juan who is looking over the cruiser.

Dewight's curiosity gets the best of him. "Juan, what are you looking for?" Juan doesn't look up. "Anything that might help Dave. Hair, blood, pieces of meat."

Dewight keeps watching him, not fully trusting him.

The officer comes out with the kit.

Dewight takes the kit and collects the samples of blood. Juan shows him some hair to collect, as well. They find nothing bigger than the blood and hair.

They all go inside and Dewight asks. "Are we missing anyone, other than Ben and Carl?"

Everyone else is present and accounted.

Julie asks. "Isn't that weird that the beast went after you? They don't usually attack more than once a night. They had that big attack and then still went after you."

Dewight looks at Juan. "Would you like to try and explain what happened tonight? I have only theories and don't even know how to explain them. Tonight's behavior is new to me."

Juan looks at Dewight. "Yes, I try. I do not see this before tonight either. It is new to me also. But I think that with so many in the area tonight. Many packs together and they got confused. Many pack leaders and followers. The dead dogs may also have been a difference tonight. I never see that before. May be the beasts are going to be different than what we know in past.

Maybe we need to change also. Time to change how we deal with them. How we hunt them. How we kill them. May be the beasts know you are police chief. Odd I know it sounds but they are smarter than we think."

Dewight thinks about the statement. "You may have a point there. Because apparently they were watching us from the dark. So, they could have seen me in charge tonight. If they are smarter than we know it could be a change we need to learn and to make for survival."

All the other officers agree. It is time to change how things are done to survive.

# Chapter 5

# A New Day

The next morning Dave and Ashley are getting ready for work.

Dave, "Ash last night from my room I saw the Wolves and coyotes that Juan listed."

Ashley's eyes light up and her excitement shows. "Really? Should we go out and collect at least one of each for study?"

Dave lowers his head. "We can't. The beasts removed them last night. I saw one stare at me then chase the cat. When I looked back the wolves and coyotes were gone."

Ashley looks at him. The confusion is obvious on her face. "I wonder why they would have removed those bodies only."

Dave looks up. "You know I didn't look out this morning. They may have removed more than just those."

They both look out the window to the street. What they discover has both of them confused. They go upstairs to get an elevated look onto the street. But sure enough, all the dogs have been removed. Including the beasts that didn't change back to human form. It even looks like there are fewer human bodies on the street.

They finish getting ready for work and see the cat on the way to the garage.

They pause to pet the cat. Dave looks at the cat's tail.

Dave, "Well, it looks like your tail will be just fine. At least you seem to be able to escape whenever the beast chases you."

Ashley looks at him, "What do you mean whenever it chases him?"

Dave shows her the cat's tail. "This was from the first time the beast chased him. The beast just missed the cat. Took hair off of the tail as the cat escaped."

Ashley looks at the cat's tail where the hair is missing. "It looks like the skin was punctured, as well. Aren't you concerned that the cat could become infected?"

Dave looks at her. "We need to get going."

She puts the cat down and they both get in the car.

Dave starts the car and is pulling out of the driveway. "I don't know if the cat can be infected from the beast. It appears to be a canine infection. Granted it infects humans, as well, but felines. I just don't know. I never even considered testing for that possibility."

Ashley responds calmly. "Don't you think we need to consider it and start to see if it is possible? Because we could have a whole new problem if it can be transferred to felines, as well."

They are heading out of town. Looking at the dead still along the street. But not a single dog or untransformed beast remains in sight.

They pass the coroners car with her police escort on their way in. Dave waves at her and continues on his way to work.

Carla calls Dave.

Dave answers. "Hello Carla. You have a lot of bodies today. You may need a truck."

Carla answers with a little sarcasm. "I hear you are the reason I have all these to collect today. Aren't you getting these bodies today?"

Dave. "Not today. I have more than I have room for now. Just send them to be cremated."

Carla, "Haven't you finished with the female body yet?"

Dave laughs. "Not yet. Last night was interrupted when we got attacked."

Carla laughs. "Here I thought Sarah demanded you get rid of the body instead of research."

Dave. "No, she hasn't gone that far yet."

Carla. "Well, I better get to work here collecting the bodies. I have a long day ahead of me. I still need to identify the bodies before I can cremate them."

They say goodbye and they both continue with what they need to do.

Ashley seems interested. "Who was that?"

Dave smiles. "Oh, sorry that was Carla. She is the coroner."

Ashley looks back out the front window. "Oh, you do know it almost sounded like she is more to you than a colleague?"

Dave thinks about it. "Really? But that is how I've always talked to her. I try to talk to everyone that way. Even you."

Ashley smiles. "I know. You do realize it makes your wife jealous, don't you?"

Dave looks at her then back to the road. "She has been jealous for a long time. I don't pay attention to it anymore. Nor do I try to explain myself to her anymore."

Ashley looks at him and he is not looking to happy. The smile is gone, and he seems super focused on the road so not to look at her at all. "I'm sorry if I said something wrong."

Dave just does not answer. The rest of the ride to work is quiet.

Dave parks the car, and they get out to walk inside.

Ashley steps in front of Dave. "I apologized for upsetting you. Will you accept my apology?"

Dave looks at her. "I forgive you. It's just that I get tired of dealing with Sarah's attitude and trying to explain her jealousy to everyone."

Ashley steps aside. "Thank you." They walk toward the entrance of the building. "I'm not asking you to explain anything about her. Or make excuses for her. I just want to know that we can stay friends and stay professional. Even when one of us upsets the other without knowing it."

Dave smiles. "I apologize for overreacting. You don't know the history with her and I."

Ashley looks at him. "I forgive you for being obnoxiously silent to me." They both laugh and continue to the Lab to clock in.

They get clocked in and proceed to the office to get their list for the day. Allen isn't in yet. But no worries the work schedule is on the desk from the night supervisor.

Frank is also there for his work schedule for the day.

Frank already has an attitude toward them. "You don't think you're just going to take whatever jobs you want do you?"

Dave looks at Frank and stays calm. "No, I was going to wait for Allen. Unless you think you know what is on the schedule for whom?"

Frank picks up the schedule and looks at it. "Well, I see here that there are samples to be tested that I usually get. I don't see anything about possible werewolf samples for you."

Allen is behind them in the doorway. He responds before Dave. And his tone is not a pleasant one. "Frank, give me the schedule and get out of my way. You also owe Dave an apology for disrespecting him. He does get other jobs, as well, and you know it."

Frank gives the schedule to Allen and apologizes to Dave.

Allen gives them jobs to start with while he looks over the rest of the list and divides the jobs to keep everyone busy.

As they walk away Dave notices that Frank is limping. He is holding his lower back as if it is bothering him today.

Ashley notices it, as well. She nudges Dave and points at Frank. Dave nods an acknowledgement.

Dave curiously asks, "Frank, what happened to your back? You seem to be in pain this morning."

Frank looks at him. "My back pain is none of your business." He is not hiding any of his anger over the question.

Dave looks at him. "Sorry for caring about you."

Frank nods in agreement. "You need to be."

They all go to their work areas. Everyone is working on the samples they were given. Dave and Ashley are not speaking any more than they need to and only about work. Frank and his assistant are doing the same. Only talking about work.

They all work and stay to themselves. Dave and Ashley look over at Frank periodically, just to see what he is doing and how the pain level is doing.

It finally is lunchtime, and Dave and Ashley head out to the cafeteria for lunch.

Frank speaks up, "Don't talk about me too much." He is being as arrogant as he can portray in his voice.

Dave stops and looks at him. Returning the arrogance, he asks, "Why would you think we would talk about you? You are not interesting conversation."

Dave leaves before Frank can respond.

Once they get to the cafeteria, they get their lunch and sit in a corner away from everyone else. They do get some odd looks from some other staff members. Some start a rumor that they may be having an affair. Others figure they chose to be away from everyone else to talk about werewolves and the theories and ideas they may have about them. Others just don't worry about them and continue about their own business. Dave and Ashley both return greetings when offered to them.

Ashley asks Dave, keeping her voice low to almost a whisper but not a full whisper, "Is it just me or does Frank's injured back coincide with where you shot the beast last night? To me it looked like you hit the one on the car in the lower back. Today Frank has a sore lower back."

Dave trying to keep an opened mind but has the same thoughts and can't hide it when talking to her. "I know, it is a very strange coincidence. Yesterday he came in with his knuckles scabbed over. That was the first day he had the injury. It was also the day after I had a beast beating on the basement door for access. He won't say how he got the injury."

Ashley says, "Yeah, like today. He just wants us to not notice."

Dave says, "Let's get through the day and not worry about Frank. If it is him, then the day, or night, rather, will come when we will know for sure."

Ashley says, "Okay, let's worry about why the wolves and coyotes were the first to be picked up and why the rest of the dogs and remaining beasts were, as well?"

Dave is thinking, "I know it is just weird. It also appeared as though they removed some human remains, as well."

Ashley is thinking about that one, as well. "Yeah, why do you think they might remove any bodies?"

Their lunchtime is about done, so they head back to the lab.

They are talking about last night and the bodies when Frank passes them in the hall.

Frank is his usual arrogant self. "What are you blabbering about beasts and missing bodies for?"

Dave looks at him and returns the arrogance. "If you explain how you got your injuries, I will explain our conversation."

Frank says, "Forget it then. I don't need to tell you anything; you are not my doctor." They continue on their separate ways.

Dave looks at Ashley and continues their conversation. "My thought is, let me know if you agree or not about the missing human remains. Is that they are not dead? At least the beast inside of them is not dead. What died was the human and not both. As far as the dogs... well, I wonder if there is a clue there to finding a cure."

They go in and clock back in and finish the day. Both of them are thinking about the beasts and what may be the reasoning behind them removing bodies.

After work, Frank asks Dave, "So, how many werewolves do you have at home to experiment on?" He lets out a little laugh.

Dave smiles and says, "Just two. Why would you like to volunteer to be another?"

Frank looks at him and gets angry. "Why would you even suggest such a thing? Do you think I am one of those demons?"

Dave smiles. "No, you asked first. I just gave you an option."

Frank looks at him and changes his tone to a more friendly one. "Unless you are asking for my help in your lab?"

Dave looks at him, remaining calm and friendly in return. "No, I think there are enough of us now. But if you really want to help, I can bounce ideas off you, and we can talk about these things and what to do and what to look for."

Frank starts laughing. "You actually fell for it. You actually thought I'd be willing to work with you and study those demons. That is just too funny." He walks away.

Ashley and Dave continue to the car.

Ashley asks, "Were you actually asking him for help?"

Dave smiles. "No, not actually. Just testing the waters, so to speak."

Ashley is a bit confused. "Okay, if he would have said he was willing to discuss the beasts and help with theories, would you have accepted his help?"

Dave unlocks the car. "Of course. He is arrogant but to have another look at these things would not hurt."

Ashley agrees as they get into the car.

Ashley speaks up, "About our earlier conversation... I'm not sure I totally agree with the theory. I mean, it makes sense and all. But the beasts that turned back to human and disappeared didn't commit suicide. So, wouldn't the beast have died, as well? If we go with the theory of suicides only killing the human side and not the beast, then they should have still been there, correct?"

Dave is heading out of the parking lot. "I understand that, and you do have a good point. Like I said, it is good to have more looking at this. But let me ask you this: How do we know for sure they didn't commit suicide? I mean, they were there, yes. But was it their choice? Did they go with the intent of dying? Were they there because they were commanded by a leader? One beast that leads them all. The alpha of the alphas."

Ashley smiles. "Okay, if they were there because they were commanded, then they would not have been able to commit suicide. They were ordered to be there. I agree if they were there of their own free will with the intent of dying, like you said."

Dave smiles. "I like you. You are willing to discuss this and work out ideas and theories."

Ashley starts laughing.

Dave looks at her and back to the road. "What is funny?"

Ashley says, "I forgot about my car in the parking lot."

Dave smiles. "Well, I forgot about it, as well. On the plus side, it will be there the next day we work."

Ashley says, "I know you're right, but it is still funny."

Dave agrees and their conversation the rest of the ride is more of the ideas they already discussed. They do more thinking out loud and not listening to the other.

They get to the house, and Dave parks in the garage.

They get out of the car and see the cat on a shelf in the garage.

Dave reaches up to pet the cat.

The cat does not reject the offer and allows Dave to not only pet it but to pick it up.

Ashley pets the cat while Dave holds it. She also looks at the tail.

Dave releases the cat and asks, "So, how does the tail look?"

Ashley responds, "The same as this morning."

Dave closes the garage door on the way to the house.

Dave says, "So, in your opinion, is there any risk of the cat being infected?"

Ashley says, "It needs to be watched. I'm not ready to rule it out."

Dave says, "Tonight the moon will be full. If the cat does not change, I think we could believe that the cat is not infected."

Ashley says, "I will agree with you on that."

Sarah overheard is curious. "What do you mean cat not infected if it doesn't change?"

Dave says, "Remember a couple nights ago when the cat escaped with its life after the beast chased it?"

Sarah says, "Yes, What about it? You don't think it is going to become one of those beasts, do you?"

Dave says, "That is the million-dollar question, dear. We don't know if the infection is strictly canine, or if it can be transferred to feline and, if so, what other animal could it infect."

Sarah isn't sure what to think. "Well, dinner is ready. I pray the cat does not become a werewolf."

Dave asks her, "So, how are you feeling today?"

Sarah looks at him. "In pain, as always. But at this moment, it is not keeping me down."

Dave says, "So, can I count on you being in the lab after dinner?"

Sarah smiles, "Well, you have Ashley. Why do you need me? I don't do much to help anymore."

They are eating dinner. When there is a knock on the door.

They look at each other.

Sarah asks, "Who are you expecting?"

Dave gets up and heads for the front door. "Nobody."

Dave opens the door. It's Brooke and Julie.

Dave is confused. "Hello. Forgive me, but why are you here?"

Brooke says, "Dewight sent us over, so you have protection tonight. So, you can do your studies and not defend yourself. We will do that for you."

Dave says, "Well, come in, then. We just sat down to dinner."

They go follow Dave into the kitchen.

Dave says, "Look who Dewight sent to protect us tonight." He sits down to continue with dinner.

Sarah looks at them. "Ladies, there is enough here if you want to join us."

Brooke looks at Julie before responding, "We are here on official business, not social. Thank you."

Sarah is already up and getting more plates for the table. "Nonsense; you can join us anyway. Now sit."

Brooke and Julie both sit at the table and join in dinner.

Brooke looks at Dave. "I wonder how long it took Carla to clear out the bodies this morning. And what would she have done with the dogs?"

Dave and Ashley look at each other. They use a look that Brooke knows they have information she doesn't.

Brooke asks, "What is wrong? I see it in your faces."

Dave speaks first and says, "The beasts removed all the dogs before dawn; some of the human remains, as well. Every beast that didn't change from beast form was also gone by dawn."

Brooke and Julie look at each other.

Julie says, "We should probably tell Dewight."

Brooke speaks before Dave, "No, let's not just yet. We can tell him later. There is nothing he can do now anyway."

Dave is a little excited. "Oh, good, so Dewight made it out last night. I saw him hit two beasts on his way out and then didn't see him after he turned to avoid a larger group."

Brooke says, "Oh, yeah, he made it out." She reaches in her pocket and removes the samples they retrieved from the cruiser. "Here these are blood and hair samples they recovered from Dewight's car at the office last night."

Sarah grabs the samples. "You will finish dinner first, then I will give you these samples."

Dave smiles. "Yes, dear."

Everybody has a little laugh.

Julie asks, "Why do you think the beasts would remove any of the dead? Do you suppose it would be for food?"

Dave looks at her. "Well, actually, Ash and I were talking about that throughout the day. We just don't have any solid idea. We do agree it most likely is not for food."

Brooke asks, "Do you think they wanted to bury their dead?"

Ashley speaks up, "Well, we didn't think about that idea." She looks at Dave. "What do you think? She has a good point."

Dave thinks and speaks at the same time, "It is a good question, true. But in order for that to be entertained as a possibility, first we would need to assume that the beasts retain enough human emotion to want to bury the dead. Then also why didn't they take the rest of the dead. Why only selected dead?"

Ashley nods in agreement. "You have a point. If they were going to bury the dead, they would have taken them all."

Brooke says, "Not if they ran out of darkness. If dawn was approaching, they may have left the rest to come back for tonight."

Dave nods in agreement since he has a mouth full of food and decides to be polite and not speak with his mouth full. He does respond when he swallows his food. "You have another good point. But again, remember there were more than could be counted last night. The number of living beasts should have outnumbered the dead greatly."

Julie speaks up, with an idea, "What if they only removed the dead that they knew?"

Dave stops eating. His fork is in the air when he stops, and he lowers it back to the plate.

Julie isn't sure what to think. "Sorry, just a thought I had."

Dave smiles. "Oh, no, don't apologize. You have a great idea. What if they knew the dead they removed?" He looks at Ashley. "That could help explain why the wild animals were the first to disappear last night. They were leaving the area first."

Ashley is thinking and responds, "But don't wolves and coyotes usually just leave their dead? Don't they usually compete for the same food? So, why would they work together here? Why would they remove the dead now?"

Dave got up and got a notebook and tried to write down the questions, but they were asked to quickly. But he got them recorded on paper.

Dave is trying to finish dinner now, looking at the clock and realizing dusk is approaching fast.

So, now he speaks with food in his mouth, although not much food so he can still be understood, "These are all questions we need to try to understand. I don't know if we will find the actual answers or not, but we can try."

They finish eating and head to the basement after loading the dishwasher. Nobody is alone upstairs.

Sarah looks at the body in the cell and stares at it.

Brooke looks at her. "What is with this body?"

Sarah doesn't look away. "It was a suicide. It was dead with no heartbeat when we hooked it to the machine. Now it has a steady heartbeat. It has gotten hairier just since last night. I don't see anything obvious about it being awake."

Brooke looks at her. "Are you serious?"

Sarah says, "Yes."

Sarah turns and goes to a chair to watch what is going on in the room. She still prefers not to help, and her chronic pain is starting to get worse. So, she sits and tries to deal with it. She does take a pain pill that she keeps with her, but it barely helps with the pain. She would prefer to be in bed but doesn't want to be alone.

Dave and Ashley start looking at the blood samples from the dead dogs. They do not remove the female body from the cooler yet.

Dave asks Ashley to start on the samples that Brooke and Julie brought from Dewight's car.

She starts the testing and separating the DNA out of it. She uses as little as possible, so they have more for other testing.

Dave has different vials of animal blood out. He has the "contaminated blood" of the wolves and coyotes. Then he has his zoo samples of wolf and coyote blood that is not contaminated. He had pulled the whole tray of zoo blood from the refrigerator. So, yes, he has many other species there, as well.

He has the tray with the "clean samples" on the edge of his worktable. Everyone knows it is there and watches it when they are in the area. Some samples are from endangered species, and he is trying to help figure out some of the medical illnesses that the vets have not isolated. But the animal's health is good, and the meds they give them help the animals greatly.

Dave puts a drop of "contaminated blood" labeled "wolf" on a slide and puts it under the microscope. He looks at it and studies it. He pulls it out and places the "clean blood" labeled wolf under the microscope and looks and studies it. He finds a difference in the samples. He calls Ashley over. She goes when she is at a point when she can walk away from her job.

She looks at the two samples and sees a difference, as well. "It is subtle, but there is a difference."

Dave is smiling. "Yes, it is subtle. But it still looks close enough to the same strand in humans to mean that this must be the beast infection. I need to check the coyote next and then the other dogs." He looks at Ashley. "We may not get to the body in the cooler tonight."

Ashley doesn't sound disappointed. "No problem; we need to get these checked and studied. She isn't going anywhere."

Dave agrees as he is getting the coyote samples on a slide to look at under the microscope.

Again, he looks and studies the sample. Beginning with the "contaminated" and then the "clean" samples. Again, he finds the same anomaly in the "contaminated blood." He moves on the other samples of the domestic dogs. He doesn't have clean samples of each breed to check against the "contaminated' samples. He keeps looking in his blood vial tray for a "clean" sample with each breed he grabs of "contaminated."

Those that he does have "clean' samples for he again compares the samples. Again, he finds the same anomaly. He even sees it in the samples he doesn't have a "clean" sample to compare, too. But the anomaly isn't exactly the same in each breed of domestic dog he checks. It isn't exactly like the strand in the wild dogs and the human strand is just a little different, as well.

But each strand is similar enough to leave him with no doubt that he is looking at the werewolf infection in each sample of blood. He figures that the slight difference is most likely due to the host of the disease. It is different because, as he figures, of the transformation needed. Human to canine, canine to human, wild, and domestic. But the domestic is transformed to a human wolf from whatever breed they are. This is also why the wolf's strand is different. It just needs the human aspect of the disease for transformation. The smaller breeds of dog also need to gain some size with the human side of the infection to be as powerful as the others in beast form. He figures this is some of the reasoning for the difference in the way the infection looks under the microscope.

Ashley needs to wait until the DNA is completely separated before they can see the strand in beast form.

Ashley looks at the samples again that Dave checked. She agrees with him that they must be looking at the disease in the sample. "Granted, we need to test it to know for sure."

Dave agrees and they begin testing the samples of canine blood they have.

The night is still and quite outside, which has Brooke and Julie both on alert. They have both been doing the night patrol long enough to figure it is too quiet, especially after last night.

Dave and Ashley are too busy with their work testing to even acknowledge the officers. But Sarah is fully aware of the officers pacing and watching the windows to the street, watching the surveillance cameras and all.

Sarah's pain med has lessened her pain enough she gets up and walks over to Brooke. "What are you guys nervous about?"

Brooke looks at her. "To be honest, we don't know as yet. It could be nothing, but we need to be watching out for any possibility."

Carla has been busy all day, trying to identify the dead that is at the morgue.

She had a few that were locals and wasn't too difficult for her to identify. But those from out of the area are a little more challenging. She needs to check federal data bases to identify them.

For those that she identified her colleague has notified the family. So, the body is in the freezer waiting to be cremated.

The bodies she has not yet identified are in the cooler not the freezer. Just in case she needs to get anymore samples from them.

She does not feel as safe as Dave with known werewolf bodies in her morgue. But she has a job to do, and she has no reservations about doing her job to make sure the family of each of the dead knows about their loved one.

By law she has no choice but to tell them that their loved one was a beast when they died. She has to inform them that they cannot have the body of their loved one, that by federal law she is required to cremate the remains.

Granted there are families that want their loved one returned so they can bury the body. But Carla reminds them of the law and has to decline their request. She informs them they can have the ashes once finished.

Carla gets involved with notifying the family, only if her colleague is having issues with the family. Some families are better at taking the news than others. As expected, no family wants the hear that their loved one was killed and definitely do not want the hear they were killed as a werewolf.

There is one body in particular that has Carla's attention. She doesn't understand why this one body is on her mind. She has not yet gotten the identity of this individual. It is a female, and yet Carla keeps looking at her.

This is not the only female body she collected and is trying to identify. But this one is on her mind more than the others all combined.

Carla continues to keep processing the bodies and trying to identify them all. As she puts bodies in the cooler, she keeps this one out. Her coworker asked her if she wanted it in the cooler. She said, "No, not yet."

Her coworker is confused but does not ask questions.

The day continues on and results come in and those families are notified. This one female is the last body out yet. Carla waits until the last minute before closing for the day to put her in the cooler.

They put the body in the cooler, and on the way out as they are shutting down for the night, the computer lets them know they got a notification. Carla opens it and almost falls to the floor after reading it. Her colleague catches her, and Carla points to the email, showing the results of the female on which she is focused.

Her colleague sits down once finished reading it. They are both in shock. This is a totally new discovery. Carla isn't sure to call Dave or not. Could this female help him with his studies? He already has a female for his studies.

Carla tells her coworker to go ahead and go home. She will call the family herself.

The female's father answers the phone. "Hello?"

Carla is almost in tears herself as she begins to speak. She has found the missing person report that was filed that morning. "Hello, my name is Carla. I have bad news for you and your family."

The father asks, "Are you a cop? Have you found my daughter?"

It is harder for Carla to keep from crying. She continues to fight the tears, so she can inform the family. "No, sir, I am the coroner."

The father loses it and is crying now. "What happened? Where is she, and when can we come and get her?"

Carla is fighting the tears harder and almost losing it herself. "Sir you cannot have your daughter's body."

Understandably, the father is upset. "Why? She is my daughter. I need to be able to bury her."

Carla is starting to lose her battle with the tears. "Sir, she was a werewolf when she was killed."

The father is very upset. The mother takes the phone from him.

The mother is still in control of her anger at this moment. "Sorry, but whatever you told my husband upset him greatly. He told us that our Jenifer is dead. What happened?"

Carla is still fighting a losing battle with her own emotions. "Ma'am, I informed your husband that your daughter was a werewolf when she was killed."

The mother drops the phone. She reaches down and picks it up again. "No, you must be mistaken. She could not have been a beast. She was a good kid and only sixteen. How could she have been a beast? She wasn't old enough. Was she?"

Carla says, "I know it is hard to understand. I don't understand it myself, ma'am but, apparently, she was old enough to be a beast. Your daughter is the first person under the age of twenty-five positively identified as a werewolf."

The mother is getting emotional now and is talking through her crying. "But beasts are only male, aren't they? A beast can't be female, can they?"

Carla says, "Well, ma'am, this week we actually have other females that were beasts when killed. Your daughter is not the only, nor is she the first, female we have discovered. But she is the youngest person."

The mother asks, "So, can we come and get here and where do we need to pick her up?"

Carla says, "Ma'am, do you know about the law that all bodies that were killed in beast form must be cremated?"

The mother says, "Yes, we know about that law, but she was only sixteen. That law was for adults, not children. When that was passed, it wasn't known that children could be infected. You can release her to us, so we can bury her."

Carla shakes her head in disagreement as if the mother can see her. "I am truly sorry, ma'am, but I cannot release her body. I can only send you email photos to identify her remains, so I can get her to the crematorium. I am sorry, ma'am, but that is the law, and it does not specify between adult or child. There is no age listed in the law."

The mother says, "There has to be a way we can get her body to bury. The law was made before anyone knew about children being infected. Children are not included in that law."

Carla says, "I am sorry, ma'am. I need your email address, so I can send you the photos to identify her body."

The mother says, "So, if I don't give you my email address, we can come and get her body and bury her ourselves?"

Carla is again shaking her head. "No, ma'am. If you don't give me your email address, I will still follow the law and send her to the crematorium. There will be pictures of her with her ashes for you and your husband to claim her at that point. She will be listed as a Jane Doe with her possible name under that. But until she is positively identified, she will be another Jane Doe. And you and your family will not have her ashes until you claim them and identify it is her."

The mother gives Carla her email address. "I will be calling my senator about this. This isn't right. The law was never meant to include children."

Carla politely responds, "Ma'am, there is no age listed in the law. Until that is changed, I have no choice but to follow how it is written. It doesn't matter if I think different. The law is there to protect the public from the beasts."

The mother lets her know that she will respond to the email when it comes in. Then she hangs up on Carla.

Carla hangs up, as well, and then lets herself cry for the young lady in her cooler and the family.

## Chapter 6

# The Awakening

The chair that Sarah sat in is in front of the cell with the body in it. As nervous as she is about the body, she still placed the chair there herself. She decided it looked like it was out of the way of everybody else. Dave and Ashley are testing samples and the officers pacing and watching outside.

Brooke is in the empty cell watching out the window to the street. Julie is watching the surveillance cameras.

Julie sees the cat in the driveway. "Dave, what happened to the cat's tail? It doesn't look right."

Dave looks at the monitor from his position. He recognizes the cat enough at the distance. "Oh, that is the cat. The beast, at least we think the beast, got its tail. Just the end of it."

Julie looks at the monitor. "Aw, poor cat. Do you think the cat will change in to a beast?"

Brooke looks away from the window. She looks at the monitor and then to Dave waiting his response.

Dave keeps working on the blood samples. "We have no evidence of that being a possibility. Everything we see is canine."

Brooke speaks up, "And two days ago, we knew only men got infected. Just yesterday we knew that only humans could become werewolves."

Dave looks at her. Before he says anything, his cell phone rings.

He looks at the number, and it's Carla.

Dave, "I wonder what she wants."

Sarah asks, "Who?"

Dave answers his phone. "Hello, Carla."

Sarah is confused, as well. She doesn't usually call.

Carla, still not in complete control of her emotions, says, "Dave, I found something with one of the bodies you should probably know about."

Dave gives her his full attention. "What did you find? Why does it sound like you have been crying?"

Carla says, "I have been crying because of what I found. One of the female bodies was only sixteen."

Dave's expression goes blank. "Say again? I don't think I heard you correctly."

Carla says, "I think you heard she was sixteen. One of the female bodies was sixteen Dave; not even an adult yet. Do you think you will need her body for study?"

Dave is holding onto the counter with his free hand. "No, you got to be mistaken. Please tell me I didn't kill a sixteen-year-old kid last night."

Carla says, "No, you killed a beast that was a sixteen-year-old kid."

Dave is starting to get emotional. He fights it. "No, I don't see any reason I would need her body for study. Do what you need to and get her to her family."

Carla says, "Okay, I will do that. But I thought you should know about her age to expand the knowledge of the beasts."

Dave, "Yes, thank you. We have learned a lot the last couple of nights. Just last night that dogs of all breeds are capable of being infected."

Carla, sounding surprised, asks, "What do you mean? I didn't see any dogs when I was out there."

Dave says, "Yeah, we think the living beasts removed them for some reason."

Carla responds, "Well, dang. You mean every breed no matter the size of the dog?"

Dave says, "Correct."

Carla, "Okay, well I'm going to go. I was going to go home and decided to call you first in case you wanted the girl."

Dave, "Thanks, but I don't need her. You go home and enjoy your time off."

Carla lets out a little giggle. "Really, you think I can relax since you told me about the dogs. Now I'm not going to trust my little chihuahua."

Dave says, "You're welcome. I never trusted those little dogs." He lets out a little laugh.

They end their call.

The others are looking at him.

Sarah speaks, "What was that about a sixteen-year-old?"

Dave lowers his head and does not make eye contact with anyone. "Carla identified one of the female bodies as a sixteen-year-old."

Sarah sits back in her chair and slides down a little.

Ashley lowers her head.

Brooke and Julie are looking at him.

Brooke is curious. "There would not have been a sixteen-year-old out there alive. Not with all those beasts. Dave there is no way you shot a kid... unless the kid was a beast."

Dave looks up at her. "Yesterday we knew only adults were infected. Today we know children can be infected."

They all look at him and nod in agreement.

Julie asks, "Do you think kids younger than sixteen could be infected?"

Dave looks at Ashley then to Julie. "I don't see why not. I believe at this point it is possible."

Everybody goes back to what they were doing. The officers looking outside. Sarah sitting. Dave and Ashley testing samples.

Everybody is thinking about the kid that was killed as beast. But nobody is willing to discuss it.

Darkness is coming on faster now.

Julie watches the cat leave her line of sight from the surveillance camera.

Brooke is watching the street. She watches as far as she can see. Her distance of vision is reducing as it gets darker. Some of the streetlights aren't coming on, so her vision is limited from that, as well.

Ashley speaks up; she sounds excited and confused at the same time. "Dave this sample reads 'fox.'" She hands him the sample.

He looks at the sample. Then looks at Sarah. "This looks like your writing, dear."

Sarah doesn't get up. "Yeah, I took a sample from a red fox last night. So, what of it? You said you wanted a sample from all the canines out there."

Dave looks at her, "But you didn't say anything knowing how I was looking for the wolves and coyotes from Juan's samples."

Sarah stays calm. "You were looking at his, thinking he made a mistake. Why would I have given you a chance to think the same about me?"

Dave looks at the sample and back to her. "Do you really think I would have questioned you?"

Sarah is letting a little anger show. "You are now."

Dave just lets it go. He gives the sample back to Ashley. "Test it and let's see if it is infected, as well."

He looks through his zoo samples and pulls the red fox sample from the tray.

He and Ashley look at both samples and decide the sample that Sarah collected was in fact infected.

Ashley says, "Well, so far, we have more to test farther then to not count on testing."

Dave looks at her and at the samples yet to go through. "Yes, I bet we will find the same in all these samples."

Ashley agrees.

Dave says, "Maybe we should just start testing these, then we can pull the body out of the cooler and examine her. See if she can help with any of this mess."

Ashley agrees and they start to test the samples. They already have the sample from Dewight's cruiser running.

Nobody is aware of the body in the cell.

Since dark fully arrived, the body has transformed slowly into a werewolf.

The beast is just lying there. It hasn't awakened yet. It is laying there, breathing quietly.

Brooke sees movement outside. She lets the others know the beasts are out there.

Julie is keeping her eyes on the surveillance monitors. She sees a beast come into view in the driveway. She lets the others know about it.

Dave looks at the monitor. "Watch that one. That might be the same one that tried to get in a couple nights ago."

He looks back to his work. The officers look at him.

Brooke has fear in her voice. "OH, MY GOD!"

Everyone looks at her.

The beast in the cell is not only awake, but also standing behind Sarah and reaching for her.

Sarah goes to move out of reach, but the beast is faster. It grabs her shoulder. She screams as it is holding very tightly to her.

Dave grabs his .44 mag revolver. Brooke is also taking aim with her service pistol.

The beast digs its claws into Sarah's shoulder. She screams in pain as the blood starts to flow out of the wounds.

The beast leans its muzzle out over her.

It appears as though the beast is getting ready to bite her.

Sarah is telling them to kill the beast: "Shoot it! Kill it!"

Brooke asks Dave, "Is it safe to kill it over her?"

Dave tells her, "Take body shots. All I have is a head shot, and it would infect Sarah from the blood of the beast mixing with her blood through the open wounds on her shoulder."

Brooke takes the body shot as instructed. The beast howls in pain. She fires again. The beast again howls in pain.

The beast in the driveway is now at the door and starts to beat on the door.

Another beast appears at the window of the cell. It does a test touch and figures out the power isn't on. It grabs the bars and pulls. The beast in the cell throws Sarah and jumps at the window. The bars give and the beast is out.

Sarah lands on the zoo samples. The tray is upset when Sarah hits it. Dave tried to catch Sarah, but she still hit the tray and dumped the samples. Many vials are on the floor. A few stayed in the tray. There are a few vials that got broken. None of the "infected" samples got broken as they were on a different tray more in the middle of the work area.

The beast at the door is gone, as well. All is quiet again.

Dave never fired a shot. Brooke is the only one that had a safe shot at the beast without the risk of hitting anyone else.

Dave and Ashley are tending to Sarah's wounds.

Brooke looks at the window space with no window and no bars on it now. "Dave what do you have in mind about the missing window and bars?"

Dave looks at Brooke and then the window. "Oh, that isn't good."

Brooke looks at him. "I know, that's why I'm asking if you have any ideas."

Dave looks at Ashley. "Will you continue with Sarah? I will go figure out how to fix the window."

Ashley goes to respond, but Sarah beats her. "You go she can handle my shoulder. That window needs fixed, or they will get in."

Dave goes to the cell and slips in the drool. "Oh, he was a droller." He unlocks the cell door, and he and both officers enter the cell.

There appears to be nothing around the opening of the window. The bars are not too far from the window opening in the yard.

Dave looks at the window opening as the officers keep watch to protect him.

Dave is still looking at the window opening as he speaks, "It looks like if we just get the bars and put them in place it may work. I would need to use screws to reattach the bars and need to be careful of the wiring for the electricity into the bars. But I think I can do it." He looks at the officers. "If you two will cover me while I get the bars out of the yard and reattach them."

Both officers agree, and he crawls out the window to retrieve the bars.

He grabs the bars and is trying to work his way back in backwards. He sees the shadows moving across the street. "Ladies, some help, please. The beasts are watching."

The officers grab a leg each and begin to pull him in when he continues speaking, "No. Correction… the beasts are coming straight at me now."

They get him back inside before the beasts reach the house. He ducks as the officers take aim and fire at the beasts.

They drop a beast each and the rest of the beasts run for the shadows across the street again.

Dave looks at the officers as they holster their weapons signaling it is safe again. Dave gets up. "Thank you, ladies. Now let's see about reattaching the bars."

The officers look at each other and Julie offers her help as Brooke goes to the other window to cover them as needed.

Dave asks Brooke, "Brooke, would you like a rifle to use?"

Brooke smiles. "No, thank you. I appreciate the offer, but I don't know your rifle and don't know how it is sighted in. I don't want to miss my target or just wound it because I am not familiar with the rifle."

Dave gets his drill, screws, and a bit to reattach the bars over the window opening. As he is getting the things he needs, Julie stays at that window to help secure the house.

He returns with the items he needs to reattach the window bars.

As he is reattaching the bars, Ashley got done with Sarah's wounds. She had some cuts on her hand, as well.

Sarah goes back to her seat as Dave and Ashley start to clean up the samples from the zoo.

Once they have all the samples picked up and on the tray, Dave gets the list so he can verify the broken samples. Some of the labels are no longer legible because of the blood covering the lettering.

The officers are watching movement outside. So far, it is all across the street.

Dave and Ashley do their inventory of the zoo samples. They are missing a few vials. They already knew about the gray fox vial because the label could still be read. The labels they couldn't read are the ones they need.

Their list of broken vials is longer than they wanted but not as long as it could have been, considering Sarah was thrown into the tray.

The list of broken vials, including the one they could read, include: grey fox, wolf, bald eagle, golden eagle, raven, and bobcat.

There is one label that is harder to read, and Dave is sure it reads "axolotl."

Brooke asks, "What is that?"

Dave explains it is a Mexican salamander that is able to regenerate any body part it loses, including its brain.

Brooke says, "That would be nice."

Dave and Ashley are talking about Sarah's injuries. They are concerned that she may need to get to the hospital.

Ashley assures Dave she got the bleeding to stop on Sarah's shoulder. She also informs him of the glass she pulled out of Sarah's hand. She suspects it was a vial from the tray but couldn't be sure which one it would have been.

Dave thinks, "Well, if it were the wolf or fox vial at least they were not infected, so she should not become infected herself."

Ashley agrees, "And we shouldn't need to worry about the others, as well, since this is a canine issue."

Dave agrees with that statement, as well.

They clean up the blood as the officers keep watch, and Sarah stays seated.

Dave asks Sarah how she is feeling occasionally, just to check on her and to be sure that she is staying conscious after losing the blood.

Sarah is sitting there and gets more irritated each time Dave asks her how she is doing. But at the same time, she understands his reasoning for asking. So, she tries to be patient.

They get the cleanup done. All the glass is cleaned up, all the blood is off the floor.

Dave has already has access to wolf DNA, the uninfected strand, and can get another sample from the zoo, if needed for other studies. So, the loss of that vial isn't a big problem. And the animal that came from at the zoo was not sick anyway. The zoo had supplied him with that sample at his request to assist him with his studies.

Ashley asks, "I wonder why the beast decided to attack? And why Sarah?"

Sarah asks her, "Are you jealous it grabbed me and not you?"

Ashley looks at her, "No, I'm just thinking out loud. I am just wondering why it would have decided to attack at all. We weren't paying attention. It could have gotten out before we knew it even woke up."

Dave looks at her. "You have a point."

Sarah smiles. "Maybe they are not as smart as Dave likes to think they are."

Dave looks at Sarah and smiles. "Apparently you are feeling better."

Sarah smiles. "The pain is manageable. Let's leave it at that, shall we?"

Dave agrees. "So, would you like to be part of this discussion?"

Sarah nods. "I thought I already was part of it."

Brooke speaks up, "Heads up. We have movement headed this way."

Julie had stayed at the other window to keep watch and protect the glassless window. She already has her weapon out and ready.

Brooke is ready, as well.

The beasts are coming toward the house.

One of them looks at the officers and makes eye contact with each of them as other beasts separate from the pack and surround the house.

Julie asks, "Why do they keep attacking your place now? They didn't used to. What changed?"

Dave looks at her. "You remember the female in the cooler? That is when the beasts became interested with this house."

Brooke is a bit surprised. "Oh, my, there is the one that was in here. It has the blood stain on its side. I could have sworn I hit it well enough to kill it."

Dave says, "Remember, it is a full moon tonight. We need to hit them directly in the heart or the head. Anywhere else is no guarantee it will die. So, a lung shot will not kill it tonight?"

Brooke says, "I thought I did hit it in the heart. Apparently not."

Dave goes to the cooler and removes the female body.

Sarah asks, "What are you doing?"

Dave responds, "We need to figure out why they are so persistent to get in here since she arrived."

Ashley helps him.

Ashley looks at the body. "Dave, doesn't she look like she may be pregnant?"

He looks at the body. "That is what I thought the first night. But I have not had a chance to verify it."

Ashley, still looking at the body, says, "Yeah, it isn't really obvious, but we need to find out."

Dave looks at Ashley. "I don't have an ultrasound machine. The only way we can verify is to cut her open."

Ashley helps gather the equipment needed to do the autopsy.

As Dave takes the scalpel to cut her open, he says, "Well, we already know how she died and why."

Nobody laughs. Dave gave a slight smile until he realized nobody else thought it funny.

Dave loses his concentration on the body when the beasts start to howl.

Then again at the door, the beating on the door begins.

There are beasts looking in through the windows at them, including the one that just woke up.

The officers are aiming at the beasts in the windows.

Dave tells them not to shoot.

Sarah says, "Are you mad? Kill them. Before they kill us."

Dave doesn't look at her. "They would have already been in here if that was their intent."

He looks at the monitors.

He sees a beast sitting in the driveway.

He walks over and turns on the electricity to the door and windows for the entire house.

The beating on the door stops as the voltage increases. The beast doesn't get a full charge of electricity tonight. Leaving, Dave thinking the beasts are learning.

The beast from the door is seen at the driveway level. It has its head down as it approaches the one sitting in the driveway. The one in the driveway barks, and the other one runs for the street. The beasts at the window back off and are not near the window anymore, confusing everybody.

Dave figures it is time to continue with the experiment and see if the beast can understand him and perhaps get some answers tonight.

Dave figures the glass is missing from a window and the beast should be able to hear him, maybe better than the other night.

Dave begins, "Are you the same one from the other night that I talked to?"

The others look at Dave like he lost his mind.

Ashley asks, "Do you expect it to answer?"

Before Dave answers her, the beast nods its head yes.

Dave asks everyone to stay quiet now and let him ask the questions, so he doesn't get confused as to which question is being answered.

Everyone agrees to stay quiet and just watch the monitor and the windows.

Dave looks at the monitor. "I am going to take it that you answered me and not her. So, you were here the other night. You never did tell me how this lady on my table is important to you."

The beast nods in agreement.

Dave smiles. "I believe that we figured out why she is so important to you. She appears to be pregnant. Is that why she is so important to you?"

The beast turns its head to one side as if thinking about the answer or trying to hear better. The beast does not answer.

Dave gives a little laugh. "You think we don't know? We will find out for sure when we cut her open."

The beast just stares at the camera. It appears to start growling after Dave mentions cutting open the lady on the table.

Dave asks, "You don't like to know about that do you?"

The beast keeps showing teeth and nods no.

Dave asks, "Well, are you going to tell me why you and your pack are here?"

Again, with teeth still being bared, the beast answers no.

Dave shakes his head in disapproval as if the beast can see him. He looks at the windows and the other beasts are sitting there watching and appear to be listening.

Dave smiles and looks back to the monitor. "So, you are the leader of the pack that is here, aren't you?"

The beast releases it snarl and tilts its head again as if not understanding. But again, does not answer the question.

Dave laughs out loud. The beast hears him laugh, and the women all look at him not understanding what he found funny.

Dave says, "You already admitted you are the pack leader when I asked why you and your pack are here. Or are you going to say you are not the pack leader?"

The beast begins to growl again. It also answers no.

Dave is very curious and continues, "You surprise me tonight. Being a full moon tonight and you still seem to be able to communicate. So, you still retain some of your human qualities even in a full moon… at least enough to communicate."

The beast is still growling, even though the people cannot hear it.

The beast tilts its head again.

Dave believes it appears to be thinking, but he keeps that thought to himself.

The beast gets up and begins to leave.

Dave says, "Okay, then, we will get to work on your lady friend and figure out for ourselves why you want her back so bad you would risk death to get her."

The beast stops and looks directly at the camera. Growling loud enough, they can hear it inside. It barks and the other beast stand on all fours and approach the windows growling now, as well.

The officers take aim at the beasts, with one officer per window.

Dave says, "Don't shoot."

Sarah is about to hit him. "Why not? They are getting ready to come through the windows."

Dave looks back to the monitor. "He wants her back. He is not going to risk losing her." He looks at the monitor. "Are you?"

The beast answers no.

The beast barks and the other beasts lay down, stop growling and just stare in the windows.

Dave looks at the windows and back to the monitor. "So, you do want her back?" The beast nods its head yes.

The beast has not sat back down, it is still standing upright on two feet. It has stopped growling… at least for the moment.

Dave tells the beast, "You know, I have to finish with her first, and we still haven't figured out who she is. These things need to be done before her body can be released. You do know that, right?"

The beast growls and takes an aggressive stance. It nods no.

Dave shakes his head disapprovingly again. "Her body will not be released before we know who she is, and we are done examining her. If you continue to attack, then it will take longer for her body to be released. You will lose many more members of your pack of various ages and sexes. Do you want to continue to attack and lose more pack members and take longer to get her back?"

The beast stops growling and answers no.

Dave has a serious look on his face. "So, you will take you pack and leave us alone?"

The beast stares at the camera.

Dave says, "I am waiting."

The beast nods yes.

Dave lets a little smile show. "So, you and your pack leave and let us do what we need to and nobody on either side needs to die tonight. Agreed?"

The beast nods its agreement. It gets up and barks a few times.

The beasts at the window get up and join the one from the driveway in the road.

Many more beasts appear that were not visible before. There are more than they can count and still coming out of the dark.

Everybody is amazed at how many beasts are out there. And that they are still coming out of the shadows.

The beast from the driveway is separated in the front of the rest. It howls deep and long.

Other beasts respond with a howl, and they begin to leave the area.

The pack leader is standing alone, staring at the house.

Dave thinks out loud, "Leave; just leave, and don't try anything."

The beast leaves, slowly walking away and looking back to the house occasionally.

It finally disappears into the darkness.

Chapter 7

# The Autopsy

Dave looks at Ashley. "Let's get started on the autopsy before they change their mind."

Ashley looks at him. "How did you know it would leave?"

Dave walks to the table with the body on it. "I didn't. I just took it for granted and prayed that it wanted her back more than it wants to kill any of us."

Sarah hits him on the back of his shoulder. "You know they could have come through the windows and killed all of us?"

Dave looks at her. "I figured if it wanted in here, we weren't going to stop it. I took a gamble and prayed that its entire attack was to get her out of here."

Julie responds, "It apparently worked. They left."

Brooke and Ashley are nodding in agreement.

Dave says, "For now, it worked. No guarantees how long they will give us." He looks at Ashley. "Let's get this done and pray that Carla has an identity on her by morning." He looks at Sarah. "Would you help us, please?"

Sarah sits in her chair. "No, I will not help you. I am in pain and don't want to move any more than I absolutely need to."

Dave asks her, "Is it your shoulder or your chronic pain you feel more?"

Sarah looks disgusted that he would even ask. "Why would it matter? I'm in pain, and I WILL NOT help you."

Dave and Ashley begin the autopsy without Sarah.

They begin with cutting into the abdomen, wanting to answer the question if she is pregnant or not.

Nobody is ready for what they find inside of her.

They find that she is pregnant with multiple fetuses. They count four as they remove them. All are dead, of course.

Aside from the number of fetuses they find, which surprises all of them alone, the appearance of the fetuses surprises them even more. Sarah is horrified to say the least. She wants to leave but doesn't want to go upstairs alone and figures it is too late as she has already seen the fetuses.

They estimate that she is about ten weeks into her pregnancy because of the size of the fetuses. But the development of the fetuses appears to be eighteen to twenty weeks.

Sarah is holding a .357 magnum pistol in her lap and has her hand on it.

The fetuses do not look completely human. They have human like appearance but are hairy. Their faces are longer, more canine but not fully developed as a canine; they have a look of being a cross between canine and human.

Dave sees Sarah holding the pistol. "Why are you holding it like that? Like you might need it quickly?"

Sarah doesn't change her gaze off of the fetuses when she responds, "Look at those things. Those things you pulled out of her are not human. They are more beast than human. You gonna tell me otherwise?"

Dave looks at one of the fetuses, picks it up, and turns to Sarah. "I can't say exactly what it is until we look at blood samples from it, but I see how you would think it is beast."

Sarah pulls the pistol up and points it at the fetus when Dave turns to her with it in his hand.

Dave looks up from the fetus he is holding. "Why are you pointing that at me?"

Sarah says, "I am pointing it at that thing you are holding. You just happen to be behind it."

Dave turns back to the table, and Sarah puts the pistol down.

Dave works until he gets as blood sample from each of the fetuses, so he has more than one sample to look at.

Ashley asks if he wants to open her stomach to see what she ate recently before dying.

Dave tells her to go ahead. She opens the stomach while he is putting the blood samples away after listing where the samples came from on the vial.

Ashley gasps and jumps back from the table after opening the stomach. Dave isn't finished listing the vials.

Dave turns around. "What did you find?"

Ashley says, with fear in her voice, "You need to look and make sure it is what I think it is."

Dave puts down the vials he had left. He returns to the table and reaches in to separate the cut in the stomach, so he might be able to see what is in there without pulling everything out.

He sees but isn't sure and really doesn't want to accept what he sees.

He reaches in and pulls out a human finger. There are other parts of human flesh in her stomach, as well. He also retrieves parts of animals that are unidentifiable without DNA testing.

Sarah is again horrified at what is being pulled from the stomach.

Brooke and Julie are watching the windows and monitor, but they look at the table occasionally, as well. They both look at each other.

Julie says, "Well, I guess they kill humans for food and not just to kill, like was suspected."

Dave doesn't look at her. "Would appear that way, wouldn't it? I would say that the beasts are feeding on humans and anything else they catch."

Ashley steps back in. "Do you think the pieces of human flesh are all from the same person?"

Dave says, "Without DNA testing, we can't say for sure. That is providing the pieces aren't degraded by being in the stomach."

While Dave and Ashley were removing the fetuses, Dewight calls Brooke. Brooke answers here phone. "Hello, Dewight."

Dewight asks, "Haven't heard from you, Julie, or anyone out there tonight. How is it going? It sounds quiet."

Brooke answers calmly, "Oh, yes, it is quiet here tonight. The beasts did show up, and the body in Dave's cell woke up as a beast. It got out and one sat in the driveway. Dave spoke to the one in the driveway, and it did respond like it understood him. They made a deal, and the beasts all left and haven't been back."

Dewight is surprised; not sure if he is more surprised or if he is mad. So, he keeps his anger in check and is more curious when he asks, "What do you mean Dave spoke to a beast and they made a deal?"

Brooke stays calm as if nothing is abnormal. "Oh, yes, he asked yes and no questions to the beast and it shook its head yes or no. You didn't think I meant the beast actually responded verbally, did you?"

Dewight lets out a small laugh. "Of course, I didn't think that. But I was confused when you said they spoke. What do you mean about the deal they made?"

Brooke said, "Oh, yeah, Dave told the beast that if it continued to attack the house, it would take longer to get its lady back and many more of its pack would die. The beast called off the pack, and they haven't been seen or heard again."

Dewight does not allow any anger into his voice as he says, "Did Dave tell the beast it would get the woman back?"

Brooke responds, "No, he told it he could not release the body without examining her and not without knowing who she is. He told the beast the longer it attacks, the longer the examination will take. He never told the beast he would release her to him."

Dewight is relieved. "Good. Dave can't make the call to release the body to the beast. The body will need to go to Carla for cremation and identification if she hasn't gotten that information yet. The federal law is very clear on that."

Brooke says, "I understand. He didn't say anything to the beast about releasing the body or where it would be going when he is done. He wanted to buy us some peace tonight, so we aren't fighting for hours, trying to survive."

Dewight says, "Well, it sounds like he achieved that tonight. I don't hear any gun shots. We haven't had a single call tonight, either, which is very strange on a full-moon night. Usually, the phone is ringing non-stop."

Brooke says, "Yeah, very strange. I won't tell you what they found in the stomach of the woman when they cut her open. I will let Dave tell you that if he wants."

Dewight says, "Okay, is everything else okay tonight? No problems with anyone in the house?"

Brooke responds, "No problems; we are all getting along nicely. Well, the body that woke up as a beast did injure Sarah, but she is okay. No need for a hospital."

Dewight interrupts her there and says, "What do you mean woke up as a beast and injured Sarah?"

Brooke, not sure about his tone, says, "Yeah, you know the body Dave had in the cell. It was dead, and it woke up tonight as a beast. It grabbed Sarah's shoulder drawing blood, but they stopped the bleeding, and she is doing fine. I shot the beast to release her. Dave only had a head shot and didn't want to risk infecting her if its blood hit her open wounds."

Dewight, allowing concern to show in his voice, asks, "So, the beast never bit her?"

Brooke answers, "Correct; only claws in the shoulder. She can still use her shoulder, as well. She says it's sore and that's it."

Dewight says, "Okay, as long as she wasn't bitten and is doing good. Okay, I'm going to let you go and keep guard there."

They both say their goodbyes, and they return to their jobs.

Dave and Ashley are finished with their observations of the fetuses and the stomach contents by the time Brooke is finished with her phone call.

Dave askes Ashley to finish closing the body up, so Carla can have it the next day.

He turns to Brooke. "I suppose that was Dewight that called you."

Brooke looks at him. "You would be correct with that assumption."

Dewight continues, not showing any emotion, "What did he want?"

Brooke gives a small smile. "He just wanted to know how it was going here with the beasts. If we are holding out or if he needed to send back up. He was surprised to hear it was quiet here. He said the phone is quiet there tonight."

Dave starts thinking as he speaks, "So, mayhaps the agreement with the beast is more meaningful to it than expected. It may believe it will get her back."

Brooke says, "Yeah, Dewight was surprised to hear that you spoke to the beast and made a deal with it."

Dave, still thinking, says, "To be honest, I am surprised, as well. I didn't expect to be able to have a conversation with one the other night let alone during a full moon. I always figured that the beast was in complete control during a full moon and the human side was buried deep, no say in its actions at all. Granted, a lot of that theory was from werewolf movies I have watched over the years. I never had reason to doubt that about the beasts before."

Brooke is curious and gets the question out before Julie does. "So, how much more do you think is wrong about what we were taught about the beasts growing up? You with what is written in books and how they are portrayed in movies."

Dave, "Well, we already know that they kill humans for food. We know they will run in a pack, although there was a movie that suggested that from a long time ago. There is a movie that claimed to be able to cure the beast of its curse. They used wolf bane to create the cure. I have not been able to get it to work. I don't know if I am doing something wrong or not."

Ashley is done closing the body and speaks up, "I know that movie. That is why I believe it can be cured. The character that created the cure was a drug dealer, and he made his own drugs to sell. I don't remember what drug he made. Maybe that drug needs to be involved somehow."

Dave looks at her. "You may be onto something with that thought. I think I have that movie here; I don't remember the drug that was being made either. I think it may have been meth. But even if that drug isn't involved to activate a cure, it may have something to do with the way they manufactured the vaccine as they did with the drug that was being made."

Sarah speaks up, "You are all nuts. The only proven way to 'cure' the beast is to kill it."

They all look at her disapprovingly. Even the two officers want to believe that it can be cured.

Julie speaks up, "I saw that movie, as well. That movie also suggested that the infection can be transmitted sexually."

Dave agrees with that idea that the infection can be transmitted sexually since it is known to be transmitted by bodily fluids. So, he does not argue with that theory. But does add that there is no evidence as yet, and then he decides to take a vaginal swab of the body before releasing her to Carla for cremation. The hope is to prove if the disease is evident in her vaginal fluid.

The four of them continue discussing werewolf movies they have seen and how these are different than the "traditionally" known beasts.

Dave and Ashley put the body back in the cooler and get things packed up and put away for the night.

Dave tells the officers they are welcome to watch T.V. upstairs if they are staying their entire shift.

The officers agree to go up to the living room for the remainder of their shift.

Dave, Ashley, and Sarah all go to bed for the night.

Dave and Ashley do not work the next day, so the night was longer since they didn't need to worry about getting up in the morning. It's about 1:30 A.M. when they all head up to the living room and on to bed.

The officers keep watch through the night from the living room windows while the others sleep.

The officers head into the office after sunrise to end their shift and file their report for the night.

## Chapter 8

# Carla's Discovery

In the morning when Carla arrives at her office, she realizes the door is gone. She calls the day shift supervisor for the Hughesville Police using the office number listed in her cell phone.

Dispatch tells Hope that Carla is on the phone for her.

Hope answers the phone in her office, not knowing how much privacy the call would need.

Hope, sounding cheerful, says, "Hello, Carla. How may I help you on such a good morning?"

Carla isn't cheerful with her response, not angry either, just concerned and curious why Hope thinks it is a good morning. "Why do you say it is a good morning?"

Hope, still sounding cheerful, "It was a quiet night, and I didn't have anything to deal with when my shift started."

Carla still not angry, just staying calm, says, "Well, I am about to change that for you. I got to the office this morning, and the front door is missing or at least kicked in. I didn't go look, I just called you, so hopefully you will send officers here to check it out for me?"

Hope is less cheerful now. "Oh, I am sorry to hear that. I will get officers heading your way right away."

Carla thanks her and waits in her car for the officers to show up.

Hope leaves her office to see who is available in the office.

She finds Bill and Jerry sitting at desks doing reports.

Hope calls out to the officers.

Both officers respond, "Yes."

Hope tells them to get their cruiser and head to the coroner's office. She had a possible break in and they need to get there to investigate.

The officers both agree, then save and close the computers to continue later.

The officers head to the coroner's office.

Once they arrive, Carla exits her car.

She approaches the officers as they exit their cruiser.

Bill says, "We were told you had a possible break in."

Carla points to the front door as she speaks, "Yes, the door was already open or missing when I got here."

Bill tells Carla to wait there, and they head to the door with weapons drawn.

Carla gets back in her car and waits for the officers to clear the building.

Carla has stopped her staff as they arrived, so they didn't just go in and discover someone in there.

After the officers clear the office and ensure it safe for the staff, they go back out to Carla.

Jerry is the first to speak this time: "Carla you and your staff can go in. We will go with you, and you can let us know what is missing."

Carla agrees and waves to her staff in their cars to go in.

The officers split. One leads the group and the other follows the group into the building.

As they enter the building, Carla notices the door is broken and against the wall opposite of the doorway.

One of the staff members mentions about the amount of strength needed to achieve something like that.

Carla heard the comment and doesn't respond. She does, however, think to herself that it was possibly a beast. Then she begins to wonder why they would enter. They never attacked her office before.

They continue to the morgue.

The doors are not in good shape there, either.

The doors are still on the hinges but very damaged and not working correctly.

They go on in, and Carla notices multiple cooler drawers open; some didn't have bodies and others that did.

Carla says, "There appears to be bodies missing." She looks at the officers. "Will you wait until we get a count and see which bodies are missing?"

Both officers nod in agreement.

Bill says, "We will take note and put it in our report. We will also need to know if anything else is missing."

Carla agrees and splits her staff, having some inventorying the office and others helping her inventory the bodies.

Carla has her list of which body was in which drawer. As she has a staff member read the open drawer number, she looks at the body listed and if it was identified as yet.

When they are finished with the inventory, she notices that the missing bodies are all female. Other open drawers had a body in it but some were already identified and some were already cremated.

The other staff members inventorying the office return and say nothing missing from the building.

Not every drawer that had a body still in it was open. The drawers with male bodies were not all open. The only bodies in there at this time were all killed as beasts. But every drawer that had a female in it was open, whether the body was in there or it was already identified and cremated. The drawer was open either way.

The officers look at the drawers individually with Carla to see how it was opened.

Every drawer appears to have been opened from the outside; no scratches inside the drawer pocket to indicate someone alive trying to get out.

Carla goes out to her car and gets her laptop to hook up since the desktop computer has been broken.

Once she has her laptop hooked up, she goes into the security camera recordings.

The officers and her staff stand around her and watch the footage.

What was suspected was confirmed on the recording.

The saw multiple beasts come through the front door after it was forced open.

They even got to see how the beast opened it on the exterior camera view, which showed many more beasts outside than what went inside.

To open the door, one beast hit it with what appeared to be a closed fist. One hit and the door went flying into the wall opposite of the doorway.

The beast that opened the door was first to go in. Others followed and kept a short distance from the lead beast.

Once in the morgue, one of the beasts grabbed a random door and opened it, breaking it in the process.

The beast that led the group in barked as it grabbed the other and threw it across the room. Landing on the desk and the desktop computer.

The beast that got thrown got up and the lead beast barked again and the other left the building with a different beast replacing it.

The beast that led the group in seemed to let the others know what to do. How to open the doors without completely destroying the door and breaking more than needed. It also appeared to teach them to sniff the doors before opening the doors.

The lead beast was sniffing doors much faster than all the others combined; so much so that it barked, and the others just stood back while it sniffed and opened the doors.

The other beasts removed the dead women as the doors were opened for access.

What was really intriguing to everyone watching was there was one beast per female body they removed, minus the one that led them into the building. That one beast was the only one that left without carrying a body. It did, however, look straight into the camera on the way out, as if it knew the camera was there and recording.

The officers finish with the information they need for the report and head back to the office. There is nothing they can do knowing it was the beasts that broke in during the night.

Carla calls Dave after she checks her email. She has the identity of the lady in his basement.

Dave's cell phone is ringing as they finish with breakfast.

Dave slept in since he didn't work and is wondering who would be calling at nine in the morning.

Dave answers after looking at the caller I.D. "Hello, Carla, hope you have good news this early today."

Carla tries to keep a calm tone. "Some is good. I know who you have in your basement."

Dave says, "That is great. Who is it, and what do you mean some good news?"

Carla says, "The lady you have is Maria Bears."

Dave is surprised. "Well, that is interesting, I thought I knew her. Dewight and I went to school with her. Now, how about the rest of your news?"

Carla looks down like Dave can see her as she speaks with the depression and fear in her voice. "The beasts broke in here last night. They took all the female bodies and only the females that I didn't get identified and cremated yet."

Dave's voice has concern in it as he speaks, "You mean even the sixteen-year-old?"

Carla says, "Yes, we watched the surveillance recording, and she was the first to be removed. I don't know what I will tell the families of these unfortunate souls."

Dave sits back down in his chair. Sarah and Ashley are looking at him because he did not put the call on speaker.

Carla says, "Dave, the one beast looked straight at the camera on its way out. It was the one sniffing and opening the doors. It threw another beast across the room and destroyed the desktop computer."

Dave had put the phone on speaker, so the ladies could hear the conversation, as well.

Dave says, "Did the one bark at all? You do have sound on your recordings correct?"

Carla responds, "Yes, we do record sound and, yes, it barked at the others."

Dave is sitting there, looking at the ladies.

Carla says, "Dave, I can't explain how the beast knew how to open the doors to the bodies, how it appeared to know it was being recorded. Dave that thing is much stronger than I ever imagined. It didn't struggle at all to pick up and throw the other beast. It was like you or I picking up a small child."

Dave returns to scientist mode, perhaps more to separate himself from the emotional state of what happened. "I figure the full moon is when the beasts are at their strongest. Granted, I have no way to test that theory."

Dave has a small pause and continues speaking before Carla responds, "I also thought that the beast would be all beast and no human qualities on the full moon. You know, like the werewolf movies we watched before studying the beasts. We now know that to be incorrect. The beast has human capabilities to think and communicate, even on a full moon. What we knew from movies is not correct. Some are, but a lot are just wrong."

Carla asks, "What do you mean?"

Dave responds, "Earlier in the night, the beasts were here. I spoke to the one I believe is the leader. This was the second time it sat and responded to my questions. We made a deal that it was going to leave us alone, so we could get our work done with Maria. The beast, I think, thought it would get her back. Maria is pregnant, and we believe that is why it wanted her back. But the fetuses were all dead when we removed them. Carla, do you think that mayhaps the other women were pregnant?"

Carla thinks, "Well, I didn't check for that. I suppose it is possible. You don't think the beast took them because they were pregnant, do you?"

Dave says, "It is the only thing that makes sense to me."

Ashley voices her agreement.

Carla asks, "Do you think the offspring will survive, even though the mother is dead?"

Dave answers, "I wouldn't suspect they would survive. If they are close enough to birth, perhaps. But very unlikely. Oh, by the way, you can come and take Maria's body today. I believe we have everything we need from her."

Carla says, "Okay, I will be out this afternoon."

Dave says, "Okay, I am going to take Ashley to get her car this morning, then we will be in the basement lab the rest of the day."

Carla, sounding curious, asks, "Who is Ashley?"

Dave says, "Oh, sorry, I forgot you didn't meet her. She is my new co-worker at the hospital and my new assistant at the house."

Carla doesn't know Sarah is in the room with him, but she does know the call is on speaker. "What does Sarah think about that? I assume you talked to her first?"

Sarah speaks before Dave: "Yes, Carla Dave spoke to me about her, and I agreed to give her the spare room. After all, with her helping him, I don't need to nor do I want to help anymore."

Carla says, "Good to hear that he checked with you first, Sarah. I didn't know you were with him on the call. Happy to hear your voice. I do miss our girl chats."

Sarah lets out a little smile. "I miss those chats, as well, Carla. But I don't want to even help moving the bodies anymore. I don't know how you and Dave can still do it, with known beasts getting younger now. It would finish me from doing the job if I were still in it."

Carla says, "I admit it isn't easy, same reasoning you quit, and now younger humans killed in beast form. But someone needs to do the job, and the families need to know what happened to their loved one. So, I try to be patient and compassionate with the families even when they don't return the understanding."

Sarah says, "Well, it was nice to talk to you this morning. But I'm going to let you and Dave get back to talking business."

Carla says, "Thank you. I enjoyed talking to you, as well. Maybe we can all get together sometime and chat."

Sarah says, "I would like that."

Dave asks, "Is there anything else you want to talk about in reference to the beasts in your office last night?"

Carla is thinking as she speaks, "Not that I can think of right now. Have you had a chance to see how powerful the beasts are?"

Dave says, "We had one break out of here. Without the power to the bars, they pulled the bars off the windows, like they weren't even secured with anything. Their speed is incredible, as well."

Carla says, "I didn't get to see their speed on the surveillance footage, but I did see their power… at least some of it. I can bring a copy of the footage if you want to watch it."

Dave responds, "No, that won't be necessary. You have told me enough when we put it with what we know and have observed the information is very helpful."

Carla thanks him, and they end the call.

## Chapter 9

# Bodies Found

Dave and Ashley say goodbye to Sarah and head out to get Ashley's car from the hospital parking lot.

They have small talk to pass the time for the ride, but the ride is uneventful.

They get her car, and she gets in and follows him back to the house.

Ashley pulls into the driveway first, and Dave backs in so his car needs moved before she can leave since his car is larger and usually the one used if they both need to go anywhere. If Ashley would want to go somewhere by herself, he would simply move his car, so she could leave.

Dave and Ashley go to the basement lab when they go back inside. Sarah decides to stay upstairs in the living room and watch T.V.

Sarah tells them that she is a lot of pain this morning and she would just prefer to stay in one place. She also tells them she already took a pain pill, and it isn't helping much.

Dave has gotten use to her painful days and doesn't push for her to join them in the basement.

Ashley does ask, "Are you sure you won't join us?"

Sarah looks at her. "I will not join you. I already told you I am in pain today and not moving."

Dave looks at Ashley and shakes his head no as she was getting ready to continue with the request. Sarah was not looking and did not see him shake his head.

Dave and Ashley go down to the basement.

The first test they do is the vaginal swab. They both want to know if the infection is present in the sample.

As the test is being run, Dave looks at a small sample of the swab under the microscope to see if he is able to see the infection.

Dave asks Ashley to look because he isn't one hundred percent positive. Ashley agrees it might be there, but the sample isn't blood, and the infection is not as obvious.

Once all the steps are done for the test. They look at the results.

Neither one is actually surprised to see that the infection is in fact in the sample.

Dave says, "So, now we can be sure that the infected can infect new people sexually."

Ashley agrees it looks that way. "But that would mean that people that do not know they are infected can pass it to new people without knowing it."

Dave says, "Yes, and that also means that the number of infected could be many times more than we would have ever guessed."

Ashley says, "Not to mention, that the women are able to give birth to more beasts."

Dave responds, "Yes, that adds countless more to their population. I am beginning to think this battle has become a war for survival."

Ashley asks, "Do you need to call the police chief or anyone else?"

Dave answers, "No, they don't need to know anything yet. The night shift are the ones that need to know, and they are sleeping at this time of day."

Ashley nods her agreement.

Carla is coming down the steps as they finished their conversation. Her curiosity is obvious in her tone. "What does night shift need to know?"

Dave and Ashley are surprised to see her.

Dave asks, "Why are you coming in that way?"

Carla smiles a little. "I visited with Sarah a little. She told me to come down this way and surprise you."

Dave introduces her to Ashley and then answers her question.

Carla says, "Yeah, I agree night shift needs to know what you discovered."

They retrieve the body from the cooler and put her in a body bag.

Dave and Carla are carrying the body to Carla's car when Dave's cell phone rings.

Dave asks Ashley to answer the phone.

Ashley says, "The caller ID says it's Greg."

Dave responds, "Answer it, please, and I will get to him as soon as we have this body loaded if he won't speak to you."

Ashley answers the phone. "Hello, Dave's phone; this is Ashley, his assistant."

Greg looks confused. "Is Dave available?"

Ashley says, "Dave is helping Carla load a body right now. Can I help you?"

Greg responds, "No offence, miss… Ashley, was it?"

Ashley says, "Yes."

Greg says, "No offense, Ashley, but I need to speak to Dave. I don't know you and would prefer to speak to Dave directly."

Ashley keeps a calm tone in her voice. "No offense taken, I understand, and he said he will speak to you as soon as the body is loaded. I am actually behind him waiting for him to be available."

Greg says, "Thank you for understanding."

Dave and Carla get the body in the car, and he turns and takes the phone being offered. "Hello, Greg. To what do I owe the privilege of your call today?"

Greg smiles. "Now, come on, Dave. You don't like to hear from me." They both have a short laugh.

Dave says, "Actually, I don't want to hear from any of you officers. Because none of you call to chat. It is usually in reference to the beast in some way."

Greg says, "Well, I won't surprise you then. We had a phone call that some hunters found a pile of bodies."

Dave tries to stop Carla, but she was already pulling out of the driveway.

Dave asks, "Did you call Carla?"

Greg answers, "Left a message on her voicemail."

Dave's confusion is showing in his voice. "So, why call me? Are they dead beasts?"

Greg says, "I saw a report of what happened the other night. Multiple beasts killed at your place. Some were human; many females, and even canines were killed."

Dave lowers his head. "Yes, but everything dead was beast when I shot it." Dave has the speaker phone on, so Ashley is hearing the conversation, as well.

Greg says, "I am not doubting you on that. I thought you'd like to know that the missing bodies were found."

Dave looks surprised. "Where? I didn't think we'd ever see those bodies again." Greg tells him where the bodies were found.

Greg asks, "Do you want to head out there and see if you can learn anything new or if you need any of the bodies?"

Dave answers, "Yes, we will head out there."

Greg says, "Great. Carla is calling me back. I'll see you out there."

Dave says, "Great."

They end their call.

Dave is almost in a full run going inside to get his keys.

Ashley asks if they need any testing equipment or anything for samples.

Dave tells her to grab anything that might be needed as he runs upstairs to get his car keys and let Sarah know what is going on.

Sarah tells him to just go.

Dave is torn with her comment. He knows her well enough to know that attitude and comment is usually the opposite of her words. But at the same time, he has this rare opportunity to go to the scene and get information.

Dave decides to go. He tells Sarah, "I love you and will be back as soon as I can."

Sarah looks at him as he runs down the stairs and she doesn't even try to say anything or to stop him. She just figures he made up the whole thing to go out with Ashley.

Ashley is finishing getting what she thinks may be needed and runs out the door behind Dave.

Dave makes sure she closes the door then they get in the car and leave.

Dave and Ashley get to the site before Carla.

Greg is already there.

Greg takes them to the site.

Ashley is astonished at what she sees. "Oh, my God."

Dave doesn't look at her. "God had nothing to do with this."

The bodies are thrown about; some on top of others, both canine and human.

Carla is escorted to the site by one of the state police officers working the site for security.

Carla recognizes one body particularly. "Oh, my God."

Ashley speaks up, "Dave told me God had nothing to do with this."

Carla looks at her and smiles. "No, this body." She walks over to the body. "This is the sixteen-year-old Jennifer that went missing from my office. And most of these other bodies, as well."

They all look at the bodies and start loading body bags and hauling the bodies to vehicles for transport to the county morgue.

Dave and Ashley tell them which bodies to take. As they finish examining a body, it gets loaded.

Dave and Ashley are photographing the bodies more than anything else for an exam.

One of the officers asks, "Don't you need more than photos?"

Dave says, "Not at this point."

Greg mentions the time. "Dusk is about an hour and a half away. We need to get this done or it waits until tomorrow to finish."

Dave, Ashley, and Carla have a meeting and discuss the options.

Carla says, "We load bodies for the next half hour, and then we finish tomorrow if the bodies are still here."

Greg looks at Dave. Dave agrees with a nod.

Greg relays the order to the officers, and they focus loading as many bodies as they can.

Every available vehicle is used to load bodies. Every living person is used to load bodies.

They manage to get all the human bodies loaded.

They stopped using body bags and just loaded bodies. Even before they ran out of body bags.

When they get to the coroner's office, Carla's staff comes out and the police cruisers are unloaded first, then Dave's car, and last is Carla's coroner van.

They do not have enough gurneys for everybody that was brought in.

Carla is looking around. "Holy cow, we were never equipped to receive this many bodies. I'd have to count, but I'd guess we have fifty bodies here now; not counting what was already cremated."

Carla asks a staff member to take a count of bodies and asks another to count the cooler drawers that are empty.

The staff members count forty bodies and thirty-five cooler drawers available.

Carla tells them, "The bodies not in bags go in first, then we will start on the body bags."

Dave asks, "Do you need me to take a few bodies for the night?"

Carla says, "No, we have nine we still need to get to the crematorium. So, we can do that tonight, and we will be okay."

Carla asks, "Dave, before you leave, why do you think these bodies are torn open? It looks like the beasts used their claws and opened the stomach of only the women."

Dave looks at her, "Some of the canines at that location looked the same way, like the stomach was sliced open. The only thing I can think of is the beasts were looking to see if the females, human and canine, were pregnant and if the fetuses survived."

Ashley nods her head to agree.

Carla looks around the morgue. "If all the women... sorry, all the *females* were pregnant, then that is a lot of young with the potential to be beasts."

Dave says, "Sorry, Carla, but the young is most likely already beast when they are born. If what we are understanding what we found out with Maria. She was pregnant when killed and the fetuses looked like a canine human hybrid."

Ashley says, "Dave is thinking that the beasts were attacking the house the last couple nights because she was pregnant. They wanted her back."

Carla looks at Dave. He nods to agree.

Carla says, "We already cremated Maria's body, as well as the others we already had claimed. Good thing the door got fixed today."

Dave looks at Ashley and back to Carla. "If they want in, your door won't stop them. You even said the power they displayed on the video was incredible."

Carla smiles. "I had a heavier steel door installed and had and electrician wire it with an electrical charge. It worked for you so hopefully it will keep them out of here."

Dave says, "My place is wired with 150,000 volts. How much did you have them charge this with?"

Carla looks at him. "Two hundred thousand volts."

Dave smiles. "That should work. Well, if you are done with us, we will head home and hopefully get inside before any beasts show up tonight."

Carla thanks both of them and gets to helping her staff putting the bodies in the coolers.

On the way to the car, Dave tells Ashley, "Like before, just sit down and hold on; we are out of daylight and need to get to the house."

Ashley gets in the car, and they head to the house.

Dave is going well past the speed limit to get back to his house as soon as possible.

## Chapter 10

# Angry Pack Leader

Dave left his phone in the car and never checked it to see if he missed any calls.

Dave's phone starts ringing after they leave the morgue.

He answers the phone with his wireless Bluetooth.

Dave didn't look to see who is calling. "Hello."

Sarah, sounding very angry, asks, "Where the blazes are you?"

Dave replies, "Sorry, babe, we are on our way back. The location had more bodies than Carla could haul by herself. The officers and I used our vehicles to help get the bodies to the county morgue in one trip."

Sarah has her head moving side to side just wanting him to hurry up with his explanation. "I don't care. You need to be here. I am alone and the beasts are already here."

Dave's Bluetooth is through the vehicle speakers, so Ashley hears the conversation, as well.

Ashley gets a surprised look and then fear starts to appear on her face as the conversation continues.

Dave says, "I was afraid of that. I lost track of the time helping unload the bodies."

Sarah is not letting up on her anger. "I don't blooming care. You need to get here now. I can't defend myself properly while in pain."

Dave says, "I know babe. I didn't do this on purpose."

Sarah rolls her eyes in disbelieve. "I don't care. You left me alone and now you may get your wish the beasts will kill me, and you can move on to someone else."

Dave shakes his head disagreeing with her statement. While he is picking up speed, he says, "I don't know why you think that. You know I get sidetracked on these cases. You know I how easily I lose tracked of time."

Sarah says, "I don't care. You seem to not want me around or want to be with me anymore since I stopped helping you in the lab, and my chronic pain has gotten worse."

Dave is trying his best to stay calm. He knows that he cannot allow anger to show while talking to her. She will lose the composure she has, and the conversation will be useless. "Babe, I still love you. I want you around. I try to respect you when you are in pain and can't do much. I help out when I can, as much as I can. You know that."

Sarah hangs up on him.

Dave gets on the radio, calling for Dewight.

Dewight responds, "Hello Dave. Why are you still out at this time of night?"

Dave replies, "I was helping Carla and the state police collect bodies to go back to the morgue."

Dewight says, "Oh, yeah, I saw a report where the morgue was broken into last night. Good to hear the bodies were recovered. So, what can I do for you?"

Dave says, "Sarah is home alone right now. I am travelling as fast as I can safely in the dark to get back. Do you have anybody in the area of my house to check on her? She said the beasts are already there."

Dewight says, "I don't know. I had to rework routes since we lost Ben and Carl. Brooke and Julie had asked to run the route that has you on it, but I don't know where they are in their route tonight."

Julie picks up the mic before Dave responds, "We are less than two minutes from Dave's house. We will head there now."

Brooke was already turning the car around and speeding her way to Dave's house as Julie responded.

Dave responds to Julie, "Thank you both. I should be there soon. I am going as fast as I can."

Julie replies, "No worries, Dave. You are welcome, and we will be there when you get to the house."

Dave thanks them again then puts his full focus on the road.

Dewight calls Diane and informs her of Dave and him trying to get to the house as fast as possible.

Diane agrees to inform her officers to not stop him and to offer escort if they see him.

Dewight turned down assistance offered by Diane to send more officers to help at Dave's house.

Dewight is hoping it's similar to the previous night and nothing is going to happen… at least nothing more than they can handle.

Dewight leaves the office and heads toward Dave's.

When he gets to Main Street, a car went through the intersection at a very high speed.

Dewight uses his radio to contact Dave, thinking it might be him. "Dave, you there?"

Dave takes his mic. "Yeah, I'm here."

Dewight is entering onto Main Street. "Was that you I saw going through the intersection heading out of town, toward Picture Rocks?"

Dave is a little confused by the question. "Yeah, it was me."

Dewight says, "Good. I will be behind you all the way to your house."

Dave asks, "Why? I thought Brooke and Julie were going to be there."

Dewight replies, "You had mentioned the beasts are already at the house. I am going to back up my officers, so you can get back inside safely."

Dave says, "Thanks, man. I do appreciate it."

Dewight says, "Just wait for me to get there before anybody gets out of a vehicle. That goes for you too Brooke and Julie."

Dave agrees and Julie responds an agreement, as well.

Dave gets to the house and Brooke and Julie are there waiting as expected.

Dave backs into his driveway, as usual.

His headlights shine across the street and show beasts in the area that was shadows.

One beast is standing upright, in front, and the other beasts are sitting.

They don't have to wait long for Dewight to arrive. He is pulling in as Dave puts his car in park.

Dewight gets on the radio. "Okay, Dave, Brooke, Julie, and I will get out of our cars and you get inside. We will cover you."

Dave says, "I will cover you from the house so you can leave."

Dewight says, "Get inside and don't worry about me."

Brooke and Julie look at each other. Dewight answers their question before it can be asked. "Brooke, Julie, I want the two of you to stay here and help defend the house. So, you will follow Dave to the house after he is in."

Brooke answers, "Okay, we can cover you from the house when we get in there."

Dewight, "No, I will be in the car and moving as soon as you make it to the house."

Dave says, "The beasts might go after you again tonight. They may try something different to get you. You can stay at the house and stay safe."

Dewight replies, "I'm getting out now. I will be fine. They change what they do, and I will change accordingly. Let's go."

Dewight is out of his car.

Brooke and Julie get out of their car.

Dave and Ashley get out and head for the front door.

Dave is carrying a pistol that he keeps in the car.

Nobody can see the beasts in the shadows at this time. No lights are pointing in that direction.

A beast does come out of a different area behind Dewight. It steps into the lit area on the street.

Dewight turns and starts to aim at it.

Dave yells, "Dewight! Do not shoot it unless it comes at you or us. They will attack if you shoot."

Dewight is thinking his friend lost his mind. But he respects the request because of the previous night when they didn't attack. He is hoping his friend knows something about these beasts nobody else does.

Dave and Ashley enter the house.

Brooke and Julie make their run for the front door.

More beasts appear with the other one in the street behind Dewight's car.

By the time the officers are at the door, the road is packed with beasts behind Dewight. But the road in front of him is clear.

Dewight jumps in his car when the officers reach the house, and he takes off as quickly as he can.

Dave and the others watch from the living room as Dewight leaves the area and is out of site.

Dave turns to Sarah. "How are you doing now?"

Sarah looks at him angrily. "How in the blue blazes do you think I am? You wouldn't answer my call for a long time tonight. You finally decide to answer after I see beasts outside. I am in pain and you ask how I am doing. What in the world is wrong with you?"

Dave looks at her. "I'm going to the basement. Brooke and Julie, would you please stay up here with Sarah? Ashley, do you want to work on samples tonight?"

Ashley is confused at Sarah's attitude and figures it might be because of her pain why she is so unreasonable.

Ashley says, "Yeah, I'll help with samples tonight."

Sarah says, "Oh, course you will."

Ashley looks at her. "What are you implying?"

Sarah looks at her. "Oh, nothing. Just didn't think you would pass up the chance to do some testing."

Brooke looks at Ashley and shakes her head no.

Dave is already in the basement.

Julie talks to Sarah and Brooke talks to Ashley.

Brooke says, "Ashley, just go downstairs and don't keep this going with her. She is a very jealous type. None of us understand why Dave is still with her."

Ashley agrees to go downstairs and not continue the argument with Sarah.

Julie looks at Sarah. "Why are you so mad tonight? And why in pray tell are you taking it out on Ashley?"

Sarah looks at her. "They left me here alone to go to some area that apparently had bodies. Besides, Dave already went downstairs; she didn't."

Julie sees Sarah look at Ashley when she started down the stairs. "Sarah, don't say a word to her. Let her walk away and you talk to me."

Brooke joins Julie with Sarah.

They get Sarah to settle down and talk to them and leave Ashley go downstairs.

They tell Sarah that they need to watch the outside for any potential risk the beasts may present.

Brooke takes first watch at the window while Julie sits with Sarah.

Brooke still participates in the conversation but keeps her eyes on the area outside.

Dave has already turned on the external surveillance cameras before Ashley gets downstairs to help.

They begin with the vaginal swab from Maria to determine if the infection can be transmitted sexually.

Ashley looks up at the monitor and points it out to Dave.

The beast is sitting there, in the driveway, staring at the camera.

Dave sees the beast and remembers he didn't turn on the electricity to the door and window bars.

Dave writes on a piece of paper telling Ashley to turn on the electricity to the door and window bars. The note also tells her which breaker switches to flip to turn on the electricity. He points to his ears, then to the monitor, and then makes the quiet sign with his finger to his lips.

Ashley nods and goes to the breaker box while Dave stands in front of the monitor and begins to speak to the beast.

Dave isn't sure what to ask the beast and how it will react when it finds out the female is no longer there.

Dave says, "Hello."

The beast nods a greeting, a "yes" motion.

Dave responds, "Thank you for not attacking us last night."

The beast again nods yes.

Dave says, "I learned you attacked the morgue last night."

The beast tilts its head and then nods yes.

Ashley has the breakers all turned to electrify the door and window bars.

Ashley joins Dave at the monitor.

Dave continues, "Did you find what you were looking for at the morgue?"

The beast nods yes.

Dave asks, "Were all the women pregnant?"

The beast tilts its head but does not answer.

Dave asks, "Did you take all the women from the morgue to see if they were pregnant?"

Again, the beast tilts its head and does not give a yes or no.

Dave responds, "You probably already know that we found them and removed them from where your pack left the bodies."

The beast nods yes.

Ashley is surprised.

Dave is a little surprised because he didn't expect an answer.

Dave asks, "Are you here for Maria's body? Yes, we found out whom see was in life."

The beast tilts its head and again yes.

Dave isn't sure if he wants to tell the beast that she is no longer there, so he stalls a little more trying to make sure the door and bars have a full charge just in case it decides to try to enter.

Dave says, "We found out she was pregnant, as well."

The beast tilts its head again, giving no definite answer.

Dave says, "Sorry to tell you, but the young inside of her did not survive."

The beast lowers its head, then goes into a sorrowful howl.

Other beasts join in with the sorrowful howl.

Once all is quiet again, Dave continues, "Are you here to get her body back?"

The beast nods yes.

Dave asks, "Would you like to have just the young that was inside of her?"

The beast nods no.

Dave is getting more curious and begins to forget about the threat the beast poses.

Dave says, "I am sorry, but she and her young have already been cremated according to state and federal laws."

The beast is obviously upset.

It stands upright with teeth showing. The beast barks loud enough that everyone inside the house heard it.

Julie yells down the stairs, "Did you hear that?"

Ashley yells back, "Dave is talking to one in the driveway."

Brooke is surprised, "I never saw one come across the road."

Julie says, "Maybe it was already over here, and we didn't see it."

Dave tells Ashley to let them know to stay alert up there.

Ashley relays the message.

Other beasts run across the road to the house. They are faster than Brooke ever imagined.

The officers don't shoot, not sure about what is going on as yet. Since Dave told Dewight not to shoot earlier.

Julie relays the information to Dave about what Brooke is observing.

Dave is fixed on the monitor, and the beast in the driveway.

The beast grabs Dave's car by the front bumper, lifts the front of the car, and lets it drop.

The beast is still growling. By the show of teeth, it is presumed and is looking around for something, anything.

Dave is curious; he left the officers know not to shoot and that power is on the window bars and be careful.

Dave and Ashley both watch the beast in the driveway. It is pacing as other beasts arrive at the basement windows and some in the driveway.

The beast that was already in the driveway attacks another and throws it at least thirty feet.

Dave estimated the distance with land markers. The beast is about center of driveway and the other landed in the road.

The other beasts lower their head and body. Dave thinks it may be an act of submission.

But the beast Dave was talking to didn't appear to care and attacked them anyway. If one tried to run, it was grabbed by the tail and was forced to fight. The one was fighting at least three others at the same time. It threw as many as it could grab.

One of the beasts is laying there in the driveway in front of Dave's car, badly beaten. The first beast sees Ashley's car parked behind Dave's car. It wasn't in the garage but in front of the garage door.

The apparent leader goes to Ashley's Hyundai Accent.

The beast approaches her car. Ashley is watching and hoping it isn't going to do what it did to Dave's car.

The beast reaches down and grabs the front bumper. It lifts the front of the car. It works its way back the under carriage of the car, finally lifting the entire car.

It carries the car to the other that is laying in the driveway.

The one laying there appears to be submitting and possibly whimpering. It holds up its hands as if to stop the car from crushing it.

Just as the beast holding the car begins to slam the car down, the other beast laying in the driveway rolls out of the way. The car is slammed into the concrete driveway front first.

The little car just seems to fold like an accordion.

Ashley is almost in tears seeing her car get destroyed.

Dave is in scientist mode and wonders if the beast couldn't lift his Crown Victoria.

Dave puts his hand on Ashley's shoulder. She in return puts her hand on his.

The beast that rolled out of the way gets up on all four feet and runs across the street away from the apparently angry beast.

The beast turns to Dave's car and picks up the front of it and then pushes the car back to the garage.

Dave is impressed with the beast's strength.

The beast barks, and the beasts at the windows reach out and grab the bars and get electrocuted. The begin howling in pain.

The beast in the driveway is pacing and looks at the door. It works its hands in and out of a fist when it looks at the door.

Another beast appears in the driveway.

The first one looks at the new one in the driveway.

It rushes the newer appearing beast, grabs it and throws it at the door.

It started howling in pain as soon as it hit the door.

The door held and did not give to the impact.

Dave is glad he had the door repaired, but the contractor told him he couldn't guarantee how well it will hold. The wall needs to be redone where the frame attaches for better strength.

Dave didn't let anyone know about the weakened state of the wall around the door.

Dave is wondering how long the door will hold. How many more will the beast sacrifice to gain entry?

No other beasts are entering into the driveway.

The one in the driveway does not appear to be calming down.

The beast sees the cat in the backyard.

The beast goes for the cat.

The cat runs for the garage. Again, the cat barely escapes the jaws of the beast.

The beast isn't happy about losing the cat again.

The beast runs from the garage on all fours and launches itself at Ashley's car.

It hits her car and pushes it over onto its roof, then pushes itself off of the car and lands in the road. This was all done in one move.

The beast stands in the road and looks at the house.

Dave is trying to understand the beast, trying to figure out what it is thinking.

Dave thinks it looks like the beast might be looking at the front door.

The front door is not steel; it has no steel bars or a steel exterior door. It has no way to have electricity protecting it.

Dave yells up the stairs to the officers, "Brooke, Julie, get Sarah and yourselves down here now. I will meet you and lock the door from this side and electrically charge the door."

Dave runs up the stairs as he is calling to the officers.

They all pass on the stairs, and Dave slams the door and locks the door as fast as he can. Then he flips the switch to electrify the door.

He is almost at the bottom of the stairs. Sarah began to ask why he needed them down there, but she barely started to ask when they all heard a crashing sound upstairs in the living room.

Ashley watched the beast start running on two legs and drop to all fours while running and gaining speed as it ran to the house and to the front door. She watched it jump but couldn't see it go through the door. But everyone heard it break through the door.

Now the beast is inside. They can hear it walking around upstairs.

It sounds like other beasts enter the house, as well.

They hear the beasts walking around and things breaking as the beasts knock over objects and flip furniture.

Dave is wishing he would have installed surveillance cameras inside the house now because he cannot keep track of the beast's movement in the house.

Dave and Brooke are watching the door at the top of the stairs.

Dave is thinking to himself that he is happy that he had a steel door installed.

Julie and Ashley are watching the basement windows.

Sarah is the only one not holding a firearm. She is still in pain and is not shy about letting anyone know it.

Sarah is complaining about the beasts inside the house. She is blaming Dave for the beasts being in the house. She is screaming every time she hears a beast walking above her. She is complaining that her pain medication is upstairs. She is yelling at Dave for not putting a steel door on the front of the house.

Dave turns and reminds her that she was against that idea.

That just made her angrier.

The leader of the pack is sniffing the air after entering the house. Other beasts enter the house, as well, being careful not to cross the leader.

The leader barks, and some beasts head upstairs to the bedrooms.

The leader looks at the steel door leading to the basement. It goes to all fours and sniffs the floor.

It stands up and grabs the nearest beast and throws it against the steel door.

The beast hits the door and begins howling in pain from the electrical charge. It didn't bounce off of the door as most would expect. The beast hit at the bottom of the door and maintained contact and was electrocuted to death.

Dave and Brooke saw the door move when it was hit. They were ready with their pistols to defend the basement if the door didn't hold.

Everyone in the basement heard the howling and nobody questioned the tone if it was pain or sorrow or just communication.

The leader is growling. He just sacrificed another of the pack and is no closer to getting the people inside.

The beasts are destroying the living area of the house, destroying furniture, breaking lights, lamps, tables, and chairs. This is the things they are hearing in the basement.

The leader of the pack sniffs the chairs as they are destroyed.

The leader barks and howls and all the beasts leave the house.

Julie and Ashley see the beasts exiting the house and relay the information.

Dave tells Julie to trade positions.

They switch and, to Dave's expectation, the pack leader is the last to leave the house.

The beasts all stand in the road and into the shadows across, up, and down the street.

The leader turns and faces the house, looking the house up and down.

It seems to spot Dave in the basement window and stares at him.

Dave is waiting and wondering what its next move will be.

The beast howls, long and deep.

All the beasts that can be seen leave into the shadows. The pack leader again being the last to leave.

Dave gets his cell phone and calls Carla.

Carla answers, "Hello, Dave."

Dave staying calm, says, "Hello. We just had an incident here where the beasts came inside through the front door. I believe the pack leader was wanting to get to us and try to find Maria's body. I did speak with the leader again, and it seemed to get very angry when told she was already cremated."

Carla is surprised. "How many did you have to kill tonight?"

Dave says, "We didn't kill any tonight. They have left now and may be heading to the morgue. I think the leader killed at least two of his own tonight. I can't verify until morning, though."

Carla says, "The morgue is empty now. We finished and left an hour ago. The front door is charged and hopefully enough to stop them from getting in tonight."

Dave responds, "Glad to hear."

They end their call.

Dave tells Julie to take over at the windows and Brooke to stay there at the door to the inside of the house. He and Ashley return to the testing.

They confirm what was suspected—that the infection is found in the sexual reproduction fluids and can be transmitted sexually.

## Chapter 11

# The Dog Man Theory

Julie overhears the conversation about the infection being able to be sexually transmitted.

Julie says, "Hold on. You mean that an infected person can infect an uninfected person simply by having sex?"

Dave looks at her. "Exactly. The infection is in the sexual fluids. It is in the bodily fluids—blood, saliva, and now we know for sure the sexual fluids, as well."

Julie says, "So, people have a new reason to avoid sex. Is there a blood test available to the public to see if someone is infected?"

Dave replies, "Sadly, there is no such test for the public."

Brooke asks, "How did the infection ever get started?"

Dave responds, "Well, that is an interesting question. There are a couple popular beliefs. One is the curse from Satan; another is that it started with a rabid wolf biting a person. I have never been able to verify the bite theory. But, in my opinion, the bite theory would make more sense. So, the actual origin is still a mystery."

They all spend the night in the basement for security reasons since the front door has been broken through.

Sarah is so mad about the beasts entering the house that she doesn't speak to anyone the rest of the night.

The officers stay awake while the others get some sleep.

In the morning, Brooke wakes Dave to let him know they are leaving. He helps them force the door open at the top of the stairs; after turning off the electricity to the door first, of course.

It takes the three of them working together to push the door open with the dead body of the werewolf against it.

The beast is one of those that didn't transform to human form after death.

Julie looks at the remains. "That looks like a dog man."

Dave looks at it. "It does. I believe that is what people have seen for many years in the wild and called it a dog man. In reality, what they have seen was a werewolf. But at the time, nobody believed the beast existed. So, they simply called it a dog man."

Julie looks at him. "You do know that makes the legend of the dog man even scarier?"

Dave calmly explains, "That is partly, if not mostly, the reason the dog man has been more aggressive than the average Sasquatch… or Bigfoot, if you prefer. Which would also make it an older being than anyone ever thought. It will also make it harder to find a cure and even learn the history of the werewolf… how it first appeared and why."

Brooke says, "I liked not knowing that the dog man was a werewolf. I have family that has seen a dog man. I guess they are luckier to be alive than any of us ever thought."

Dave says, "Yes, my friend, they and everyone else that ever saw one is luckier than they ever knew. Look at the size of the beast—what? Three to four hundred pounds, seven to eight feet tall. It could very easily be mistaken for a Sasquatch at a distance."

Brooke looks at Julie. "Let's get out of here before he destroys our ignorance about the beasts any more than he already has. I'd prefer not to know this much let alone more."

Julie agrees and Brooke heads out first.

Julie looks at Dave. "Maybe we can continue this conversation another time?"

Dave agrees and Julie joins Brooke in the cruiser. They then take off and head for the office to end their shift.

Dave returns to the basement and closes the door on his way down as a precaution but does not turn the electricity back on to the door.

Ashley wakes up shortly after Dave returns to the basement.

Ashley asks, "What test do you want to run this morning?"

Dave looks at her. "I've been thinking about it for a while now. I think we need to test the samples from the fetuses. Let's map their DNA into the system and see if it is new or some kind of hybrid of human and canine."

Ashley looks at him. "You do have the DNA code of the werewolf in beast form, right?"

Dave smiles. "Of course."

Ashley says, "I figured but thought I'd make sure."

Dave says, "The test usually shows a contamination with human DNA, but I still have the structure saved any way."

Ashley asks, "So, what have you been looking for in your research?"

Dave replies, "I have been trying to find evidence of the change, scientifically. But I have not been able to find a sample that shows the change occurring. The samples I get are either all beast or all human, nothing during the transformation; part human or part beast, different portion of each not equal or dominant one way or the other."

They begin the testing on the samples. First is the DNA sequence to see which side of the beast, human scale it is on.

Sarah wakes up as they are doing the testing.

Sarah is still in a miserable mood. "What are you doing? Okay, I can see you are testing samples, but it is still early."

Dave calmly responds, "If you can see we are testing samples, than you already know what we are doing. Yes, it is early, but we were not going to go upstairs without you."

Sarah doesn't let any kindness show. "You don't need to be rude. Am I supposed to be flattered that you would care to wait for me to go upstairs?"

Dave says, "Actually, I didn't expect that from you. I just wanted to be sure you are okay and can make it up the stairs alone."

Sarah says, "My back is sore this morning because I had to sleep down here instead of in my own bed last night. My shoulder is sore from the stinking beast grabbing me. But I will make it up the steps just fine alone, without either of you helping me."

Sarah starts up the stairs alone.

Dave and Ashley wait in the basement until Sarah reaches the top of the steps.

Sarah asks, "Why is the power off to the door?"

Dave replies, "I turned it off to let Brooke and Julie leave, dear."

Sarah rolls her eyes and speaks softly, so Dave doesn't hear, "I should have guessed."

Dave asks, "Do you want help opening the door?"

Sarah replies, "No!"

Sarah manages to push the door open by herself without using her injured shoulder.

Once she walks through the doorway and around the door, she sees the dead beast and screams as loud as she can.

Dave and Ashley run up the steps as fast as they can.

Once upstairs, Dave asks, "What are you screaming about?"

Sarah gets behind him and points to the dead beast.

Ashley sees it and jumps back, as well.

Dave says, "That is the beast that hit the door last night. It is dead."

Ashley replies, "But it didn't change back to human form. Okay, I remember some the other night that didn't change after dying. But how many of those can there be?"

Dave says, "I couldn't guess how many there is that won't change. But I believe their human side, or perhaps their other side, since we now know that canines can be beasts, as well, has died and only the beast side is alive. So, when it dies, it doesn't change back."

Ashley asks, "But when it is killed in beast form, both sides die, correct?"

Dave responds, "That is how it has been so far."

They are in the kitchen for breakfast.

As they are eating breakfast, Ashley looks up quickly. "What if the beasts that don't change after death were never human or canine? What if they are and always were a beast?"

Dave thinks for a moment. "You mean the 'dog man,' what has been seen and labeled dog man?"

Ashley smiles. "Yeah, it's a theory."

Dave says, "I like the theory. Guess we should see if we can prove it. We have a body here now for testing."

Ashley agrees.

As they finish breakfast, Dave's cell phone rings.

Sarah rolls her eyes and gets up from the table.

Dave sees it's Carla. "Hello, Carla. Hope this is a social call."

Carla lets out a chuckle. "You're funny. I found a body against the door to the morgue building this morning. It is still in beast form. Appears to be dead; hope has officers on the way. I thought I'd call you to see if you want the body."

Dave says, "Actually, I have the same type of dead beast here. We will use this one and hopefully get some more information about the beasts."

Carla replies, "Well, I offered, but if you don't want or need it, how am I supposed to identify the body for a family to claim?"

Dave says, "That is a problem that we are going to try to answer with the body here. I suppose you can try DNA and see if you get a match with any missing persons."

Carla replies, "I was hoping to avoid DNA testing. It isn't too bad if the individual was in the military or criminal background with DNA on file. But those that aren't on file can be a pain to find the identity."

Dave says, "Well, we have a new theory that we are going to test and will let you know what we find out."

Carla asks, "Do I even want to know your new theory?"

Dave smiles. "No."

Carla laughs. "I thought so. Hey, the officers are here to verify the beast is dead. Gotta go."

She hangs up before Dave responds.

Dave says, "Okay."

He laughs when he goes to end the call and sees she already ended the call.

Ashley looks at him confused at his laugh.

Dave says, "She already hung up. Let's get this body to the lab and see if we can get some blood to sample. Either way, hopefully this body will answer more questions than it creates."

Dave and Ashley put their dishes in the dishwasher and grab the body… carefully, of course, making sure that it is dead and there is no electrical charge left in the body.

Sarah looks at both of them and does not offer any help.

Sarah asks, "What exactly do you think that dead beast will tell you?"

Dave replies, "Well, that is what we need to find out."

Ashley and Dave manage to get the body to the lab with just the two of them. Getting it loaded onto the table for testing is another challenge, but they manage to work together and get it onto the table. They both lift the upper body onto the table, then the lower body. They made it work.

Dave says, "Oh, we have another body outside. If it died at the door like this one did."

They open the exterior door and discover another body. This body transformed back from beast to a beagle.

So, they again check for electrical charge in the body before handling.

Dave carries the dead dog to the cooler and places it inside. He doesn't have a chip reader to see if the dog is chipped or not. There is no collar, which is to be expected with the size of the beast. A collar would have broken off during the transformation.

Dave mentions how much lighter the beagle is compared to the werewolf.

While Dave was putting the dog in the cooler, Ashley started working on getting a blood sample from the beast. She pokes around and finds an area that gave blood without trying to stab the heart.

She does get a little concerned that she got blood, and it is supposed to be dead.

Dave is beside her when she gets the blood.

Dave asks her to see if she can get anymore.

She mentions how creepy it is to her to get blood in a syringe from a dead body.

Dave looks at her and at the body. "If you don't see the area still bleeding when you are done, then it is a good indication the heart is not pumping blood through the body."

She looks at him as if to tell him she isn't stupid. But she agrees and goes on trying to get more blood without saying her thoughts.

Dave begins running a DNA test to see if it is human, canine, or what it is.

Dave goes back to the body and begins a physical exam while Ashley gets the last of the blood they believe they should need.

Dave says, "Well, we know it is a male body."

Ashley looks and then looks at Dave. "You had to make me look, didn't you?"

Dave says, "Yep."

They both laugh.

Dave uses his stethoscope to see if he can hear a heartbeat.

Ashley says, "Hold on. Shouldn't that have been one of the first things we did?"

Dave replies, "I suppose you are correct. But on the plus side, I don't hear a heartbeat."

Ashley says, "Well, that one that we brought in had no heartbeat on the machine when we hooked him up. But he sure enough woke up and escaped."

Dave says, "Yes, you have a point, but that was a different scenario. That was a suicide and in human form. The beast was not dead. This was killed in beast form and that usually means they stay dead."

Ashley says, "I hope you are right with this. We are way too close to it to be wrong. It is still in beast form, and we don't know why, not for sure."

Dave agrees with a nod. "That is why we are testing the samples you collected. So, we can hopefully find out why it is still in beast form. If your theory is correct, that could also help explain how this has spread. But will be harder to figure out the origin of the disease… not to mention it could change the theory of it being curable."

Ashley looks confused. "How would that help explain how it has spread?"

Dave says, "Well, we would have a good lead on how the disease started spreading. By the people that survived being attacked by a dog man. They would have, most likely, gotten their infection from the attack, but it still wouldn't help us figure out how the original came to exist, or how to go about finding a cure. If the infection is that old, we will need to look at dog men to help find the cure if we can find a cure."

Ashley looks at him, still confused. "So, are you thinking there may not be a cure?"

Dave says, "We need to figure that out. If we can get the right information from the tests, we can find a cure… at least for those that were infected. If the dog man is a different creature, on its own, then we won't be able to cure it, as it would be a 'naturally' occurring creature and therefore could not be cured."

They take some hair samples, that has not been burnt by the electrocution.

Dave and Ashley agree that neither of them can see any evidence of the body healing, so they keep watching the body as they are working on tests.

Sarah had called a carpenter to replace the front door.

She seems to be feeling good today; her pain is tolerable, so she is cleaning the house as the carpenter does the repair and Dave and Ashley are working in the lab.

The carpenter had made the comment that it looked like a car went through the door, minus the width of the car. He also asked about the car in the driveway that is nosed into the concrete.

Sarah explained to him that it was a werewolf that smashed through the door and put the car in its current position.

The carpenter is amazed and does eventually ask why it would do that much damage. He mentions how he has repaired houses before a beast damaged, but nothing even close to this extent.

Sarah politely explains that Dave is the scientist that examines the bodies and last night the beast was, apparently, angry, so it destroyed the car and entered the house.

The carpenter decides to leave it at that and finishes his job and leaves after getting a check for his work.

Sarah feels better knowing that the door is fixed.

The DNA test is complete, and Dave takes it and looks at it with Ashley.

Ashley says, "It does show human contamination."

Dave replies, "Yes, but look. The contamination isn't to the same degree as with the other tests."

He pulls up the results of other tests on the computer to look at side by side.

They look at the results and compare the similarities and the differences at the same time.

The result of this one is more predominately canine than human. Or human contaminated, by comparison to the other test results they are looking at.

They check the body again and agree it still appears there is no healing happening.

Dave looks at a blood sample under the microscope while Ashley begins the test to find the infection.

Dave thinks he sees the infection; it isn't as obvious as in other samples he has seen. He asks Ashley to look at it. She looks at the sample and agrees it is hard to see. She tells him he has more experience looking at the infection than she has and can see it easier than she can.

Dave does not argue with her and is happy to have someone else look at the sample to see if they can see it or not.

Sarah yells down the stairs that lunch is ready.

They leave the lab and go upstairs for lunch.

Dave compliments Sarah on how well the house looks.

Sarah says, "Well, it would go faster if I had help."

Dave looks at her. "Do you want us to help you?"

Sarah looks at him like he lost his mind. "No."

Dave asks, "Are you sure? We can stop in the lab and help with cleaning the house."

Sarah says, "I said I do not need your help, nor do I want your help. I need to clean this up, so I know what the beasts destroyed. If the two of you help, I will not know what needs replaced or if it is something that can be replaced."

Dave says, "Okay, I just wanted you to know we will help if you wanted."

Sarah glares at him. "I said no help. How many times must I repeat that before you understand or accept it?"

Dave is trying not to lose his temper. "Okay, it won't be mentioned again."

Sarah says, "Good."

After lunch they put their dishes in the dishwasher and go back to the lab while Sarah goes back to cleaning the house.

Once they get in the lab, Ashley asks, "Is she usually like that?"

Dave says, "Not all the time. I am used to her jealousy, her pain, how she speaks to me at times. But some reason this is different; mayhaps it has to do with the beast coming into the house."

Ashley says, "Well, I am confused why anyone would say they could use help then refuse the help when offered."

Dave smiles. "Welcome to Sarah's mind; it does not always make sense."

Ashley smiles, and they check the body and again agree it appears to not be healing.

They go for the test results about finding the infection in the sample.

Upon reviewing the results, neither of them is surprised to see the infection present. They are, however, surprised to see that it is not as strong as the other samples. The numbers involved just are not as high as other samples.

Dave is comparing the results to previous results and is trying to figure out why the numbers are so different in terms of the overall percentage of infection in the blood.

Ashley is also looking at the results. "If this is a dog man and not a werewolf that used to be human, wouldn't that infection rate be different?"

Dave says, "You have a good point. If this is a creature that never was human, the results would, most likely, be different."

Ashley says, "Yes, and if this is the creature that started the infection in humans and other canines, the results would be different, as well."

Dave sits on a stool in front of the computer.

He calls Carla with his cell phone.

Carla answers, "Hello, Dave. Hope this is a social call."

They both laugh.

Dave says, "Now you know I don't usually make social calls."

Carla said, "I know."

Dave has his call on speaker phone so Ashley can hear it, as well.

Dave replies, "We have some news about the beast here that didn't change from beast form after death."

Carla says, "Okay."

Dave continues, "We did a DNA test, and it is not a typical werewolf; half-human and half-canine."

Carla says, "I know. I believe I have the same results with this one."

Dave asks, "Really? The one you have is not showing up as human contaminated?"

Carla replies, "No, it still shows as contaminated just not as strongly as the usual werewolf does."

Dave says, "Amazing. We have the same results here."

Carla says, "Well, I have this one scheduled to go the incinerator as soon as possible. I don't like having one that is still in beast form."

Dave and Ashley both agree with her to send it as quickly as she can.

Dave says, "If what we think is right, these were never human and were always this werewolf… or as they have been called in history, dog men."

Carla's mouth drops. "You are not serious."

Dave nods his head. "I am very serious."

Carla says, "I saw a dog man long before werewolves were known to exist. When I was hiking as a kid with my parents. We got out of there as fast as we could."

Dave says, "We believe they are where the werewolf legend started, as well as being a source of the infection."

Carla asks, "You mean if we would have been attacked, we could have become a werewolf?"

Dave answers, "You would have needed to survive the attack first, including a bite. The one here has the infection; it just isn't as easy to see. Like it might be in a dormant stage."

Carla asks, "Why did we never hear of these dog men attacks before?"

Dave replies, "Well, one would have needed to survive the attack to describe their attacker. Most bodies that were found in the wilderness before werewolves were known to exist were classified as bear attacks. If they found them before the body decomposed and then they blamed the scavengers for the teeth marks on the bones."

Carla says, "You are right. Nobody ever questioned any of that back then."

Dave says, "Unlike Sasquatch, or Bigfoot, if you prefer, we have not only one body but two for DNA verification. We don't have that for Sasquatch DNA verification. So, that one is still the few samples they get to test occasionally."

Carla replies, "Yeah, it is nice to be a part of science history. I never expected that with this job. Why haven't we ever seen these before?"

Dave responds, "I think the bodies that disappear in the night after a mass killing of the beasts might be the pack removing these bodies, so we wouldn't find them. Last night the leader may not have been thinking and sacrificed the dog men instead usual of the werewolves from the pack."

Carla says, "Well, I will email you my DNA results, so you can compare to your results. Let me know if they are similar."

Dave says, "I will do better than that. I will email you my results, as well. If they are similar, destroy the body as soon as you have the crematorium open."

Carla responds, "Count on it. You don't think the beast will heal and wake up do you?"

Dave says, "I don't suspect it will, but at the same time, we never have had one of these bodies before. There is a reason why. Mayhaps it is only because the others remove them, but then what do they do with the bodies?"

Carla responds, "This is where I tell you I am only a coroner and you are the scientist. I don't have to answer the question, you do."

They all laugh and end the call.

The emails are exchanged, studied, and compared to the results on hand.

Dave and Ashley decide the results look the same.

Dave texts Carla what they decided. She responds with the same findings and that the body is on its way to the crematorium.

Dave and Ashley examine the body again, looking for signs that it might be healing. They agree there does not appear to be any indication that it is healing.

Again, that raises the question: What are they doing with the others that get killed?

Dave asks Ashley, "Do you think we could produce a vaccine from this sample?"

Ashley responds, "I don't think we should even try. If this is where it started, the vaccine from this could make the situation worse. This isn't a 'typical' disease like the world is used to now. The vaccine could cure the victim of their human side, not the beast."

Dave agrees with her. "It isn't 'typically' correct, but we can still create a vaccine from the sample, the same way we do from other hosts that have it but are not affected from it. We locate their antibody for that disease and duplicate it. We won't know if we don't even try; trying is better than doing nothing. That is also why we will test it before we put it out to the public."

Ashley agrees. "Do you have the equipment we need to locate the antibody, providing the specimen we have has the antibody, then separate it so we can duplicate it?"

Dave looks around. "If we can find the antibody in its blood, we can duplicate it here. Just may need to do it a little differently than how we are used to doing it."

They begin testing for the antibody.

While they are waiting for the test to run, Ashley asks, "Who would we try the vaccine on if we are successful at making it here?"

Dave thinks, "That is a good question. We would need a living specimen to try it on. How about Frank?"

Ashley says, "That could work, but we need to be sure he is a beast before injecting him, though."

Dave says, "Of course, if he isn't, the vaccine could make him, at least, part beast before curing him. Like the flu vaccine, it makes you sick to get you immune to the infection. At least that is how it works for me."

Ashley says, "Same for me."

Dave is looking at the body. He doesn't think it is healing. But he does have thoughts going through his head while waiting for the test to finish.

Ashley looks at him, looks at the body, and back to Dave. She asks, "What are you looking at or thinking?"

Dave responds as he is thinking, "What if… I mean, we think this creature could be the source of the infection. What if the original infection happened from someone getting poked by a tooth from a dead dog man?"

Ashley thinks as she is looking at the body. "You mean, like how a poisonous snake still has the ability to envenomate after death? It still has venom on or in the fangs, and if someone or some other living being gets stabbed by the fang, they get infected by the remaining venom?"

Dave says, "Exactly the same way."

Ashley adds, "I think it would be worth testing."

Dave takes a Q-tip and wets one end with a little water. Then, wearing gloves, he carefully pulls back the jowls of the beast and slowly swabs the teeth for the sample. He repeats this two more times, so he has three samples to test from different areas of the mouth. His first sample is from the fangs of the beast, then the back molars on both sides to the mouth.

They begin testing the sample from the fangs first. They get the Q-tip broken down and begin with the test. They follow with the other two samples, as well, making sure to keep the samples separate and labeled where in the mouth the sample is from.

The day is wearing on, and it is getting close to supper time, so they put the body in the cooler and continue discussing ideas while waiting for the test to complete running.

The antibody test is ready just as Sarah yells down the stairs that supper is ready.

Dave doesn't want to wait to look at the results, but he doesn't want to anger Sarah any more than she already is. So, they put the test aside and go up for supper.

Dusk is moving in as they sit down, and there is a knock on the door.

Sarah says, "You two sit and eat. I will answer the door."

Dave responds, "You okay? How is you pain today?"

Sarah replies, "If I were in too much pain, do you really think I would answer the door? Make lunch and supper? Do all the cleaning while you hide in the basement?"

Dave looks at her. "Sorry to care. I just asked a simple question. So, apparently, you are having a good day; pain wise, anyhow."

Sarah heads toward the door. "Duh."

Ashley looks at Dave, and he nods his head no. So, she doesn't say anything to keep Sarah going with her condescending trip.

Sarah answers the door, and it is Brooke and Julie.

She invites them in, and they all head to the table.

Once they get to the table, they all greet each other, and the officers sit down with them and join in for the meal. They are not willing to argue with Sarah and still end up sitting down and eating anyway.

Julie starts to ask about the body and if they did any testing on it.

Sarah says, "Julie, please not at the table. You can go downstairs with them and talk 'shop' all you want, but not at my table. Okay?"

Julie agrees and apologizes.

After supper, Dave and Ashley clear the table. Sarah doesn't argue and she goes into the living room to sit down and watch T.V.

Brooke says, "I guess since she said Julie goes downstairs, I will stay up here with her and watch the windows tonight."

Dave agrees but warns her that Sarah has been in a bad mood all day, even for her, and they all go their way.

Brooke nods her acknowledgement. Dave had kept his voice low so Sarah wouldn't hear him warning Brooke.

Brooke joins Sarah in the living room as the other three go downstairs.

Brooke says, "How are you doing today?"

Sarah looks at her. "I am doing okay. I had to clean all this up by myself today while they hid in the basement. So, I ain't happy about that."

Brooke asks, "They didn't even offer to help?"

Sarah says, "Oh, they offered."

Brooke replies, "So, why are you mad? Did you accept their offer to help?"

Sarah looks at her. "No, I didn't. I shouldn't have to ask. Dave and I have been married long enough he should just help whether I ask for or refuse the offer to help. He should just help."

Brooke is looking a bit confused. "Why would he or Ashley help if you refuse the offer?"

Sarah is starting to let anger show a little. "He should know to just help. I shouldn't have to ask, and he should just help."

Brooke gives up; she has known Sarah long enough to know continuing the conversation will not do anything but anger Sarah more. So, she takes a chair to the window and watches out the window as Sarah watches T.V.

Once they get into the basement, Julie asks, "Did you do any testing on the body? Have you figured out why it didn't change from beast? Is it a dog man?"

Ashley looks at her, and Dave smiles. "We do believe it is what is referred to as a dog man. We have tested it today. We have some tests to look at and see about our theories."

Julie asks, "What are your theories?"

Dave replies, "Well, we are testing to see if it has antibodies to fight the infection. We are testing to see if it can infect after death, similar to a venomous snake. So far, that is all we have come with on theories."

Julie takes her position at the window to watch outside. "So, what are you thinking if it could pass the infection after death?"

Dave says, "It is possible that could be where the entire outbreak started."

Julie says, "Wow."

Ashley takes the antibody test and looks at the results with Dave.

Ashley adds, "Holy smoke, it looks like it has the antibody."

Dave agrees.

Julie doesn't respond but does listen to their conversation.

The testing from the teeth is getting ready to read.

It is getting later into the evening as they begin reading the tests from the teeth swabs.

As they take the first results to read, Julie mentions that there is a beast in the road. She mentions it looks to be alone at the moment.

Dave asks if it is the leader.

Julie says she can't tell the difference.

Dave leaves the results to Ashley while he goes to the window to look out at the beast.

Dave says, "That is the leader."

Julie asks, "How in the world can you tell?"

Dave points out the markings on the fur. "He is the only one that I have seen with that color pattern."

Julie says, "It looks like a calico color of a cat, or perhaps the traditional saddle of a German shepherd."

Dave says, "If that is how you can identify him, then use whatever comparison that works for you."

Dave goes back to Ashley and continues with the results as Julie watches the leader.

They find out that the infection is still viable on the teeth after death.

Dave adds, "Too bad we don't have one has been dead and decomposed and just the skull, so we could find out if it would still infect."

Ashley says, "Yeah, if we process this one to just the skull, it would, most likely, wash away any traces of the infection."

Dave agrees.

Julie asks, "Do you think someone might have a skull that was naturally cleaned?"

Dave replies, "It is possible, but the individual may not even know what they have. They may think it is just a skull of a wolf; granted, a large wolf, but that might be what they would think."

Julie says, "The beast is walking this direction; it is upright." Brooke asks about shooting it.

Dave says not to shoot it. "Let's see what it might do."

The beast walks to the driveway. It's looking at the car that it slammed into the driveway and was not removed.

Other beasts appear in the street and along the side, coming into the light.

Dave turns on the surveillance cameras and watches the monitors.

The beast does not go to its usual spot to communicate.

Dave asks Julie what the other beasts are doing.

Julie says, "Just standing there, watching this one that came to the house."

Dave turns on the power to the doors and windows.

He tells Ashley to go upstairs and have Sarah and Brooke come down.

Sarah is not happy and lets it be known. "Maybe I should just sit here and let the beasts take me. Then Dave won't need to deal with me anymore, and I won't need to deal with him."

The beast in the driveway seems to hear Sarah; she made no attempt to speak calmly or at a regular tone.

Brooke tells Sarah, "We need to get to the basement. The beasts seem to have heard you; they are looking at the house now, not the other one. We are safer in the basement."

Sarah says, "I just had the door replaced today; the beasts can all go back to hell where they came from."

Brooke says, "If you don't go to the basement, I will have to carry you. We told Dewight we would protect you, Dave, and Ashley.. with our lives, if necessary. Are you going to make me die for you?"

Sarah looks at her. "No… not today."

Brooke looks at her, not sure she wants the explanation behind that comment.

Sarah looks at Ashley. "I would be okay with you dying for me tonight, though."

Ashley looks like she wants to punch Sarah.

Brooke steps in between them and tells Ashely to go downstairs and she will get Sarah down there, as well.

Ashley agrees and walks away without saying a word, but her body language leaves no doubt she is mad. Okay, mad is an understatement.

Ashley gets back in the basement without the other two.

Dave asks Ashley, "Where are the others?"

Ashley glares at him, and he steps back as this is a new look from her.

Ashley, anger obvious in her voice, says, "Sarah isn't sure she wants to come down. Brooke asked if she wanted her to die protecting her. Sarah said, 'not today,' then looked at me and said she would be okay with me dying for her tonight. So, yeah, right now I want to feed her to the beasts."

Dave tries to add a little humor by saying, "I don't think the beasts would even deal with her, let alone feed on her. She is too bitter, even for their taste."

Ashley lets a little smile show.

Julie smiles and keeps watch out the window.

Dave says, "I suppose I will go up and see what her problem is this time."

He turns and goes upstairs.

Sarah looks at him. "What do you want?"

Dave says, "For you and Brooke to come down to the basement where it is safer."

Sarah asks, "Why do you think it is safer down there?"

Dave replies, "The doors are steel; the door here isn't steel."

Sarah asks, "What if I don't believe the beasts will attack tonight?"

Dave looks at her, confused. "Then I would like to know why you think that."

Brooke is still watching out the window.

Sarah questions, "And I would like to know why you think a beast will break in again tonight? Who decided you are the 'expert' on anything about the beasts?"

Dave shakes his head. "The state and the federal government agree that I am one of the leading scientists in regard to the beasts. I wouldn't refer to myself as an expert; there is still more to learn about the beasts. Besides, the beast ran straight through the front door, including the electrified screen door with the steel bars. Whether the beast even felt the electricity in that exterior door last night is not even worth guessing. It knows it can get through at that point and might try again. We need to all be in the basement when the beasts are here and posing a threat."

Sarah gets up and walks over to a window. "They don't seem to be a threat tonight; they are just standing there."

Dave says, "So, are you going to make Brooke stay up here with you and sacrifice her, as well as yourself, if a beast decides to run through the door again tonight?"

Sarah looks at him. "No, she can go down. Send up your little playmate. I have no problem giving her to the beast."

Dave says, "What in the world are you talking about?"

Sarah responds, "Ashley, send her up to protect the upstairs with me."

Dave asks, "Why do you do think anything is going on with her or anyone?"

Sarah says, "You haven't wanted anything to do with me for a long time now. So, you must have someone else."

Dave shakes his head again. "You must have hit your head when the beast threw you the other night. You are talking a lot of nonsense. I don't show you affection when you are in pain. The first time I did, you flipped out on me demanding to know why I would think you would be interested in intimacy when you are in pain. So, I quit showing you affection, physically, even with a hug or kiss when you are in pain. So, you take that as me having interest in someone else, when the whole thing is because you started it?"

Sarah says, "Yes, you want nothing to do with me."

Brooke had turned around to look at them, more to be sure the argument wasn't going to get physical. When she turns back to the window, she screams and jumps back, raising her weapon at the same time.

The pack leader is at the window, just staring in at them. Dave looks at it and thinks it might be listening.

Dave looks at Sarah and points to the window. "See? Arguing with you and this one walked right up to the window without being seen. Hope you are happy now."

Sarah looks the beast in the eyes.

Dave and Brooke both just stare at her and the beast, switching their gaze back and forth, from Sarah to the beast and back to Sarah.

Dave puts his hand over Brooke's weapon and applies downward pressure, so she lowers her weapon without being asked. She does look at him like he lost his mind as she lowers the weapon.

Dave tells Brooke to go to the basement door and wait.

Brooke is wondering what he has in mind but doesn't need to wait long.

The beast turns away from the window and looks at the others in the road.

Dave takes that instant to pick up Sarah using a fireman's carry, putting Sarah over his shoulder, and runs for the basement door. He tells Brooke to close the door and lock it and turn on the switch as he passes her.

Sarah lets out a scream when Dave picks her up.

The beast turns and sees Dave carrying her away. It reaches for the window bars but doesn't grab the bars. Instead, it pulls back and sniffs the bars without getting close enough to get shocked.

Dave is heading down the stairs as Brooke closes, locks, and turns on the electricity to the door.

Brooke goes down after she secures the door.

Dave puts Sarah down after getting to the basement.

Sarah looks at him. "Why did you do that?"

Dave says, "Because I still care whether you believe it or not."

Sarah says, "I thought you would just leave me to the beasts."

Dave replies, "That would make me no better than the beasts we fight and try to understand."

Sarah says, "Well, if even one beast comes through upstairs tonight, I am going up there and shooting every one of them that is in the house or coming in and you ain't gonna stop me." Complete with the attitude.

Dave says, "Well, if that is what you want to do, then go for it. I am tired of arguing and you thinking I am against you, no matter what I do or say. But how will you shoot even one beast when you are right-handed and your right shoulder isn't healed yet?"

Sarah looks at her shoulder. "Well, I will use my left hand. I should still be able to take out a few before they take me out."

Dave says, "Well, you can watch the door while the officers watch the windows."

Sarah says, "No, I will sit here and watch you." She takes the chair and sits in front of the cell again.

The leader of the beasts is still at the window. It watched Dave carry Sarah to the basement door and the door close.

The beast taps the window bars with the back of its hand and gets shocked.

It goes to the front door and taps the exterior door with the back of its hand and again gets shocked.

The beast goes back to the street and sits down in the street, looking at the house.

It is looking at every window and the front door, as if it is trying to find a weak spot or another area where it can get in.

Julie lets Dave know the beast is in the street, and it is just sitting there, like a dog, staring at the house.

Dave and Ashley are working on separating the antibody to replicate.

Dave walks over to the window. He watches the beast as it is looking around the front side of the house.

Dave is curious but cautious at the same time.

Dave is wondering if the beast isn't breaking through the door because it remembers the charge in the door and it must have felt the charge, or it would most likely have already entered the house.

Dave asks the officers to keep watching it and to let him know what it does.

Both officers agree and both keep their weapons drawn for quick use, if needed.

Dave looks at Sarah. "Since when do you look at a werewolf face to face? You usually stay as far away from the window as you can, but tonight you went up to the window and faced the beast. Why?"

Sarah tilts her head a little. "Why not? You watch them as long as you can. The window bars were on and electrified. If it would have grabbed the bars, it shouldn't have been able to get past the window. I wanted to look it in the eye and see what would kill me if you would have left me upstairs to wait for it to come in. What were you thinking? That I am one of them?"

Dave says, "Don't be ridiculous. I just didn't know why you would go from a deathly fear of the creature to staring it in the eye."

## Chapter 12

# A New Pack Leader Rises

Dave and Ashley continue with the antibody tests. They test a sample from the fetuses and find the same strand of antibody.

They also test the fetuses to map their DNA structure and compare to the other strands and see how human they would be as a result.

The DNA results on the fetuses do come back as human contaminated. More than the dog man but less than the "typical" werewolf, making them think this could be another creature.

The fetuses test positive for the antibody. The strand is different to the antibody in the dog man.

They continue testing into the early morning hours. Again, not needing to worry about going to work at the hospital.

They run tests to find the difference between the two antibody samples they found.

They begin working on duplicating the antibodies, both strands, as soon as they have the samples separated and have the samples ready to duplicate.

It ends up being a quiet night; the beasts only sit and watch the house.

Dave is confused why the beasts are not attacking tonight. He asks for any ideas as to why the beasts are not attacking.

Sarah says, "You're the expert; figure it out."

Brooke looks at her. "That is just rude and uncalled for."

Sarah replies, "Get used to it sweetheart. This is me, and he knows it."

Dave nods his head yes. "But it still doesn't make it any better. I've learned to not acknowledge her when she gets like that; I go to work down here in the basement and give her the space."

Brooke says, "Well, she doesn't need to take it out on everyone around her just because she is mad about something and won't talk about it."

Sarah smiles and doesn't respond.

Ashley asks, "What if the beast outside is expecting the one in the cooler to wake up and join the pack outside?"

Dave gets a thoughtful look. "That could be possible. I was thinking that and wondered if anyone else was. But the leader would then not realize which type or kind of werewolf breed it killed last night. That would mean the leader thought it killed, or didn't kill, one that would be able to wake up and walk out to join them."

Ashley asks, "Could it also mean the leader was acting more beast like and less human? It wasn't using its human ability to think; instead, it was more beast and less human… at least less than normal."

Dave answers, "Could be if it were so grief stricken, it acted and didn't think. Sometimes humans do that, as well."

They all agree, minus Sarah, that it is interesting that the beasts are just sitting out there and not attacking.

Dave and Ashley wrap up the tests that they can and then they all agree to go upstairs to go to bed.

Sarah asks, "Are you sure it will be safe?"

Dave, "No, but we have two officers here to protect the house, if needed. If the beasts were going to attack, they would have done so by now."

Sarah asks, "You don't think that the human side is trying to trick us into letting are guard down and go to bed, so they can come in and kill us all?"

Dave answers, "Interesting theory, my dear, but we have two officers that will be able to defend the house, if needed. I am sure they will be able to hold off any advances made by the beasts until we are able to join them. I doubt any of us would be able to stay asleep if they start shooting."

Again, Sarah is the only one not agreeing.

They all go upstairs and go to bed while the officers stand guard at the windows in the living room, watching the beasts in the road and those they can see in the light.

Dave goes to bed thinking and trying to figure out why the beasts are different tonight. Why are they not attacking like they have the last few nights?

Brooke and Julie talk while they keep watch through the night.

The night finishes with no attack, and the beasts leave the area before dawn, like usual.

Brooke and Julie wonder what daylight will reveal. Did the beasts attack somewhere else like when they attacked the morgue?

Brooke and Julie leave the house after dawn and go to the office to clock out for the end of their shift.

Dave wakes up first. He looks out the window and sees the officers already left and no sign of the beasts destroying anything in the night.

He goes downstairs to the kitchen and starts the coffee.

He sits at the table and drinks his coffee when it is done.

He has thoughts going through his mind and doesn't realize Ashley came into the kitchen until she sits down at the table with her coffee.

Ashley asks, "What is on your mind so early?"

Dave responds, "Still confused why they didn't attack last night."

Ashley says, "Perhaps it might have something to do with the agreement you made the other night."

Dave answers, "Good theory, but they attacked after that agreement and actually entered the house."

Ashley says, "Oh, yeah."

Dave says, "The beasts were quiet last night, as well; usually they can be heard all night."

Ashley responds, "I wonder if it could have something to do with the one in the basement. They remember the other body disappeared when they didn't cooperate. Perhaps this is a way they think they can get this one back."

"That is possible; the night we made the agreement they didn't attack."

Ashley responds, "They didn't attack us, but they attacked and entered the morgue."

Dave says, "That is true; you have a good sense for this. I appreciate having someone to bounce ideas off of and that will contribute to the discussion."

Ashley responds, "I appreciate you taking my ideas and considering them and not just dismissing those ideas but talking about them like you accept my ideas as possible."

Dave says, "We need to look at every idea, even the ideas that come from the officers or even the occasional idea that Sarah would have; an idea that she would share."

They continue their discussion as they eat breakfast.

Dave says, "You need to call your insurance company to look at your car and then get it towed out of here today, so we can go to work tomorrow."

Ashley says, "Thank you for reminding me. You need to get your car checked out, as well, to make sure the beast didn't damage it when it pushed your car."

Dave replies, "I will check it out and after your car is towed away, I will drive it to make sure it is still working."

Ashley asks, "You don't have someone do all that for you?"

Dave replies, "I take it to a garage for the things that I can't do myself. Sometimes I will take to a garage for work because they can have it done before I can get it done."

Ashley says, "Wish I would have learned to work on cars."

Dave smiles. "Well, you are welcome to help me."

They both smile.

They finish breakfast and have their dishes in the dishwasher by the time Sarah comes into the kitchen.

Dave says, "Morning, dear."

Sarah looks at him. "What are the two of you planning?"

Dave looks at her. "What do you mean planning?"

Sarah says, "Your secret meeting in here this morning."

Dave replies, "There was nothing secret about it. She came in after I had sat down with my coffee. We discussed the day and the vehicles, about getting hers towed away, so we can go to work tomorrow. Why would you think it was a secret or planned meeting?"

Sarah says, "Well, you are both done with breakfast and heading out of the kitchen as I walk in. What else am I supposed to think?"

Dave says, "That we got up at different times and we discussed the day before you came in so not to upset you by talking about the lab."

Sarah replies, "Whatever. Just go to your lab and hide all day. I will continue with the cleaning in the areas I didn't get finished yesterday."

Dave shakes his head, and Ashley follows him to the lab.

On the way to the basement, Dave mentions that they might take the beast's body to Carla for cremation, so he can make sure the car is running correctly and save Carla a trip if she is too busy.

Ashley agrees verbally, so he can hear her since she is behind him on the stairs.

They continue their testing on the antibodies and separating them for duplication for a possible cure.

Ashley makes the phone call to get her car towed. She and Dave meet the tow truck operator at the car when he shows up.

The driver has a helper with him.

The driver asks how the car ended up like that.

Ashley explains what happened and the driver and the helper both are surprised.

They get the car loaded onto the roll back and leave.

Dave and Ashley go inside and check on their tests.

Dave calls Carla about the body he has in the cooler.

Carla says she has families scheduled to pick up the ashes of their loved ones all day and can't get away today.

Dave tells her that it's no problem; they can bring it to her. It will be a good test drive after all and a chance to escape Sarah for a while.

They all laugh, and they end the call.

They try to rush the tests as much as they can, but the tests still need a minimum amount of time to show the results.

Dave goes upstairs to get his keys and let Sarah know they are taking the bodies to Carla for cremation.

Sarah just gives a wave to acknowledge him.

Dave and Ashley load the werewolf (dog man) into the trunk of his car and the beagle, as well.

Ashley asks, "What will we do with the dog?"

Dave replies, "It is going to Carla, as well. She will have a vet check for a chip and then cremate the remains. She or the vet will contact the owners if it is chipped."

Ashley says, "Oh."

Dave had looked the car over before loading it and had decided nothing was obviously wrong with it after the beast pushed it, besides the rear tires getting flat spots from not turning when pushed. But the tires will last a while yet, providing he doesn't spin them off.

They leave and head for the county morgue.

They do not have the radio on and are not talking, so they can listen for anything that sounds wrong with the car.

Sarah had never learned to drive, and they do not have another vehicle if this one needs repaired, especially since the beast destroyed Ashley's car.

They arrive at the county morgue and go inside to ask for assistance with the heavy body.

Carla sends out a younger man with a muscular build with a stretcher to move the body once out of the car.

It takes Dave, Ashley, and the younger man to get the beast out of the trunk.

They are estimating the weight of the beast to be at three hundred pounds, at least.

Dave puts the beagle on top of the beast to go inside. The young man says, "Carla didn't say anything about a dog."

Dave smiles at him. "I will talk to Carla. I forgot to mention it to her. But she will know what to do with it."

The young man nods and then pushes the stretcher inside.

The young man says, "Sir, Carla said this body is supposed to go straight to the crematorium for immediate cremation."

Dave agrees and helps push the body to the crematorium.

Once they get to the crematorium, they thank each other for the help.

The young man picks up the beagle and places it on a different stretcher to the side out of the way. He then begins to unzip the body bag to remove the beast from the bag to be cremated. He jumps back and is startled when he realizes it's another body that is still in beast form.

Dave and Ashley turn quickly when the young man let out a surprised sound; not a scream, but a noise that got their attention. It sounded to them like the young man said, "Oh, shit," but they weren't sure.

Dave asks, "What's wrong?"

The young man replies, "Sorry, I wasn't aware this was another one still in beast form. I just thought it was a heavy person."

Dave shakes his head. "Sorry. I thought Carla told you."

The young man doesn't take his eyes off of the beast. "Oh, no, sir, she didn't tell me anything except to help you and take the body straight to the crematorium and that it is to be the next body in the furnace."

Dave and Ashley walk back to the stretcher. "Would you like us to stay and help you with the body?"

Dave and Ashley are looking at the body while talking to him, not wanting to worry him as to why they would be looking at the body.

The young man respectfully turns down the offer for help. "All I need to do is slide it over the rollers to go into the furnace. I managed with the other one."

Dave and Ashley agree and let him to do his job.

After they are out of the room, they talk about the body.

Dave asks, "Did it look like the body was healing?"

Ashley replies, "I wasn't sure. I thought maybe but then another angle looked like it wasn't."

Dave says, "Yeah, I had the same opinion but thought it was just me."

They stand outside the door and watch the young man move the body over and push it into the furnace. Once he closed and locked the door, they continue on to talk to Carla and let her know about the dog.

They get to Carla and let her know about the dog. She isn't happy about the surprise but has known Dave long enough to not let it get her too angry.

While Carla is on the phone with her vet friend, they all hear a horrific howling.

It sounds like it is coming from the crematorium.

They all run to the crematorium as fast as they can.

The howling gets louder the closer they get.

Dave mentions how it sounds like it is in pain. The sound is similar to the others he heard while being shocked.

Ashley agrees.

Once they get to the crematorium, the sound is deafening.

The three of them go in, and they all have weapons drawn.

The young man is covering his ears the best he can.

The door to the furnace is still closed and locked.

The source of the blood-curdling, painful, horrific howling is coming from inside the furnace.

Dave walks over to the furnace. Everyone else is covering their ears as best they can.

Dave looks through the window into the cremation furnace and sees the beast moving around as it is burning. He sees it actively howling in pain as it is being burned alive.

Dave is mortified that they made such a gruesome mistake, but at the same time, his scientist mode kicks in and can't stop watching the beast burn alive.

He is amazed that the beast survived the electrocution.

The beast does die and finishes burning without any more sounds of pain. At that point, they all put their weapons away.

Carla smacks Dave on the back of the shoulder. "Why would you bring in a live beast to be cremated?"

Dave replies, "We didn't know it was alive. It had us believing it was dead. It was in the cooler all night and never moved and never made a sound."

Ashley says, "Even the ride here it never made a sound, never gave any indication it was still alive."

"What if the one we cremated yesterday wasn't dead? It would have been burnt alive, as well. But it never howled out in pain, so it must have been dead."

Dave says, "Unless we are now learning something new, bear with me. What if the leader 'sacrificed' these 'dog men' knowing they would survive the electrocution?" He looks at Ashley. "That could be why they didn't attack us last night. It was waiting on this one to wake up and join them outside."

Ashley and Carla are surprised, but Ashley was thinking similarly.

Ashley says, "Dave checked for a heartbeat on the beast yesterday and couldn't hear one."

Dave agrees, "Correct, but the guy that woke up after a death like sleep, if you want to call it that, had no noticeable heartbeat, even that the machine could find. Then when it did appear, it was like a heartbeat the hibernating animals have—very slow and very few beats per minute. What if the beasts can take so much abuse and then hibernate until their body heals? At least the dog men, providing they were not shot, of course."

Ashley says, "Interesting theory. How would we prove it?"

Dave answers, "I don't know." He thinks a little. "Well, not to sound disrespectful, but that is two less 'dog men' out there for the leader to use to gain entry it wouldn't normally get in."

Carla says, "Yeah, but we need to be certain they are dead before burning them."

Dave asks, "Are you suggesting shooting them before pushing the body into the furnace?"

Carla says, "No, that would be a waste of ammunition. But we need to figure out a way to make sure before burning the body. What if one gets out while on fire? The whole building will burn."

Dave and Ashley agree but have no ideas about how to check the body before cremation.

Carla says, "How about whenever we get a dog man, we send it straight to the furnace? All other bodies in human or dog form will wait. We need to burn the dog men as soon as we can, so they don't wake up while burning."

Dave agrees that sounds like a good solid plan.

Carla looks at him. "That means anything you want from those bodies you get for your testing and then the body comes straight here for cremation. No holding the body overnight or longer."

Dave agrees, "You have a great idea. The risk of one escaping the furnace is too high to risk."

Dave and Ashley leave and head back to the house and the lab.

Carla and her staff go back to their job.

Dave and Ashley go to the kitchen for lunch.

Sarah has already eaten lunch and says she figured they would have gotten something while they were out.

Dave says, "That is okay, babe. But if I would have known that was your expectation, we would have gotten something to eat."

Sarah just blows them off and goes back to cleaning.

With no Sarah for lunch, they talk about lab stuff and ideas on how to verify any future dog men are actually dead before burning the body. They also mention how grateful they are the beast didn't wake up while in the house or in the car or even while being moved to and into the crematorium furnace.

After lunch, they clear their plates and go to the basement.

They have a sample of the antibody separated and they are both excited about testing it on a "contaminated" blood sample.

They continue with another sample to separate the antibody. This time they use a sample from the fetuses.

Then they take the sample they have ready and apply it to a small sample of the contaminated blood.

They watch the sample of "contaminated" blood after the antibody is added.

Under the microscope, they can see it attacking the infection. They are hopeful that it will destroy the infection and be usable as a vaccine.

They find other things in the lab to occupy their time; everything from cleaning to looking at other samples.

Dave still has samples from the zoo he needs to work on and determine the infection and how he can use it to help in his research for curing the werewolf.

They check on the sample they added to the antibody to see how it is progressing. They are both hopeful with what they are observing.

They put things away and go up for supper when Sarah lets them know it's ready.

With Sarah at the table, they do not talk about any tests or theories about anything.

There is a knock on the front door.

Dave goes and answers it.

Brooke and Julie are there for their shift to help keep them safe for the night.

The officers follow Dave to the kitchen, and they all sit down for supper.

Brooke asks about the beast that was at the door and if they still have it or if it went to the crematorium.

Sarah looks at her but doesn't say a word.

Brooke sees Sarah's look and apologizes.

The rest of the meal is quiet.

Everyone puts their own dishes in the dishwasher, and Brooke goes downstairs with Dave and Ashley this time.

They get into the basement, and Brooke asks again about the body.

Dave tells her it went to Carla and got cremated right away.

Ashley adds the part about the beast waking up and howling in pain as it burned.

Brooke says, "Remind me to make sure you kill me if I turn into a beast. I don't want to be burned alive."

Dave looks at her. "As far as we knew, it was dead when it went into the furnace. It showed no signs of life." He looks at Ashley. "At least none that we could identify for sure."

Ashley agrees with a nod.

Brooke takes her position at the window as Dave and Ashley continue with other testing samples. They occasionally check on the antibody test in the contaminated sample and both still are hopeful about the results they are seeing.

Brooke lets Dave know the beasts have appeared in the street.

Dave goes to the breaker box and turns on the power to all the windows and doors for the entire house; he doesn't want to take any chances tonight.

Dave asks Ashley if she would be comfortable doing the testing herself.

Ashley reminds him that she is not knowledgeable in the specific tests he wants done. She continues explaining that she doesn't know the exact tests he wants done and on which samples he wants what test done. She does ask why he is asking.

Dave tells her that he wants to watch the beasts tonight and see what he can learn new about their behavior.

Ashley offers her observation, as well.

Dave agrees, and they put the samples away that haven't had any testing started.

They see the one Dave has figured and calls the leader standing in the street, just staring at the house.

It starts to walk toward the driveway and other beasts line up in the street behind it.

Dave has the surveillance system turned on and watches the beast as it enters the driveway and continues to the area outside of the basement entrance.

The beast stands there, looking around. It sniffs the air and then bends over to sniff the ground, as well.

It sits like a dog again and stares at the camera.

Dave looks at that and says he can't believe it wants to communicate again.

Before Dave begins to speak to the beast, the cat appears out of the garage and goes back in after seeing the beast, but not before the beast seen it. The beast does not chase the cat this time; instead, it returns its gaze on the camera.

All three in the basement turn their attention to the monitors.

Dave asks the beast if it wants to communicate tonight.

The beast stares at the camera.

Brooke asks, "Do you actually expect the beast to answer you?"

Ashley speaks before Dave, "It has responded in the past. It shakes its head or nods its head as if saying yes or no. So, Dave tries to keep it to yes and no questions. It is very remarkable, actually."

Dave continues as the women watch the monitor, "Are you here looking for the dog man you threw against the door the other night?"

The beast looks at the camera and nods yes.

Brooke is amazed. She just stands there, watching the monitor.

Dave continues, "Do you think it is still here?"

The beast nods yes, then turns and looks at the garage and back to the camera.

Dave says, "You seem to be unsure. Do you think it was already moved?"

The beast looks at the camera, taking longer to answer. Dave isn't sure if it heard him. The beast nods yes.

Dave says, "Okay, I need you to be more specific please. Do you think he is here?"

The beast sniffs the ground around the door opening from the basement. It looks at the garage and sniffs the air in front of the garage door. Then it returns to sit in front of the camera and shakes its head no.

Dave responds, "You are correct; we already had him cremated. He was dead, and we are not permitted to hold on to the body any longer than absolutely necessary. So, I am sorry, but the one that was here and the one you threw at the morgue have already been cremated."

The beast lowers its head, giving the impression of grief.

The beast raises its head to look at the camera again. Its teeth are being displayed as if it is growling, although it cannot be heard in the basement.

Dave tells Brooke, "Get to the window and be ready to fight for your life and ours."

Brooke turns to the window and tells Dave, "It's too late. The beasts are already at the windows."

Dave looks at the windows. "Oh, crap, it was a distraction, and we fell for it."

Brooke asks, "You mean the beast had this planned?"

Dave answers, "Yes, contrary to popular belief, the beast retains a lot of its ability to think from its human form. We have been learning that the last few nights. I have learned more in the last four or five nights than I have in the previous six years. Ever since the female was killed and brought here."

Brooke asks, "Why do you think that is?"

Dave replies, "At that time, when she was here, the beasts arrived, and I could study them closer than ever before." He looks at Ashley. "I also now have someone here to help me and work on theories and get her input on observations."

Dave looks back to the monitor, and the beast is gone.

Dave grabs a rifle and tells Brooke to be ready.

Ashley asks about the two upstairs.

Dave tells her to go warn them, and to be ready to fight tonight.

Ashley goes upstairs and relays the message.

Julie thanks her and is ready to defend the house and those inside of it.

Sarah asks, "Dave never thought the beast would want the others back, did he?"

Ashley responds, "It was dead… at least as much as we could tell. It wasn't until it was in the cremation furnace that we found out otherwise."

Sarah asks, "So, he had the crematorium burn the beast alive?"

Ashley replies, "Not intentionally. The beast had no heartbeat, wasn't breathing, and showed no signs of life."

Sarah says, "I bet you and Dave stood there and watched it burn."

Ashley responds, "No, we had gone to talk to Carla. Then we all heard the beast howling and ran back to the crematorium."

Sarah says, "I still think Dave did it intentionally."

Ashley asks, "Why do you have to be so negative?"

Sarah says, "Because that is who I am, like it or not. I don't care. I worked with him and have known him way longer than you and have seen a lot more than you most likely ever will. When I was helping him, our results helped shape the current laws that help keep people alive and not on the menu."

Ashley says "But you act like it is Dave's fault; like he was the one killing the people."

Sarah shakes her head. "He used the dead to be able to justify killing another living being. So, it hunts and kills people. Only those that are dumb enough to be outside in the dark."

Ashley asks "What about when the beast breaks into a house and kills the people? So, you are okay with the beasts killing people?"

Sarah responds, "The beasts don't normally break into a house. I suppose Dave sent you up here to get us to go downstairs?"

Ashley says, "No…actually he asked me to come up here and let you both know to be ready for a fight tonight. He is thinking the beasts may attack tonight."

Julie watches outside. She saw the beasts approach the house, and they stayed away from the front door and went toward the basement windows and driveway.

Sarah says, "He has been thinking that the last few nights. Why would tonight be different?"

Ashley shakes her head. "He has not been thinking that each night that I have been here. He has been watching the beasts and didn't expect them to attack, even the other night he didn't expect them to attack. Until he observed that potential from one of the beasts."

Sarah says, "Yeah, and I am surprised he didn't feed me to the beast; at least leave me up here alone to face it when it ran through the door."

Ashley replies, "Well, I delivered the message. Do as you want." She looks at Julie. "Julie, you are welcome to come downstairs if you would feel safer."

Julie thanks her and looks at Sarah. "I will stay up here until Sarah decides to go down. I will not leave her alone."

Ashley says, "I understand and respect your decision."

Ashley goes downstairs, leaving the door open. She relays the message when she gets back to the basement.

Dave shakes his head.

Brooke asks if he wants her to go talk to Sarah.

Dave says no, she will decide for herself.

Brooke reminds him Julie is still up there, as well.

He acknowledges the reminder but does not respond verbally.

Ashley picks up a rifle and stands watching the door to the driveway since both windows are covered.

The beasts are moving around outside. Some are pacing in the street, some are sitting in the street in the yard, some are standing, and others are staring at the pack leader.

The leader is staring at the house. It walks out to the street and looks at the house. It looks at the door and each window separately.

Julie recognizes the behavior and tells Sarah, "We need to get to the basement NOW!"

Sarah asks, "Why?"

Julie is already heading to the basement door. "Because the beast is doing the same thing it did the other night when it came in. It is staring at the house and the door and windows."

Sarah stands up and looks out the window to see the beast looking over the house very carefully.

They all hear the leader bark, and Sarah sees a beast running from the street toward the house. It started on two legs and lowered itself to all four as it is running.

Sarah tells Julie, "Basement, now!"

As they enter the stairway, the beast is crashing through the door. The storm door is taken with the interior door, as well. The sparks can be seen from the electrified storm door where it is in contact with the beast, until the doors charge is gone.

Julie is the last one down the stairs to protect Sarah.

Sarah told her not to worry about closing the stupid door.

Dave hears that comment and hears the beast crash through the front door again. He turns to see Sarah and Julie coming down the stairs into the basement. He asks about the basement door: "Did you close the basement door?"

Julie says, "Sarah said to not worry about the door and to get to the basement; the door is still open."

Dave shakes his head and runs to the steps. As he gets to the bottom of the steps, a beast appears at the top of the steps and is cautious about crossing the threshold into the basement.

Dave stops and raises the rifle and shoots the beast.

The beast falls backward away from the door.

Dave passes the rifle to Julie, then he runs up the stairs with a pistol in hand.

Once he gets to the top of the stairs, he sees the beast he shot already changing to human form. He looks where the front door used to be and sees the leader in the doorway.

Dave raises his pistol to take aim, and the beast watches him.

As Dave pulls the trigger, the leader dives, and the bullet hit a beast behind him and drops to the ground. After the leader stops rolling, it turns and looks at the beast that fell to the ground. It then turns and looks at Dave.

Dave grabs the door and is closing it as the leader gets up and runs toward him.

Dave manages to get the door closed and latched before the beast reached him.

Dave also manages to lock the door before the beast starts to pull on it. He turns on the electric switch and is charging the door as Dave walks backward down the steps as he watches the door, fully expecting the door to open. So, he has his revolver up and ready to fire, if needed.

The beast realizes the door is electrified; it feels a shock as the charge is growing in the door. It backs off away from the door.

Another beast approaches the leader and lets out a small bark.

The leader turns and looks at the other beast.

The leader grabs the other beast and throws it against the now-electrified door.

Dave is at the bottom of the steps when the beast is thrown against the door and sees the door move inward and return to its position.

Julie and Ashley are there at the bottom of the stairs, as well. They also witness the doors movement.

Dave turns to Sarah. "What in the blue blazes were you thinking by telling her not to at least close the door?"

Sarah says, "I didn't think we had time to close it and both of us make it down here safely." Her voice is emotional and sounds like she is close to crying.

Dave says, "You almost fed all of us to the beasts tonight."

Sarah, still sounding like she is about to cry, says, "I know. I thought we could get down here and you could close the door. I didn't know if you had the electricity turned on or not. I didn't want to get electrocuted and didn't want Julie to get electrocuted, either."

Dave shakes his head.

They hear another loud impact on the door.

Dave turns to face the door and raises his pistol at the same time.

Dave turns back to Sarah and lowers his weapon. "You know that is powered by a switch on the wall next to the door."

Sarah says, "I forgot."

Dave speaks as he turns back to the door. "I thought maybe you wanted to get rid of me tonight. Sorry to disappoint you."

Sarah says, "I didn't want that to happen."

Dave asks Julie to guard the other window. He asks Ashley to watch the door to the driveway, while he watches the door to the living room.

Sarah takes her seat in front of the cell.

Another impact on the door to the living room.

Dave is wondering if the beast is hitting the door or throwing others against the door. He thinks that if the beast is hitting the door itself, then the electric isn't working on the door. But if the beast is throwing others against the door, what is the delay between impacts?

Dave reloads the one shot that he used in his pistol and puts it in the holster and takes a rifle, making sure it is fully loaded.

Another impact on the door. Dave sees the door move again. He is trying to gauge how far the door is moving and praying that it holds.

Dave is wishing he had surveillance cameras inside the house.

The beast is throwing other beasts against the door as they come in, and it is running out of others willing to come inside.

The beasts it threw are all laying against the door after being electrocuted to death.

The leader is looking around and sniffing the air and the floor, as well.

As it looks around it doesn't see a surveillance camera. It lets out a growl.

The pack leader sits in Dave's chair and looks at the basement door.

Another beast appears in the doorway. The leader sees it and barks.

The other beast growls.

The leader stands and approaches the other beast.

The leader barks again and points to the basement door.

The other beast shakes its head no as it growls.

The leader is not happy, to say the least. He grabs the other beast, and it stands its ground, and the leader is having problems moving it. The new beast is fighting back and resisting.

The leader is getting angrier. It growls and faces off with the other beast.

The challenger grabs the leader and throws him into the yard over its own shoulder.

Brooke tells Dave the leader just appeared in the yard. Didn't look to be voluntary, either.

Dave goes to the window. The others join in watching, as well.

The challenger is on the leader before he can stand up again.

The leader is able to roll and defend himself, laying on his back, as his challenger is coming down the leader is able to catch him and throw him farther toward the street.

Dave is thinking about what they are witnessing. He is wondering if this is a battle for dominance. Is this just a less dominate saying it has had enough? What exactly is happening? How closely is the werewolf behavior and their pack structure related to that of other canines?

Dave doesn't know it, but Ashley has the same thoughts in her mind and is watching as enthusiastically as Dave, although she is a lot more animated than he is.

The challenger hits a group of beasts and knocks a bunch of them to the ground.

He fights his way back to his feet as the leader is charging toward him.

The challenger throws beasts after he gets up and even throws some at the leader.

The leader is on all fours running at the challenger and easily dodges the beasts that are thrown at him.

The leader jumps at the challenger and grabs him by the shoulders and tackles him. When they hit the ground, the leader rolls and keeps his claws dug into the shoulders of his challenger and throws the challenger as they roll.

The challenger lands in the street. Other beasts separate to stay out of the way of the landing area. He rolls onto his feet and turns in time to catch the leader in the air and throw him into a large tree.

The leaders back slams into the trunk of the tree. He was upside down when he hit the tree. He falls to the ground and lands on his head.

The challenger goes to a Ford F150 that is parked along the street. He picks it up and throws it at the leader.

The leader sees the pickup flying his direction and rolls to the side, escaping the impact of the pickup landing on him.

Dave and Ashley are both impressed with the amount of physical strength the challenger is displaying.

The leader is still dazed from the impact of the tree and landing on his head.

Brooke asks, "Which one to shoot?"

Dave tells her, "Neither; let's see what happens."

They watch the battle as it continues.

The leader stands up and is a little wobbly.

The other beasts are starting to get excited. They are barking and moving around like people watching a sporting event, although Dave is not sure if the beasts are happy about the battle, or if they are hoping for a certain winner. He just isn't reading the body language very well.

The leader is standing and growling. It reaches for the pickup that was thrown. He picks it up, but Dave realizes not as easily as the challenger. The leader throws the pickup truck at the challenger.

The challenger catches the pickup and throws it back at him.

The leader didn't move fast enough, and the pickup lands on him.

The challenger runs over and jumps on the pickup with the leader under it.

The leader howls in pain.

The challenger looks down at the leader and barks.

The leader turns his head and lets out a soft bark, like a whisper.

The challenger is still standing on the pickup and lets out a long deep howl.

The other beasts all bow their head toward the challenger.

The beasts all leave and disappear into the shadows. The challenger is the last one to leave the area.

The leader is still under the pickup. All the other beasts are gone.

Dave and Ashley start comparing observations. They agree the most likely outcome of the battle is the challenger is now the new pack leader.

The new leader is a solid red color.

They continue to watch the beaten leader struggle to get out from under the pickup. It manages to lift the pickup and get out from under the pickup.

They watch the beaten leader limp into the darkness across the street.

Dave and Ashley are still excited and are comparing observations until everyone lays down for the night. Except the officers of course; they stay up and stand guard the rest of the night.

The rest of the night is quiet… at least as quiet as it used to be before the female was killed.

## Chapter 13

# The New Moon

The next morning, Dave and Ashley wake up and go to work.

The officers go back to the office to end their shift.

Sarah stays asleep.

The drive to the hospital is a quiet ride. Dave is listening to the car and how it is running, so the conversation is kept to a minimum.

Of course, they want to talk about what they witnessed the night before, but Dave is concerned with the car and doesn't want the car to breakdown on the way home later because they were talking and not listening for a potential breakdown.

They get to the hospital and, after parking the car, they head inside.

They do talk on the way in.

Ashley and Dave agree that neither of them heard anything to be concerned about with the car. Ashley did point out that he is more familiar with the car and would be a better judge about any abnormal sounds.

They start their shift, and Allen has their work waiting for them.

They take their samples and go to their workstation. They do talk about the previous night while working.

Frank walks in, a few minutes late, and Ashley points out to Dave that Frank is limping, like the beast that was beaten last night.

Dave observes Franks walk and agrees the limp does resemble the beaten leader.

They observe Frank the rest of the day, and he is slumped over, as well, like he has back pain. His knuckles are healed.

Frank overhears. Okay, he was listening to their conversation about the previous night and the fight they observed.

Frank asks, "So, what do you think about the fight?"

Ashley looks at Dave surprised.

Dave says, "Well, it appeared that the pack has a new leader."

Frank asks, "So, you think they have a pack mentality like wolves or coyotes?"

Dave replies, "Yes."

Frank shakes his head. "Sometimes I think you are crazier than that guy that walked among the beasts trying to study them."

Dave says, "I got to meet him and will say he has some different insight to the beasts and their behavior that I can't accomplish by occasional observation."

Frank shakes his head again. "You still believe you can heal the beast?"

Dave answers, "Yes. We have not found anything to suggest anything else. What happened to you that you are limping today?"

Frank looks at Dave. "Why, are you concerned?"

Dave says, "Curious more than concerned, but if it is hard for you to move around, mayhaps you should have stayed home to recover."

Frank says, "So, you could accuse me of being one of those beasts?"

Dave says, "No."

Frank replies, "I know a lot of people think that, and I really don't care. Actually, I like it that way; they leave me alone. Except for you, you don't leave me alone."

Dave says, "That is because you start the conversation; besides, I like you."

Frank says, "Knock it off; I know better."

Dave answers, "What? You started the conversation."

Frank says, "You don't like me; nobody likes me."

Dave responds, "Wrong… I do."

Ashley speaks up, "I like you, too. You remind me of my departed father."

Frank looks at her.

Dave says, "See? Even a cute younger lady likes you."

Frank says, "You set her up to say that."

Ashley responds, "Oh, no, I make up my own mind."

Frank says, "Bug off and get back to work."

They all go back to their job, and Frank stays out of the conversation.

Dave turns his phone on at the end of the shift and has a text message from Sarah.

He opens it and reads it before leaving the parking lot.

The message just lets him know the front door and storm door is fixed again.

Dave lets Ashley know and they leave and head home.

On the ride home, they do discuss Frank and how his injuries seem to coincide with the beast, how his injuries seem to mirror the injuries the beast receives in the night.

They agree that Frank is a good suspect for being the beast. Especially the one that was beaten for the leadership of the pack.

They get home and sit down for supper with Sarah.

Sarah his having a good day with minimal pain. Even her shoulder isn't very sore; her pain pills are controlling that pain.

Dave asks about the install of the new doors.

Sarah lets him know the carpenter was nice. She used the same one that installed the other doors. She tells him the carpenter was curious why the beasts would enter the house two nights in a row. The carpenter says how rare that is; he rarely has to return to a home that soon to replace a door. Sarah continues and says how she explained the night to the carpenter.

Sarah lets them know that she had to go out to the driveway and around to get upstairs because of the dead against the door to the living room. She mentions how there was only men this time and all the dead transformed back to human form. She tells them that she called Carla directly and had her come and remove the bodies.

Dave asks, "So, did you get to visit with Carla while she was here?"

Sarah looks at him. "A little. Why?"

Dave answers, "Well, she mentioned how she missed visiting with you and thought maybe you get to visit a little."

Sarah says, "Yeah, well, the visit had to be short. She needed to get the bodies to the morgue and start trying to identify them. She also said she had more families coming in to claim the ashes of their loved ones."

Dave says, "Well, at least you got to visit even if a short visit."

Sarah nods.

Brooke and Julie arrive at the end of supper.

After supper Dave and Ashley put their dishes in the dishwasher and go to the basement. Brooke goes downstairs with them.

Once in the basement, they check the antibody test.

Brooke takes her position at the window watching the street.

The results are looking promising. They can see the antibody has attacked the infection.

They test the sample for DNA structure to find out more detailed information and if the antibodies did as it appears.

The result of the DNA test is very surprising to both of them.

The result does show the antibody attacked the infection, but not as expected or hoped.

The results show less human DNA and more canine, looking like the dog man DNA structure, leaving them to believe that the dog man antibody works on the human side to cure the beast of its human side and keep the canine side.

They decide to keep the antibodies and see if they can work with that to cure the beast. The hope is that they can find some way to use the antibody to create the vaccine for the beast.

They start discussing ideas to try in an attempt to manipulate the samples to make it cure the beast and not the human and to rid the infected of the beast and keep the human not the other way like it is in its current form.

They discuss the idea of the wolf bane being used again. But this time, combine it with the antibody and see what that does.

Ashley reminds him that they still haven't figured out what he did wrong when he tried that to make his vaccine before.

Dave nods. "Yes, but hopefully this time it will, at least, get us on the right path to figuring out the cure. Hopefully combining it will make a difference."

They retrieve the wolf bane that Dave still has in the lab.

They begin to process it and get it ready to use with the antibody.

They use the lab technique instead of trying to duplicate the scene from the movie where the drug dealer made the vaccine from wolf bane.

They are careful and using as little as they can; they don't have much material to work with.

Dave mentions that if they can get this to work, he will order more and see if they can make it work again before putting out for mass production.

It stays quiet outside, and there are no beasts spotted.

The nights go on like that. The officers quit coming around to protect them. Dave is told to call if any beasts appear. The officers do continue their patrol of the area every night, driving through the streets and watching the shadows for any movement.

Dave and Ashley bounce ideas of each other as they continue with the experiments trying to get the wolf bane to work as a vaccine.

The days and nights run together when they are not working at the hospital. The nights are long, and sleep is less than when they work the next day.

The days and nights go by without another attack and leading into the night of the new moon.

The night of the new moon they have some promising signs for the wolf bane to work as a vaccine. This is also the night Dave and Ashley got bitten by the cat in the garage.

They were checking on the cat and its tail. Dave was holding the cat while Ashley looked at its tail. The hair has all grown in and there appears to be no scabbing from where the teeth from the beast scrapped the tail.

The cat is purring and seems to be enjoying the attention like it usually did when they would check on its tail.

The cat starts to get restless, like cats do when they are done with being held.

The cat scratches Dave, and Ashley tries to take the cat and gets scratched, as well, as she is trying to take the cat from Dave.

They release the cat and decide they have the information they wanted.

Ashley mentions they probably should take a blood sample from the cat and see if there are any changes to the blood. Check to see if it is infected, especially now that they have been scratched.

Dave assures her the infection is canine. The odds of a feline getting infected are nonexistent. He adds they were scratched and not bitten. The infection is in bodily fluids and is not known to be transmitted without an exchange of fluids: saliva or blood or, as we learned, sexual fluids. But he adds that the sexual transmission is theory as they have no known cases.

Ashley accepts his explanation, and they go inside and bandage the cat scratches they have. The cat has drawn blood with its scratches.

While dressing their scratches, Ashley mentions that they don't have any way to test for the infection to have been transmitted sexually, unless they admit to being infected and how they got infected.

Dave agrees.

They go back to their experiment for the vaccine.

They are making good progress with the wolf bane as a vaccine. The mix with the antibody was determined to work the opposite of what they wanted. It did work as a vaccine; however, it cured the individual of the human form and not the beast form, at least according to their samples of werewolf blood they tested. The mix only affected the human side and not the canine infection.

They have the surveillance cameras on like they do every night. They check the monitors every so often and not always at the same time the other checks.

Ashley sees the cat and points it out to Dave.

Dave is happy to see the cat on the monitor. He tells Ashley with the cat being out the chances are pretty good there are no beasts in the immediate area.

The cat appears to be calm and just sitting in the driveway looking around into the street and the shadows.

They continue to watch the cat for any signs of nervousness.

The cat displays confidence more than nervousness.

Ashley asks if the cat looks bigger or if it just the way the light is shining on the cat.

Dave looks at the cat a little differently and wonders the same thing. He admits that he can't be certain.

Sarah comes down and sees they are looking at the monitor with the cat. She asks what is with the cat. She mentions it's nice to see the cat out again.

Dave asks Sarah if the cat looks larger.

Sarah looks at the cat on the monitor. She decides it looks more like the lighting in the driveway.

Sarah has been enjoying more good days than bad days with her chronic pain. Even some days that are pain free. Her shoulder is healed, and even the bruising is healed. She still has some soreness in the muscles of her shoulder but less at this point. She had refused medical attention when she got injured because she didn't believe she had any broken bones. She has been doing more of the things she has been wanting to do but couldn't because of her pain keeping her down… or at least kept her from doing everything she wanted.

Sarah sits in her chair, as it has come to be known, and watches them with their testing. She also looks at the monitors every so often, as well. Sometimes, they all three look at the monitors at the same time.

Sarah notices the bandages on their hands and asks what happened. She is thinking it has something to do with the testing.

Dave tells her the cat scratched them while they were checking its tail.

The cat had strolled out into the street and was still visible on a different camera and monitor. It is walking around like it has no worries, which makes Dave happy seeing the cat walk with so much confidence.

Sarah looks at the monitors and sees, what she thought was, the cat running for the driveway. She looks at the monitor for the driveway and tells Dave about what she saw.

Dave and Ashley look at the driveway monitor, as well.

They all see the cat come into view and then the cat is snatched up very quickly.

Dave realizes the cat has been grabbed by the new pack leader.

The beast is solid red like the one that beat the leader.

Another beast comes into view and looks like the previous leader.

The red one has the cat and is raising it to his mouth.

The cat is struggling but not getting anywhere. The cat is clawing and biting the beast's arm.

The beast doesn't seem to be phased by the cat's attack.

The beast opens its mouth as the cat gets closer.

Sarah is sure they are going to see the cat get eaten.

Dave and Ashley are more interested in the scientific observation.

How is the beast not bothered by the cat's attack on its arm? They can see bleeding on the monitor.

The beast gets the cat to its mouth, and the cat claws the beast's nose.

The beast drops the cat and howls in pain.

The other beast gives chase, but the cat makes it into the garage.

The beast breaks off the chase again and doesn't hit the garage door.

It turns back, and the red beast hits the other and knocks it through the privacy fence.

The other beast, which Dave believes is the defeated leader, gets up and approaches Red again. This time on all fours, head down, ears back, and tail between its legs.

The red beast doesn't attack this time.

Dave, Ashley, and Sarah are all watching the behavior and are impressed with how much they resemble a pack of dogs. Whether it is wolves, coyotes or just a pack of street dogs.

Sarah does mention how grateful she is the cat got away.

Dave and Ashley agree.

The beast that was the leader sits in the driveway and stares at the camera.

Dave figures it wants to communicate but is confused if it is no longer in charge.

Dave asks, "Are you still the leader of the pack?"

The beast lowers its head and shakes no.

Dave asks, "Is Red the new leader?"

The beast doesn't raise its head and nods yes.

Dave asks, "Is he younger than you?"

The beast still doesn't look up and shakes its head yes.

Dave is thinking as he is asking questions and doesn't want to ask something that will make him leave or worse have the pack attack.

Dave asks, "Is Red able to communicate like you do with me?"

The beast raises its head and appears to smile a little and shakes no.

Dave looks at Ashley and whispers, "I wonder if there are different degrees of beast-to-human ratio in their genetic makeup when they transform. Or mayhaps this one has been able to retain more human abilities than the others and how it got to be leader and made it weaker than the others leading to it losing its leadership of the pack to a younger and more powerful beast."

Ashley agrees and tells him to ask.

Dave isn't sure how to ask that question, or even if he should.

Dave speaks up and tells the beast he is thinking of questions and hopes it will be patient and answer what it wants to and is able to answer. Dave goes on and tells the beast that he needs to figure out to ask the questions in yes and no so it can answer, and he will understand the answer. He then asks the beast if it understands.

The beast nods yes.

Dave asks it if it can wait for the questions to be phrased correctly.

The beast looks at the leader and then back to the camera and shakes no.

The beast gets up and follows the other to the street where there are now many more beasts than the streetlights can light up. They see the shadows moving.

Dave tells Ashley to go lock the basement door to the living room and turn on the electricity to the door; it's the switch next to the door.

Ashley runs up the stairs and locks the door and flips the switch and impresses herself by not turning off the lights first.

She goes back down the stairs, and Dave is watching out the window with a rifle in hand and two more next to him.

Sarah is watching the monitors holding a revolver.

Dave is watching the beasts that he can see in the streetlights.

He is mainly trying to watch the new leader and try to determine if it intends to attack.

He doesn't have to wait long.

The leader barks and beasts run toward the house.

Dave loses thought of defending the house.

The beasts have no form to the attack tonight. They are just running and looking like mindless beasts.

Ashley nudges his shoulder. Okay, she smacked his shoulder and got his attention.

Dave is in one window and Ashley in the other.

Before they start shooting, Dave tells Sarah to call Dewight and tell him they are under attack and to avoid the area tonight.

Sarah makes the call just as they begin shooting into the crowd of beasts running at the house.

Dewight understands what is going on with the sound of gun fire in the background.

Dewight radios all cruisers to avoid the area. "Let's not repeat Ben and Carl's pass down the street."

The police regroup at the office and work on a plan to go in and assist Dave, Sarah and Ashley.

Brooke says, "I like them and would like to think of how we could help them and not lose any officers in the process."

Julie agrees, and many other officers agree, as well.

Dewight says, "I understand, but we have to have a plan before we go in, or we all will die."

Dewight calls Sarah back; she doesn't answer.

Dewight figures it is because she can't hear the phone over the gun fire.

Sarah is helping with the rifles. She is loading them while the other two empty them into the beasts.

Sarah's phone dropped out of her pocket and when she picked it up to put it back in her pocket, she noticed a missed call from Dewight.

She calls him back.

Dewight answers the phone, "Hello, Sarah."

Sarah says, "Sorry, we are in the middle of a major advance here."

Dewight asks, "What can you tell me about the attack tonight? Is it possible for me and my officers to assist?"

Sarah put the phone on speaker and tells Dave to talk.

Dave looks at her. He heard Dewight's comment and tells him the beasts have a new leader and are not acting the same as they did.

Dewight looks confused. "What do you mean they are acting differently?"

Dave says, "The new leader has them acting more like beasts with no rational thoughts of their human side. I don't know what to think about them tonight. They are not acting the same as they did with the other leader."

Dewight asks, "Do you think we can come out and help you tonight?"

Dave says, "NO! Don't come out here. You and your officers will be killed tonight. The beasts are very unpredictable and irrational with their movements and actions tonight."

Dewight asks, "Do you have enough ammo to make through the night?"

Dave replies, "I highly doubt it."

Dewight asks, "Do you think you can make it through the night?"

Dave replies again, "Don't worry about us here. You keep yourself and your officers safe to protect the area."

Dave tells Sarah to end the call.

Sarah screams at him, "WHY DID YOU TELL HIM TO NOT HELP?"

Dave replies, "Because they will be killed if the show up here now. There are more beasts than we can see. If the officers come, they will be out there with the beasts with no cover."

Sarah says, "At least they would be here to help."

Dave says, "We have the house to cover and protect us."

Sarah replies, "You mean this house that they figured out how to run through the door?"

Dave says, "Honey, look at the beasts tonight. Does it look like they have the human thought process tonight?"

Sarah looks out the window as Ashley keeps firing from the other window.

Sarah agrees with Dave.

The beasts are not even focusing on the windows like they did previously.

Dave continues firing into the crowd of beasts, as well. He is hoping for one, clean shot at the new leader that he now refers to as Red.

The beasts do not give him the opening he seeks. He asks Ashley if she can get a shot at the leader. She says no.

As they keep firing into the crowd. He is thinking about what is different, why have the beasts lost their ability to think.

Dave thinks he hears a bark between shots. He believes he hears more barking as they continue to kill beasts.

The beasts retreat rapidly; the previous leader is standing in the street with Red.

Red retreats after the last beast is lost to the darkness, and only the previous leader is standing staring at the house; or perhaps the carnage left in the yard as many beasts lost their lives this night.

Dave takes aim at the previous leader. He is thinking that is the difference in their behavior. When he led the pack, they were coordinated and had focus and were more difficult to defend against their attack. If the new leader decides to listen to him, they could be in trouble again.

Before Dave pulls the trigger, the beast drops to all fours and is gone in just a couple strides and into the darkness.

They never heard the sounds of beasts coming inside or on the floor above them, but they were focused on the beast outside and consistently firing their rifles. So, the sound of beasts in the house could have been drowned out.

Dave asks the ladies to be quiet, so they can listen to see if there might be any beasts upstairs.

They listen and cannot hear any movement upstairs.

Dave tells the ladies to wait in the basement to watch if the beasts return.

Dave goes up the stairs slowly and quietly.

He turns off the power to the door and allows it time to discharge before attempting to open the door. As the door discharges, he listens for any movement that he hasn't heard to this point.

His biggest fear is that there would be many beasts on the other side of the door, and he gets ambushed and overrun with more than he can deal with. At which time he would have just given them full access to the basement and the women.

Dave double checks his revolver to make sure every round in it is live and has not been fired. He also verifies the barrel stamp that he grabbed his .44 Magnum and not the .357 Magnum that Sarah prefers to use.

Dave slowly opens the door. He watches through the crack and as it grows to a full opening.

He doesn't see any evidence of the beasts entering as he opens the door.

Dave steps out into the living room and closes the door once he is sure the living room is clear.

Dave walks through the house starting on the first floor. He checks one room at a time.

He finds no evidence of the beasts breaking in on the first floor and doesn't find any beasts. So, he moves to the second floor and does another room by room sweep of the house. Again, he finds no evidence of the beasts getting in and no beasts.

To say the least, he is relieved but also confused. They had no problem getting in before. Why did they not get in tonight?

Dave goes back to the basement and closes the door on his way back down the stairs.

He does lock the door but doesn't turn on the electricity to the door. He figures the beasts will do like they use to do and not return the rest of the night, but they are acting differently, so he isn't sure if they will be back.

Once in the basement, he informs the ladies as to his walk through the house and that he suggests they sleep in the basement anyway because of how differently the beasts acted tonight. There is no guarantee they won't return. He lets them know that was always a possibility but more tonight since their behavior is so different.

Both Sarah and Ashley agree that sleeping in the basement is the safest option.

They put the samples away. Sarah helps, and Dave doesn't say anything since she has decided to help and has not helped for a while.

They do a last check out the windows before lying down for the remainder of the night.

There are no beasts in sight, so they all lie down.

# Chapter 14

# The Next Generation

The rest of the night was as quiet as the nights use to be. The sounds of the beasts were at a distance and did not concern them the rest of the night.

The next morning, Dave and Ashley get up and go to work.

There are bodies all over the place from the battle the night before.

All the bodies transformed from beast. Some are dogs of various breeds and sizes. Some are human, both male and female. Not a single body still in beast form. Dave wonders if the beasts came back and removed those bodies or they just didn't kill any of the dog men last night.

They did need to move some bodies to clear the driveway, so they could leave.

The cat was perched on the workbench in the back of the garage when they went in to get into the car. The cat appears to be fine with no obvious signs of injury.

They go to work and have an eventless ride to work. Even the scenery seems to be dull this morning.

Once at the hospital, Dave calls Carla and leaves a message about the bodies at the house for her to collect, and he adds he doesn't need any for study.

He turns off his phone, and they head inside the hospital and to the lab to start their shift.

Frank is still limping and not wanting to be social.

Dave and Ashley don't worry about him as that is usually the way he is anyway, until he decides to give his opinion on a conversation. But today Frank stays to himself and doesn't inject into their conversation.

Dave and Ashley still have their suspicions about Frank being a werewolf but have no evidence and don't want to falsely accuse him.

They do their job and continue to discuss ideas and theories about why last night would have been different.

They are thinking that it has something to do with the new leader. He doesn't seem to be as intelligent as the other one, at least not as in touch with his human thought process and seems to be more beast and more "instinctual" with its actions, which makes them wonder if that is also how it is stronger than the previous leader. It's not weakened by retaining human traits and has given into its beast side more than the previous leader, allowing it to tap into the beast strength more than the previous leader could by holding on to the human side more.

The ride home is more of the same. More talk about how the new leader is stronger and how amazed they are at its strength and wondering how strong the beasts really are.

They talk more about Frank and even include Sarah into the talk on the way home and how her attitude seems to be usual and then nice, sometimes in the same day and can seemingly switch without warning.

As the days and nights move on toward the full moon, there are nights when beasts show up at the house. A few skirmishes have happened and, again, no beast enters the house.

Dave is grateful the beasts stopped entering the house but is also confused as to why they would have stopped entering the house. They obviously know how to enter now and for some reason choose not to.

Ashley is just as confused as Dave is and Sarah tells them to stop trying to read more into it and be happy they are not entering the house anymore.

The beasts do enter other houses across the state and all over the world. The nightly news has reports of the beasts entering houses and killing the occupants, leaving little to identify the victims of their attacks.

The only thing investigators have been able to piece together is the houses being attacked do not have electrified doors and window bars.

There is also the occasional attack on people that are out at the wrong time, usually after dusk or too early before dawn.

Those individuals are usually identified by the remaining blood stain as there are no body remains at all recovered for DNA testing to identify.

Occasionally, they have to identify the individuals in a household that was attacked the same way because they are not able to find any remains of a body, only blood.

It has been suspected for a long time that the beasts would kill and eat their victims, but that was confirmed when Dave and Ashley found the human remains in the body they autopsied. Therefore, leaving no more doubt about the beasts eating humans. They have gained some fame from the discovery.

The overseas countries that are seeing a rise in werewolf activity are getting hit hard with the beasts breaking into houses and killing anybody that is outside between dusk and dawn.

The leaders of some of those countries have reached out to the American President and asked how they are fighting the beasts.

The American President is polite and helpful when explaining how the beasts are being dealt with in his country. He tells them about policies and laws that were passed to help protect the public and how well those systems seem to work. But without doubt, the biggest help to public safety has been the national open carry laws that passed. The public now carry their firearms in the open and wherever they go, they are able to protect themselves against the beasts.

Other leaders ask about the murder rate by allowing the public to open carry.

The president tells them that the murder rate has declined. Unless you count the number of beasts killed or are beasts when killed. He also admits that occasionally someone is killed, and the shooter tries to say that individual was a beast. That is where the blood testing is done, and if the individual was not infected, the shooter is charged with murder. So, anytime anyone is shot or even stabbed, the blood is tested and determined clean or infected, and the one who did the killing is held accountable, when necessary. But usually, the samples are infected, and we have very few killing other people. Everyone seems to be willing to look out for each other and kill beasts.

Some leaders ask about how they move products in the USA now with the beasts attacking.

Again, the president explains that the truck drivers defend themselves more than the rest of the public combined because they are still moving at night and in some areas without armed protection. So, we lifted the restrictions against them carrying firearms and the do well at protecting themselves and others.

Some of the other countries are repealing their antigun laws and allowing the public to own firearms again and encouraging them to open carry like in the USA.

As a result, those countries have more werewolves being killed, and the countries that refuse to allow their citizens to own firearms are losing their citizens to werewolf kills. Their police forces are overwhelmed with the calls nightly and are also killed if they show up without sufficient backup to support the policing effort.

On the night of the full moon, Dave and Ashley checked on the cat as they normally do after getting home from work.

The cat lets them hold it for a while and has gotten better at being held but lets them know when it has had enough.

They have seen the cat come out at various times during the last fifteen nights to hunt for mice and whatever else it could find. They had started putting food out for the cat but take the bowl in at night so as not to end up feeding a beast cat food.

This night is no different. They check the cat after work and are holding it.

The cat seems to get scared and bites Dave. Ashley tries to calm the cat and gets bit, as well. The bites are deep enough to draw blood on both of them. The cat runs and hides in a dark area under the workbench.

They can hear the cat growling and hissing and are very confused as to what would have the cat so scared.

They turn around, and Sarah is standing there. They never heard her come up behind them, and she never said anything.

This is unlike Sarah as she has never come out to the garage after they got home.

Dave says, "Dang, babe, you scared the cat, and it bit us both tonight. What are you coming out here for tonight?"

Sarah sounds sweet and innocent when she says, "Oh, I'm sorry, love…I didn't mean to scare the cat. But I thought I'd come out and see if you needed any help tonight. I know I haven't been very helpful lately."

Dave and Ashley look at each other and back to Sarah.

Dave asks, "Are you okay? I mean, do you feel well?"

Sarah laughs as she starts to walk back inside. "Oh, yes, my love. I am feeling very well. No pain and can move and do things I haven't been able to do in a long time because of the pain."

Dave says, "Well, that is great news. So, the new meds are working?"

Sarah says, "It would appear so."

Sarah goes inside, and Dave and Ashley stay in the driveway and wonder exactly what is going on with her tonight.

Ashley asks if he is concerned that Sarah might try to kill them tonight by poisoning them.

Dave assures her that he doesn't believe Sarah would try to do that. "She would just shoot us and be done with us."

They decide to take the night carefully and attribute Sarah's pain-free night to the new medications she was prescribed.

They all go in for supper, and the officers still do not come around since the beasts are not attacking regularly, and the officers can be used to protect the rest of the public.

They have made great progress with the search for a vaccine.

They had to get more wolf bane and gave up on the antibody testing because it never worked to cure the canine side of the infected but cured them of the human side, according to the lab tests they were able to perform. They never had a subject to test it on and were never satisfied with the results to even attempt.

They have replenished their blood samples when they would get attacked and the next morning is when they would go out and get more blood samples as they needed and had vials for the samples.

While looking up plants on the internet one night, they found different weeds that they tried with no success.

They mixed the wolf bane with a weed called houndstongue and got promising results.

They continued to test that mix with the samples and it would cure the infected samples of the canine and leave the human host cured.

They tested the canine samples taken from domestic dogs, and the mixture attacked only the infection again, leaving the host cured of the infection.

They are very impressed with the results and are trying to figure out how to test it on a human subject.

Needless to say, there is nobody admitting to being a werewolf and therefore they have no one to test the vaccine on.

The sun goes down on this full moon night, and they have little doubt the beasts will show up tonight.

They don't have to wait long.

Shortly after dusk, the previous leader appears and sits in the street, just looking at the house. Dave sees him and is wondering when the rest of the pack will arrive.

Ashley asks if there is a way the vaccine can be shot and tested on the one in the street.

Dave says there is, but he doesn't have the dart gun or the needle to try such a task. Then he mentions that if they would shoot him with the vaccine and depending on how fast it would work would have a direct effect if the human form would survive. Because once in human form he would be attacked and killed.

Sarah, "So…then there are many more getting the vaccine as they eat his remains."

Dave and Ashley look at her and neither one argues because the vaccine would be in the very blood the others would be eating. This would, in theory, spread the vaccine through the pack.

But Dave doesn't have the dart gun and doesn't want to sacrifice anyone to spread the vaccine, although it would be a good way to spread the vaccine; spread it similarly to how the infection is spread, through the blood.

The sun sets, and the full moon rises.

The only beast is the previous leader, the one with the saddle back fur coloring.

Dave is watching the beast and the darkness for movement in the shadows.

He notices the beast stands and looks to be excited for some reason.

Sarah isn't feeling well. She tells Dave she doesn't feel good.

He asks what is wrong and she simply states that she is a lot of pain all the sudden and doesn't feel well at all.

Dave looks at Ashley, and neither of them have any idea what might be wrong.

Dave is holding Sarah, trying to comfort her.

It becomes clear as to why she isn't feeling well.

Dave backs up as she begins the change into beast form.

Dave and Ashley are confused as to why Sarah would transform. They were not aware that she had been bitten.

Sarah is screaming in pain as she transforms for her first time. The transformation takes a little time; not much but more the first time as the infected tend to fight the transformation.

Dave is close to Sarah when she reaches her final stages of transformation.

Ashley yells to shoot her.

Dave grabs his .44 Magnum and raises the pistol as Sarah appears to be transforming more.

Dave is astonished and amazed at what he is seeing, and Ashley is just frozen in fear and amazement.

Dave cannot believe what he is seeing.

The beast outside is very excited hearing Sarah's screams and is anxiously waiting for her to come out. It is at the window and watching; nobody noticed it coming to the window and still is not aware of it being there because they are focused on Sarah.

Dave looks at Ashley as Sarah finishes her full transformation.

Sarah has grown wings as a werewolf.

The very first of her kind.

Sarah stretches her wings, and before Ashley can warn Dave, he gets hit with a wing and is thrown across the basement, landing next to the workbench, where they had samples out tonight, other than the werewolf samples. His hand lands on the workbench and smashes a vial, spilling the contents onto the workbench and the floor. What didn't end up on his now cut hand from the glass.

Sarah flexes her wings and looks at Dave.

Dave is staring at her and is completely confused, amazed, scared, and curious.

Dave is on his back and looking around for his pistol.

He finds his pistol, and as he is reaching for it, he notices the tag from the vial he smashed reads Cougar. He is thankful it is not a contaminated vial.

Ashley pulls up the .357 Magnum and shoots Sarah in the heart, causing her to howl in pain.

The beast at the window now makes himself known, as well, by howling.

The beast in the window barks, and Sarah looks at him with a head tilt.

The saddle back beast barks again, and Sarah looks at Ashley.

Dave yells to Ashley to get out of there.

It's too late. Sarah grabs Ashley by the throat and picks her up.

Ashley drops the revolver and grabs Sarah's hand that she is being held with.

Sarah just holds her up in the air, staring at her.

Dave yells to Sarah to put her down.

Sarah looks at him and sees he is aiming his .44 Magnum at her.

Sarah throws Ashley at Dave with nothing more than a simple hand toss.

Ashley's hand smashes another vial of blood sample.

Dave tries to catch her and keep her from hurting herself and him at the same time when she lands.

Dave drops his pistol again to catch Ashley, and now she is on top of him, and he struggles to get his pistol back in hand.

Ashley rolls with Dave's help. They use their cut hands to help her roll, so he can grab his pistol and kill the beast that was Sarah.

They wince with the pain of their cut hands connecting and whatever glass is still in their hands being pushed deeper into their flesh. Not only from that pain but also the pain of being thrown and landing on the concrete floor and slamming against the cabinet. Ashley's pain from her being grabbed by the neck and thrown, as well.

They realize they are literally fighting for their lives tonight and getting beat very badly.

They have experienced the strength of the beast firsthand tonight; not just from observing it from the safety of the house, but actual physical contact, and neither one believes they will live if they can't get a kill shot on the beast.

Dave manages to get his pistol, and his dominate hand is the one that is injured, but his adrenaline is so high he holds the pistol with that hand anyway.

He takes aim as Sarah is standing there, looking around and barks at the beast outside.

He aims carefully at her heart, knowing Ashley already hit her in that area, looking like a good hit to the heart but failing to drop the beast.

He fires, Sarah flinches from the impact of the bullet, and lets out a howl of pain. She turns to face him, and the other beast outside is barking at her and seems to be very excited.

Dave isn't sure whether to think it is at the potential of having his body to feed on or if it just wants her to get out of there.

Dave can see the blood from both gunshot wounds on the beast and is sure both hit the heart just from the color of the blood and the amount of blood.

As he lays there, looking at the wounds, the one from Ashley's shot appears to have healed already. He is sure he is not seeing correctly. He is praying he is not seeing correctly because what that would mean to the werewolf population if she gets out alive would be catastrophic for the human race period. A beast that can heal that fast, even from a shot to the heart.

He has a thought and takes aim at her eye, hoping that a direct shot into her brain will not only stop her but kill her and prevent her from spreading the new form and healing ability.

He fires as she is approaching him.

A direct hit into her eye, and she grabs her eye and howls in pain and drops to one knee. Dave is sure this is the killing shot.

To his and Ashley's amazement and to their horror, she stands up and looks at the beast outside who barks at her. It is now continually barking at her and very franticly.

Sarah stretches her wings and folds them back again against her back.

She kneels and jumps up through the ceiling into the living room and goes out through the wall and meets with the beast outside.

Dave grabs his cell phone and calls Dewight.

Dave informs him of what just happened and that Sarah's new form is able to heal quickly and even take a shot directly to the heart; no, two shots.

Dewight is sending every officer out there hearing Dave describe the ability and the new physical change of wings, and its ability to survive two shots to the heart and a shot to the brain through the eye.

Other beasts started to show up in the street by the time Sarah got outside.

She stands there next to the saddle back beast as it barks at the crowd of other beasts in the street.

Sarah bites the saddle back beast, and it howls in pain as she has his shoulder in her mouth and lifts him off the ground as the blood runs down his body out of her mouth.

Dave gets to the window in time to witness the bite. His heart sinks as he sees the beginning of a new outbreak in the werewolf disease.

Ashley joins him still rubbing her neck where Sarah held her.

Sarah drops the saddle back beast, and as it is knelt on the ground in front of her, she opens her wings.

Dave isn't sure if she is now protecting the other beast or showing a sign of strength to the others.

Sarah tucks her wings behind her back again as Red walks up.

He looks at her and then to the saddle back on the ground.

Red looks at her and growls and barks.

Sarah stands there and doesn't acknowledge the leader.

Red gets angry with her not acknowledging his leadership.

Red reaches out to touch her wings, and she grabs his arm, and he begins to howl in pain as she tightens her grip.

Dave is in full scientist mode again, and Ashley isn't far behind.

Dave nudges Ashley's shoulder. He doesn't speak but points to his shoulder and then to the saddle back beast on the ground.

Ashley notices the beast is no longer bleeding from the bite wound.

It has been three minutes since Sarah bit the other beast.

The saddle back beast reaches out and touches Sarah's leg while she is still holding Red's arm.

She looks down at him as he looks up at her.

The saddle back begins to howl in pain again and is on all fours.

Sarah pulls Red into her with her right hand, that is how she is holding him, and then throws him to the street with her left hand pushing against his chest. She easily just threw an estimated three-hundred-pound beast at least one hundred feet before he hit the ground, then slide another thirty feet. Roughly, Dave isn't in the best position to judge the distance but is going with what he knows about his front yard and the street area; he is figuring those distances to be pretty close.

The saddle back is in the process of growing its new wings as the officers show up to defend the house. Both state and local police from the surrounding areas arrive, an actual army of officers. The National Guard has not been called in because they don't believe they need military help. Also, there is only a few on full-time duty to protect against the werewolf attacks. They, in turn, call in more soldiers if and when needed. So, the night could be over before they even arrive.

Dewight calls Dave when they get there.

Sarah turns and looks at Dave when she hears the phone ringing.

Dave answers his phone, "Hello, Dewight."

Dewight is not hiding his concern in his voice at all. "Dave, is the blonde beast Sarah, the one in front of your house?"

Dave says, "Yes."

Dewight says, "I...I...I thought you said you shot her in the heart twice and once in the eye."

Dave responds, "Yes, but we have noticed she has the ability to heal quickly."

Dewight says, "She apparently has the ability to regrow her eye, as well. She is not missing an eye. Holy...What in God's great name is that growing out of the other ones back?"

At that time, Sarah opens her wings again.

Dewight asks, "What did you create in that lab?"

Dave responds, "That is just it, Dewight. Sarah was never bitten, and her new abilities are just as confusing to us as they are to you."

The wings finish growing from the saddle back, and he stands and flexes his wings alongside Sarah.

He is admiring his new wings, watching them as he flexes them.

Red comes over to him and barks aggressively.

The saddle back beast reaches out and grabs him by the throat, lifting Red up with one hand.

Sarah moves to the side.

The saddle back starts to squeeze Red's throat.

Red is gouging and clawing at the arm that is holding him up.

The saddle back continues to squeeze and then takes his other hand and rips the head of Red, killing him instantly.

The saddle back drops the now headless body.

The other beasts in the street look to the saddle back as leader again.

Dave isn't sure what to think because this one was still able to think with human reasoning and could be even more dangerous now with its newfound strength.

Dave can't help but be curious about the difference in the color of the wings between Sarah and the saddle back.

Her wings match her fur color that matches her hair color as a blonde.

The saddle back's wings are black. The wings grew out of the black saddle patch of fur on its back.

Dewight and Dave have ended their call.

Dewight, seeing the power of the new beast, calls to all officers to shoot and take as many beasts as possible.

He tells them to shoot the multitude of beasts in the street. He designated his best sharp shooters to shoot saddle back and Sarah.

The offices have the beasts surrounded tonight, at both ends of the street.

The officers begin firing into the crowd of beasts, and they begin to drop to the ground, dead and dying.

The sharp shooters begin shooting at Sarah and the saddle back, hitting them directly in the heart.

Sarah and the saddle back take multiple shots to the chest and directly to the heart. They howl in pain with each hit.

Then questions that were formed in everyone's mind get answered.

The two open their wings and take flight.

Everyone is terrified, but they keep firing, killing as many beasts as they can.

The two separate, and Sarah is headed for Dewight. Saddle back is heading to the opposite end of the street.

Dewight dives behind his cruiser.

Sarah reaches down and grabs the cruiser by the roof, using her hands and her feet on each side of the roof, breaking the door glass as her claws penetrate the windows. Her feet wrap around the roof of the car as easily as her hands do, looking to resemble the feet of a bird.

She takes the car and lifts it and flies up with it, straight up into the air out of sight into the darkness where the streetlights end.

Saddle back does the same with a state trooper's car.

Dewight tells everyone to take cover under a tree.

They hear a bark in the darkness above them and then quiet again.

They don't wait long before the cars come crashing back to earth… only at opposite ends of the street.

Dewight's cruiser is dropped onto a state trooper's cruiser, and the state police cruiser is dropped onto a Hughesville police cruiser.

They hear another bark, and the remaining beasts drop to all fours and run into the darkness.

They officers shoot at the beasts while they are retreating but know that without a heart or head shot, they will not kill the beast but hope for the best as they fire at the crowd.

The beasts all escape.

Every officer takes their flashlight and shines it up into the air, trying to find the two in flight, but they do not see either one of them; not even eye shine.

Dewight goes storming over to Dave's house.

Dave goes upstairs to meet Dewight.

Dave opens the door, and Dewight is right there. Ashley is behind Dave, and the other officers are behind Dewight.

Dewight is angry and has no problem letting his anger show as he talks to Dave with a raised voice.

Dewight says, "I thought you were trying to find a cure for the beast, not create a super beast that can fly and use your own wife to create that beast!"

Dave is getting angry at the accusations but understands how it looks and does his best to keep his calm, but the anger does come through in his voice.

Dave says, "Hold on, Dewight, and everyone else that wants to think the same way. You had Brooke and Julie here many nights, including the night a beast woke up in a cell I had in the basement. Brooke took the shots at that beast to save Sarah because I didn't have a good shot without possibly infecting Sarah. They can tell you the intent of the experiments here were for a cure and nothing more. How Sarah got infected is a mystery and how she became this new generation of beast that is stronger, can heal faster, and fly is something else we need to figure out. You and everyone that wants to claim something else needs to get a grip on reality. If we would have known she was infected, we would have tested the vaccine on her. The vaccine that we just had confirmation tonight that it works, minus a living test subject."

Dewight asks, "Why didn't you tell us she was infected?"

Dave shakes his head. "What part of we didn't know she was infected did you not understand? Ask Brooke and Julie if they had any reason to suspect Sarah was infected."

Dewight looks at the officers, and they both shake their head no.

Dave says, "If you want to continue this conversation, you need to come inside as we don't know where they are now, and you are not safe out there in the dark."

They all move inside and continue the conversation.

The ranking state trooper asks, "If you didn't create that thing, then what in the blazes happened?"

Dave says, "That is a great question, and one I really wish I could answer."

Ashley looks at Dave. "What if we missed something when the beast had her and threw her across the basement?"

Dave says, "The only vials she broke was not infected with the werewolf disease."

Brooke steps forward. "Remember you stated you slipped in the beasts drool?"

Dave says, "Yes, I remember, but we didn't see any evidence of the drool being on Sarah's injured shoulder."

Julie said, "Her shoulder was bleeding pretty heavily from the puncture of the claws. What if we all missed that the beast drooled on her shoulder, and we all thought it was just her blood we saw?"

Dave lowers his head and drops to his knees. "Oh, God, what have we done?" He looks up at Julie. "What if you are correct? It would explain how she got the infection without us knowing. But what about the wings and ability to fly? The increase in strength?"

Ashley asks, "What if it has something to do with the vials she broke when the beast threw her?"

Dave stands back up. "She bled downstairs when we shot her. We can test her blood and see what we are now dealing with."

Dewight says, "Okay, but Brooke and Julie will stay with you and watch what you are doing and to protect you, seeing how you have a big hole in the wall and the floor now."

Dave agrees, and the rest of the officers leave while Brooke and Julie go downstairs with him and Ashley.

## Chapter 15

# A New Beast

Once they get to the basement, Dave gets the list of vials that broke when Sarah was thrown.

Ashley gathers blood samples to begin testing.

Brooke and Julie are guarding the windows, watching for the beasts to return.

Dave meets Ashley at the workbench with the list.

They begin testing the blood from Sarah.

They are breaking it down and checking the DNA first and trying to see if that will help them figure out what this new breed is and how to fight it, how to kill it.

They are looking at the list of vials that Sarah had broken trying to see if anything makes sense to them.

They see there was three different vials with bird samples. But which one would mix with a werewolf to create a flying beast?

They read the list of bird samples: golden eagle, bald eagle, and raven.

Dave says, "The increase in strength of the beast it could be a cross contamination with one of the eagles."

Ashley responds, "It could be, but think about the wings. The wing structure itself didn't look like eagle."

Dave and the officers agree.

Dave says, "So, that leaves raven."

Brooke says, "The wings did resemble a crow."

Dave smiles. "Not a crow, my dear friend; a raven. It's similar to a crow but larger."

Brooke says, "Oh, so it would be stronger, as well?"

Dave looks at her. "It would."

They already had the tests started as the conversation with Brooke was happening.

They do a quick version of a DNA test, one that Dave has developed to help him identify potential werewolves quickly.

The results are ready while they are gathering as much of Sarah's blood as possible for more testing.

Julie notices they are wearing two pair of gloves while collecting the samples.

Julie asks, "Why are you guys wearing two pair of gloves? Isn't one pair enough to protect you from a potential infection?"

Dave replies, "No, one pair would usually be enough, but we got our hands cut when Sarah threw us."

Julie responds, "We don't need to be worried about the two of you becoming beasts, do we?"

Dave says, "No need to worry. We are taking every precaution we can to prevent an infection."

Julie says, "Good. Because I would hate to have to shoot you. Thankfully, I didn't have to shoot Sarah tonight."

Dave says, "Yeah, Ashley and I both shot her, and she still escaped into the world."

Julie responds, "Sorry, I didn't mean anything by that."

Dave looks at her and gives a smile. "I know."

They now have several swabs of Sarah's blood for testing.

They check the results of the DNA test.

They are surprised with the results.

They have a total new structure and the typical human contamination: raven and one more axolotl.

Dave lets Brooke know that she was right about her guess as to the bird influence.

Brooke looks at him. "I don't know whether to be happy or disappointed."

Dave says, "Be happy because we have a place to start for looking how we need to kill this new generation of beast. But the salamander DNA will be hard to figure out. That is how she was able to regrow her eye."

Julie asks, "Do you think we need to go back to using silver bullets?"

Dave replies, "We will test that here and get an answer to forward to Dewight and the other police supervisors. That way nobody is buying silver if lead will still work."

Julie says, "Lead didn't work tonight."

Dave responds, "You are correct, but let's see what we need before we start spending the money on silver bullets if something cheaper will work. We will start with testing lead and silver to see what happens."

Brooke replies, "I can tell you lead won't work to kill these new ones. It would have worked tonight, the others still dropped dead but not the new ones."

Dave says, "I understand, but we need to know for sure what will kill them. If we use a different alloy mixture of lead with something else, will it still work to kill the beasts and be cheaper than silver? Or can we use a lead and silver alloy and still be able to kill the beasts and save money on ammo at the same time. These are things we need to test to find out."

Brooke says, "Okay, but I still say straight lead will not kill the new beasts. Our best sharpshooters were shooting them, and they still flew away. That is weird to say… they flew away."

Julie adds, "Not to mention how many times the sharpshooters hit them tonight." Dave and Ashley test the vaccine on the blood from Sarah.

They wait for the results and check the inventory of vials they had out before Sarah changed and threw them onto the vials.

They are only missing two vials: Cougar and Golden Eagle.

They found the tags from the vials, so they already knew about those two but didn't know if there was more.

While waiting for the results from the vaccine test, Dave walks over to the other window and looks out.

Dave calls Ashley to the window.

Ashley joins him and looks out the window.

Dave says, "Look at the head that saddle back ripped off Red."

Ashley gasps. "Is that…Allen?"

Dave says, "Looks like it."

Ashley replies, "I guess that means we won't see him at work anymore."

Dave says, "I guess not."

As they walk away from the window Ashley mentions she figured Frank before Allen for being a beast.

Dave agrees, and they check on the vaccine test on Sarah's blood.

They see no change in the infection.

Dave looks at his watch and mentions that they should see something for the amount of time that has passed.

Ashley agrees. She also mentions it don't look promising.

Dave agrees with that statement.

They continue running tests all night. Well, into the daylight hours.

They didn't work at the hospital that day, so they kept working on Sarah's blood samples, trying to figure out how to cure her.

The officers stayed two hours past sunrise waiting for Sarah to come home, and the plan was to try to kill her in human form. But Sarah never arrived home, even after the officers left.

Dave called the carpenter to come out and repair the house before nightfall again.

Dave and Ashley helped Carla pick up the bodies and took samples to help their studies as they helped her.

Carla tells Dave he seems to be somewhere else.

Dave explains what happened to Sarah and that she created a new generation of werewolf.

Carla mentions that she knows it won't make a difference, but she is sorry.

Dave acknowledges her, and they continue picking up bodies.

They get to the one that was decapitated.

Carla asks how that happened.

Before Dave can answer her question, she realizes who it is and is totally in shock.

Dave tells her that he and Ashley were shocked, as well.

Dave tells her how Allen lost his head and that they don't have a clue as to who the saddle back beast is.

The day goes on.

Dave and Ashley get some sleep as and the carpenter continues working on the house wall. They carpenter and his crew move to repairing the floor when done with the wall.

Dave gets up before they are finished.

The carpenter asks about Sarah and how she is doing because she usually calls him.

Dave explains to him what happened.

The carpenter apologizes for bringing her up in conversation.

Dave tells him, "No worries. We all need to learn to move on with life."

The carpenter agrees.

The construction crew leaves before dusk, so they won't be out after dark. Dave and Ashley go back to the basement and continue working on the samples from Sarah.

Dave goes back upstairs when the doorbell rings.

It's Brooke, Julie, and Dewight.

Dave invites them all inside.

Dewight says he can't stay; he just wanted to know if he has heard from or seen Sarah at all during the day.

Dave checks his phone and says he hasn't heard from nor seen her all day.

Dewight asks if he has had a chance to test the samples to see if they need silver to kill the new beasts that Sarah created.

Dave says he has not had a chance as yet, but they will test that tonight.

Dewight smiles and tells Dave the officers have silver bullets to use tonight if the beasts return, they will try the silver.

Dave agrees and Dewight leaves and Dave closes and locks the door. Then they go downstairs to continue the testing.

A few beasts appear that night but stay in the shadows and the officers can't see them well enough to get a shot at even one of them. They couldn't tell if they had wings or not.

Again, they don't work at the hospital, so they work into the daylight hours again, running different tests trying to figure out what needs to be done to change the vaccine.

The officers leave to end their shift, and Dave and Ashley go to bed separately.

Dave keeps running the night about Sarah being thrown by the beast through his mind and keeps trying to find something, anything they missed as to how she got infected. The only thing he can think of is the officers are correct, and the beast drooled on her shoulder and they all missed that.

But he is confused why and how the Raven would be able to join in the infected and make the individual stronger and add wings and the ability to fly. He is just so fixated on figuring that out, and hopefully it will help with figuring out how to change the vaccine.

While he stands there, staring out the window, lost in his thoughts, he swears he saw Sarah. It was almost like a dream, and she looked up and saw him in the window and ran away from the house. She was covered but not wearing clothes. It looked like a blanket she was wrapped up in.

He isn't sure he seen her, and he goes to bed. He is certain it is his mind playing tricks on him and that he is that tired.

Dave is only able to sleep a few hours. He is blaming himself for what happened to Sarah because he brought the suicide victim into the house. He didn't catch that the beast drooled on her shoulder; he didn't catch the beast waking up. His list is just eating at him, and he is sure he should have known and been able to prevent her infection.

It doesn't help when he talks to Ashley, Brooke, Julie, Carla, Dewight, or anyone else tells him it wasn't his fault. That there was no way of knowing that she got infected, and even if they did know, the vaccine wasn't ready in time.

But Dave still blames himself and tells them he would have worked harder to get the vaccine ready in time.

Their next day back to work, they see someone new in Allen's office. It's Frank.

They go in, and Frank greets them and gives them their jobs for the day.

Frank asks them if the rumors are true, that Allen was killed as a werewolf.

Dave admits that is true and tells Frank that he was killed by another, stronger beast—not a gunshot.

Frank is surprised. What would be stronger than a werewolf? Especially Allen as a beast the way he always worked out.

A little light goes on in Dave's head. He forgot about Allen working out; that might be what made him stronger than the saddle back when they fought for the leadership of the pack. This is a concept he hasn't thought about. The more physically fit and stronger the infected the stronger the beast. Could it also have something to do with the mental capacity of the beast? Would the beast gain more strength and be more primal, instinctive and retain less human ability? Now the only problem is how to test that theory. He thanks Frank for the insight, and Frank is confused as to what he means. Frank says he didn't have any insight.

Frank talks to Dave more when they work the same days now.

Dave asks Frank why he took the supervisor position when he swore he wouldn't take the job. Dave asks him what changed his mind.

Frank tells him that the offer was made to him to finish his time in the hospital as supervisor until he retires the following year. So, he agreed and figured it was better than having someone new come in and not understand how we work around here. They share a laugh.

Frank lets Dave and Ashley know about his back problem and how this new position helps by keeping him sitting longer than standing.

Dave and Ashley share that they had thought he might be a beast because his injuries and even his back problem matched the beast from the night before. They have a laugh, and Frank says he figured they and many others in the hospital expected he was a werewolf.

Dave shares with Frank what happened to Sarah, as well. Frank says to let him know if there is anything he can do to help.

Over the course of the next thirty days and nights leading up to the next full moon, there are a few attacks and missing people; houses broken into and families slaughtered and only blood to identify the family and the members in the household. Again, the houses do not have the window bars and steel barred storm doors electrified.

Dave and Ashley are up long hours working on different ideas of a cure. They have Frank putting in ideas, as well.

Dave was hesitant at first about accepting help from Frank, even if it is over the phone. But he has learned that with Frank's help, he and Ashley are making better progress with their testing.

Overseas, in the countries that didn't allow their citizens the rights to own firearms again are in really bad shape for the beasts.

There is nobody left alive, and the beasts are gone when the police and military arrive to defend the people that are being attacked. Sometimes half the town is dead before they arrive to kill the beasts. Other times, just the family of the house that was being attacked. Then there are those times that the beasts wait in the shadows and kill the police and military personnel when they arrive. That last scenario is happening more often as the new generation of flying beasts expand farther across the globe. Now they are all looking again to the USA to help figure out how to kill the beasts and protect the people.

In England and across Europe, there have been reports of a blonde flying beast. The color of the wings matches the fur. In the reports, they mention how this is a first for this coloring to be seen.

In the Asian countries, they are reporting seeing a beast with saddle back fur coloring with black wings. Again, the reports say this is a first for this coloring to be seen.

The reports from those areas are also making comments that the witnesses, that survive or are not seen, tell how the blonde and the saddle back beast appear to be leading the others.

Dave does his best to keep up with the world news, especially about those sightings.

Dave and Ashley even talk with Frank about the sightings overseas, and they all agree that with the ability to fly, the beasts will spread farther faster.

Frank does tell Dave not to jump to conclusions that those beasts are Sarah and the leader from Picture Rocks, Pennsylvania.

Dave mentions that it can't be ruled out entirely, either.

Frank agrees.

Dave and Ashley do continue to turn on the surveillance cameras every night.

They see the cat each night when the beasts are not nearby.

The officers take turns watching the cat, as well. Dewight has decided to keep the officers there every night, so Dave and Ashley can focus on their testing.

They have determined that an alloy of lead and silver is all that is needed to kill the new beasts. The alloy is cheaper than straight silver bullets.

The discovery makes it to the President who, in turn, spreads the word to the world leaders, so they can change the ammunition they are using, as well.

Everyone using the new alloy, and even those using straight silver are able to kill the flying beasts when they can see them.

Their ability to fly has made it even more difficult to see them.

The beasts have learned to stay higher in the air where they are out of the light and even out of reach of most flashlights.

When they decide to attack, it is usually from behind, and the victim never sees the beast until they are attacked.

The beasts have even started using the tactic that Sarah and the saddle back used when they grabbed the car and flew into the air with it.

That is now being used as a way for the beasts to attack people and pull the people from the vehicle in the air and kill them.

The beasts still waste very little of their kills.

The worst attacks that have been reported across the world are when the blonde and saddle back beasts are reported to be together.

They have been seen attacking military convoys and carrying of military vehicles of every size including semis with the trailer and, of course, the solders in the semi and the trailer if it is a troop transporter.

They are the only two beasts that have been reported to attack military vehicles in any country.

Armored vehicles have proven to not protect the solders from the beasts, either. The beasts rip the doors off of the vehicle, and they have also gone through the armor plating, as well. Granted, they usually take the doors off instead of ripping through the armor.

Dave and Ashley do not keep up with the various attacks and how they gain access to the occupants of any vehicle. Instead, they focus on the testing and trying to find a vaccine for the flying werewolf.

As expected, some nights are quieter than others.

The beasts are staying in the shadows and rarely coming into the light.

The one beast that did enter into the light one night was killed by Brooke.

A couple nights later, the blonde and saddle back were seen in the area but not at the house.

There have been reports of flying beasts entering houses that are electrified through the roof.

They crash through the roof to get to the people inside and devourer the occupants of the house. Again, leaving only blood to identify the individuals of the household.

Going into the new moon night, Dave and Ashley have discovered a weed called the black henbane, and they are trying it to modify the vaccine.

They have only just received the weed to use.

They have tried the common burdock because they could get that easily and had no luck with the experiments with the vaccine.

They officers are very alert every night but more so for the new moon because there is only the artificial light from the streetlights and the driveway light; not to mention the cat has not come out of the garage.

They don't have to wait long after dusk before they see beasts.

But the beasts are doing something new tonight. They are breaking the lights.

The beasts are moving so fast that neither officer can get a good shot to take.

By the time the officer has the beast in her sights, the beast breaks the bulb and is out of the sight window for a good kill shot.

They hear something outside in the area of the garage.

They look to the monitors and see the cat running from the garage, and a beast comes breaking through the garage doors behind it.

The beast is a saddle back.

The beast catches the cat this time.

The blonde beast appears by landing next to him.

The beast knows there is no window on that side of the house, and the only way the people inside can come out to shoot them is through the door.

The cat is clawing at the beast and biting, as well. The beast does not seem to be bothered by the cats attempt to escape.

Both beasts look at the camera.

The saddle back raises the cat to his mouth and bites the cats head off and swallows it, then eats the rest of the cat, as well.

After that, the blonde reaches up and breaks the bulb for the driveway light. The last light on the block.

Dave tells the officers to move back away from the windows. They won't be able to see a beast coming until it has them.

Julie asks, "Why would it eat the cat?"

Dave answers, "That beast has been after that cat for a while now. The cat has always managed to escape until tonight."

Brooke asks, "Do you think they will try to get in here tonight?"

Dave responds, "It is possible that they don't want us to see them and whatever they will be doing outside."

Ashley says, "We have seen reports where they entered houses with electrified window and door bars."

Dave tells her to not try to scare the officers.

They do hear a loud crashing sound upstairs.

It sounded like it was from the second floor and not the first floor above them.

They listen and watch the windows and the doors.

They hear movement on what sounds like to be on the second floor.

They continue to listen and wait to see if it will try to come down with them.

Dave and Ashley are armed, as well.

The four of them have the window and the doors covered for any potential entrance.

Brooke sees eyes reflecting the basement lights at the window. It's not close enough to see the face but she has no doubt it is a beast. She gets Dave's attention and points at it.

He nods and mouths the words to shoot it.

Brooke does just that.

After her shot, there is no more doubt about it being a beast as it let out a short howl as it died.

They hear a lot of movement upstairs and another loud crash.

They continue to listen and hear the mournful howls of other beasts.

After the howling stops, they hear footsteps above them.

They watch the doors and the windows in case the footsteps are a diversion.

Julie is the next one to take a shot at a pair of eyes.

There is no howl that follows her shot, so they are not sure if it was a hit or not; no mournful howling, either.

They hear what sounds like more than one beast on the first floor, but they aren't sure if it might be two or many more.

They can see the repaired area from the basement.

They can't see any evidence of where the beasts are stepping, other than hearing their footsteps.

They hear what they figure is scratching.

It sounds like one is scratching at the floor.

Dave has never had the floor electrified and doesn't know if that is what is being checked by the scratching.

They see a set of claws penetrate the floor above them.

They all watch, and Dave tries to figure where the body of the beast would be positioned by the claw placement.

He raises his pistol and is moving it into a position he believes will hit the beast. Brooke asks in a whisper, "What are you doing? You can't see what you are shooting at."

Dave whispers back, "Neither could you at the window. If you look at the claws in the floor, it should put its body right about there." He shoots as he finishes saying it.

The claws are removed from the floor, and a beast howls in pain and can be heard as it leaves the house and the howling stops in the yard; again, no mournful howling follows.

They hear other footsteps leave the house.

They are listening to see if that is all the beasts or if there are more in the house.

There is no more eye shine in the windows and no more sounds of footsteps above them.

Dave and Ashley go back to testing after an hour of quiet.

The officers are again watching the windows and checking the floor above them for any surprise claws coming through into it.

About an hour before dawn, they hear a loud crash outside, but without the lights they can't tell for sure what it was.

They all think it was a vehicle. But what vehicle? And why would they destroy a vehicle? One thought is they found a cruiser in the area and dropped the car close by after killing the officers inside.

When daylight finally comes, they are all relieved and begin looking outside. They don't see a vehicle in the street; the officer's cruiser is still where they parked it and doesn't look to have been disturbed.

They wait until thirty minutes past sunrise to go out the basement door to the driveway.

They get to the driveway and see Dave's car has been forcefully slammed into the driveway nose first. The finished size is close to a small compact car.

Dave is upset and considerably emotional.

All three ladies try to console him.

He does manage to compose himself and says he will need to find another car.

Ashley mentions that she still needs to get another car, as well.

They agree that they need to go car shopping before needing to go to work.

They all take a walk around to the front of the house and see three, dead beasts.

One at each window and one closer to the street.

They agree the one closer to the street is the one Dave shot through the floor.

They walk over to the bodies, one at a time.

Dave recognizes one of them; the one Brooke shot.

It is one of the guys from the construction crew that repairs his house.

Nobody knows the other two, and Dave doesn't know this guy's name, either.

Dave uses his phone and takes pics of the individual to show the carpenter the next time he comes to do repairs.

The officers leave and Dave calls Carla and leaves a message for her to come and get three bodies.

Dave and Ashley take samples to continue with the testing. Then go inside and survey the damage.

There is a hole in the first-floor wall where a beast ran through it, and a hole in the wall on the second floor in his bedroom.

They see Sarah's dressers were open and, upon looking, realize they are empty, as well.

They go to the kitchen, and Dave calls the carpenter to get him and his crew out to fix the house again.

Dave doesn't make any mention of the dead crew member.

Once the carpenter arrives with his crew, Dave tells him about his missing crew member.

The carpenter looks at the pics and agrees that was one of his crew but doesn't offer a name.

The carpenter tells Dave they will get started and should have both holes closed before dusk. He adds they may not be completely done but will be closed.

Dave thanks the carpenter and joins Ashley outside with a cup of coffee. Carla has already picked up the bodies, and they now talk about how to go car shopping.

Dave calls his insurance company and then he calls a tow truck to retrieve his car.

Then he calls for an Uber to pick them up to go car shopping.

The Uber driver shows up around the same time the tow truck driver gets there. The tow truck was first and was backing up to Dave's car.

After the driver got out of the truck, he asked Dave how in the world that happened.

Dave explains how it happened and then asks where he is taking the car.

The driver says, "Holy cow, I thought those things were bad before now they are even worse. Someday I will learn not to ask you how these things happen to you." Then he tells Dave where he is taking the car.

Dave smiles and thanks the driver and then joins Ashley in the Uber, and they head out to the dealers in the area.

Ashley decides to get a Nissan Xterra, and they keep looking for Dave.

They release the Uber driver now that Ashley has a vehicle, and they continue car shopping.

Ashley is surprised why he hasn't accepted anything he has seen yet.

Dave tells her he is looking for something specific.

Ashley asks what he is looking for.

He tells her he would like to find a vehicle similar to his Crown Victoria and swap over the parts for the engine upgrades and the suspension if it isn't a retired police cruiser.

They find a dealership with an older Mercury Grand Marquise; the same year as his Crown Victoria.

He looks at the car.

Ashley asks if he would prefer a newer model.

Dave says no.

They go inside and talk to a saleswoman.

Dave asks about the Mercury, and she looks it up on her list and answers his questions about the car.

The saleswoman gives him the keys so he can take it for a ride.

Dave and Ashley go for a ride in the car. They get back to the dealership, and Dave says he will take the car.

It has the same engine in it the Crown Victoria, and Dave is hoping to salvage some engine parts to swap over.

They get back to the house with their replacement vehicles.

Dave calls the shop where his car was taken and talks to the owner, a friend.

Dave's friend tells him the insurance person was there and has already left.

Dave asks if they checked under the hood.

His friend admits they did.

Dave then asks if the upgrades are salvageable.

He is informed that his upgrades were not salvageable. His friend tells him the impact was so hard that it split the engine block and the transmission housing.

Dave starts asking about specific parts.

Again, his friend tells him it is all broken and tells Dave to come and look for himself.

Dave believes him and apologizes for making it look like he didn't trust him. He adds it would be cheaper than starting over.

Dave calls the insurance company and learns they were going to call him.

Dave is informed his car is totaled.

He says he figured that, so now what?

He is informed what the car was valued at and the check will be getting cut and mailed within the next day or two.

Dave agrees.

The days and nights continue, with an attack every so often at random and not in the same country; one night in Canada, another in Mexico, another night in France.

Granted there are several attacks, but they are not always attacking more than one night in any place—state or country, which Dave sees as very strange. Why would they attack different countries?

The reports he and Ashley look at have the two beasts in common—the blonde and the saddle back.

Dave and Ashley continue with their testing, and they talk about ideas why the beasts are attacking the way they are.

Neither one has much to say, except that it is very weird and makes no sense.

Ashley says, "Wait… maybe that is it. It's not supposed to make sense. That way nobody can plan to kill them. If nobody knows where they will be, they won't expect them, and they get in and out with their kills."

Dave says, "You have a point. If they don't attack the same area twice, they are harder to follow harder to predict."

As the time gets closer to the full moon, Dave and Ashley both notice they have less pain after working all night.

Taking what they learned about Sarah, they draw blood from each other and check it under the microscope and do not see the infection, so they are relieved.

On the night of the full moon, the officers are not in the house. Dewight needed them in another part of the area before they could get to the house.

That night, like other full moon nights, the beasts are outside, waiting.

Dave and Ashley are working on samples and have a promising vaccine for the new generation of flying werewolves.

They are running more tests to verify the vaccine is usable and will do as intended.

They have samples running, and the beasts come up to the windows.

They make themselves known.

Dave and Ashley turn, and Dave grabs his .44 Magnum. The beasts are not in the window anymore.

Dave and Ashley are not feeling well.

The beasts have surrounded the house.

There are even beasts mounted on the roof.

Dave and Ashley see each other as they begin to change.

They now know they missed something in their blood when they looked at it.

They continue to change, and they move away from the samples before they change, so they don't knock over anything that might be needed later, especially the test with the vaccine. Dave is hoping to use it on himself and Ashley now.

Dave and Ashley are transforming, and the beasts are outside excited for them to join the pack.

The blonde and the saddle back beasts are in the street.

Dave and Ashley transform into werecats and then their wings grow in.

Their transformation is complete.

They are a completely new breed of werebeast: a winged werecat.

www.ingramcontent.com/pod-product-compliance
Lightning Source LLC
LaVergne TN
LVHW021748110725
815859LV00010B/143